Cini and the Beast

Louise Furley

Cini and the Beast

ISBN- 978-1-7363452-8-3 (Paperback)
ISBN- 978-1-7363452-7-6 (eBook)

Cover design by Pixel Mischief Design

ALSO BY LOUISE FURLEY

A Mafia Romance series

Distilled Duplicity
His Winnings
Adara
Jozadak

Satan's Brood series

Devil's Prince
Devil's Seed

Dutch Military Special Forces series

Jungle Treasure
Jancarlo

Stand alone titles

Jezábel and the Assassin

Solitar

Halo Valley

Cini

and the

Beast

Chapter One

It was broad daylight yet danger already lay in wait.

A perfect blue sky domed the two carriages bouncing and lurching over the rocky, hard-packed dirt trail.

The trail had been wide open across a vast savanna, but now it funneled into an archway of trees that rapidly thickened into dense forest. So dense, the occupants of the coaches could not see more than a few feet into the leafy woods bordering the trail.

Without warning, a nightmare sprang up right in front of them.

Bandits!

"Ya-ho!" The team master yelled, alerting the other carriage while whipping the reins. The eight horses screeched out whinnies and took off at a hard gallop, spitting clods of dirt in all directions.

They didn't get far before the bandits cut off their flight, blocking them from the front, and more came up the rear, inescapably trapping them.

In the chaos of shouts and hooves stomping, dust kicked up in clouds shrouding everything.

Bellowing commands to the carriage drivers to cease moving, the bandits waved swords and rapiers in warning, a few held rare firearms.

The men on the carriages slowed the horses and raised their hands in surrender.

An enormous black stallion, nostrils flaring, marched forward through the pack of bandits, his bold fetlocks lifting and stomping in bullying high steps.

The man atop the horse allowed the steed his dramatic, treacherous dance in front of his confined audience.

His seat arrogant, smug face streaked with filth and sweat, the bandit crowed with squalid mirth, "Good day, my friends," he leaned forward with an arm resting lazily on the short saddle horn, reins dangling in his hand.

His greedy grin nasty, he informed them, "They call me Tetek, Terror of the Spider Thread Trails. You have by now determined we are here to take your trades, your money pouches, your valuables. You will all depart the carriages and stand aside peacefully while my men divest you of your treasures."

The mean face flattened in ugly threat. Eyes narrowed at the men, he warned them, "Any resistance, *at all*, will result in your instant and likely painful, death. Do I make myself under-"

Suddenly dropping from trees and rushing out from the thicket, warriors surrounded the bandits.

Instantly hurtling into battle, they leapt off their steeds with clamoring shouts of, "Take no prisoners!" Slashing swords and daggers, the warriors were quickly and easily beating hell out of the thieves.

In the noisy turmoil, Tetek leapt up onto a coach wielding a sabre. Pressing it against a driver's throat, he shrieked in fury, "I will cut off his head if every warrior doesn't back off! Now!"

Long black hair streaming as he ran, *Dominio* Lord Kazak Adarken vaulted onto his steed. Racing the few yards, he jumped up to his feet on the saddle and launched himself onto the carriage.

He landed with a hard thud and kept moving with the blinding speed of a wild ravaging animal.

"Back! Back!" the now panicked bandit screamed. "Get back or I kill him!" Recognition of the warlord approaching him with deadly speed, the Emperor's top *dominio,* struck Tetek's face like a frightened slap leaving it stark white.

Gripping the sabre in his sweat-loosened grasp, he tried to turn keeping the driver between him and Lord Kazak.

As swift as a north wind, Kazak had his hands on Tetek's own neck before the bandit could react.

Screeching his terror, Tetek moved the sabre from the driver to stab and slice maniacally at Kazak- but in a blink, Kazak tore him to pieces with his bare hands and teeth. Like a feral beast he savaged the man until the carcass dropped in the dirt beside the carriage.

Without hesitation, Kazak jumped from the carriage and ran to the next brigand and ripped him into gristle and bones before the man could take a breath to scream.

Warrior Bo'orchu 'Bo' Targutai captured a bandit, and beat him until he barely clung to consciousness. Bo clutched the thief's collar keeping him on his feet, the battered man's head hung.

Through blood flooding in his eyes, the robber watched the bearded Kazak tear into man after armed man without raising a weapon.

The robber cried, "Who the hell is that? Is he man or savage beast?"

Bo laughed, "Both. But to be honest, I'd say more beast than man." Bo held the beaten thief and they watched the warriors viciously slay the rest of the bandits, until none was left breathing.

The sniveling male Bo restrained, shook with terror. Spitting blood and teeth he cried, "What kind of hideous *monstru* is he?"

His chuckle demonic, Bo told him, "Lord Kazak Adarken was dropped in the Black Forest they believe at three years old. They think three because when they found him, he had very few words they could understand. Some of what he supposedly said was, 'I three,' and 'I *alb tirgis.*'"

"White tiger? What the fuck does that mean?" The thief snorted up blood and spat it out. It splatted on the dirt already mottled with blood and sprawled grotesque guts.

Bo shrugged, then explained, "The legend goes that they studied his nails and hair and other things and determined he'd been all alone in the forest for around a year making him around four if what he said about being three that he remembered was accurate.

"He spoke few words, he more growled, and stalked, and preyed like an animal. On his back is supposedly a tattoo of the Siberian symbol for king, and at his shoulder there are stripes of claws, and the impression of a paw.

"They claim the Siberian symbols are not tattoos, or, henna, but birthmarks. The paw," he shrugged, "no one can tell. Looks like it was literally imprinted, clawed into him by a…" his lip twitched at the man blanching at his words, "tiger."

The bandit's mouth dropped in disbelief. "So, you're saying that- that half man half creature was…raised by…white tigers?"

Nodding with a grin, Bo replied, *"Da,* Siberian Tigers. However, he was marked by the white one, not the yellow with stripes. They named him Kazak after the Romastik word for savage, and his surname of Adarken for the words dark killer.

"He is *dominio,* prime warlord of *Împărat Radoslav's* army, Emperor Boris Radisalvo's royal league of drujinos, his elite warriors."

The bandit gasped. Panting and wheezing in pained breaths from punctured lungs, he about fainted when Kazak, wiping his sleeve across his mouth, over the thick black beard, stomped on a moaning man splayed on the ground, silencing him with death.

Kazak looked up at Bo and came to them.

Huge with cordons of hardened muscles strung across his powerful shoulders and over his thick chest, Kazak combed bloody fingers through black hair saturated with sweat and blood that hung over brilliant blue eyes.

Those merciless eyes studied the bandit Bo held, broken and bleeding, now on his knees sniveling and begging for his life.

The bandit threw himself at Kazak, frantic fingers dragging down the chainmail and leather plates sewn in under the leather vest.

Clinging to Kazak's breeches, he wailed, "Please, my Liege, I beg you for my life! I was carried along with these other fellows, I have nothing to do with-"

Whack- Kazak backhanded him, knocking the man backwards flat on his back and out cold. The warlord stood beside Bo, one of his lead warriors and his best friend, their eyes emotionless and placid on the unconscious, butchered man.

Bo said matter-of-factly, "He's the only one alive. I guess he's the one we let go free to warn the others about us."

Kazak grunted. Standing with boots akimbo, hands clasped behind his back, his face behind the thick beard and long hair a cold brutal mask.

Sighing, Bo crouched beside the bandit as the other occupants of the carriages milled about thanking the warriors for their help. He tacked a note to the unconscious man, it stated:

"Warning to all who travel the Itä Cale, the Spider Thread Trails. Thievery, kidnapping, accosting and murder will not be tolerated. Doing so will result in immediate death. There will be no second chances.

By Orders of Lord Kazak Adarken."

After every battle, the warriors left one bandit more dead than alive, to describe the horrific carnage, the bloody slaughter dealt by Lord Kazak Adarken and his warriors to any that dared disobey the Lord's written warning.

Chapter Two

Holding her long skirts up, Cini hurried down the hall praying to the good God she didn't run into anyone. Slipping into the shadowed stairwell, her swiftly pattering footsteps were muffled on the grey stone steps leading up to the towered roof.

As she stepped out to the pitch and stone floor, she chastised herself for not bringing a scarf to cover her bright hair. The corn-silk color was such a light yellow it bordered on white.

Her Aunt Marta always embarrassed her saying Cini had the flaxen curls of a toddler and could have easily blended into a field of early daffodils.

But Cini wanted to be likened to a woman, not a child. However, right now, she had to move carefully to stay in the shadows lest the sun reflect off her fair hair giving her away.

Sneaking to the side of a turret, Cini was careful to keep as much of her body hidden behind the gable while she peered over the edge. Parts of her blue flowery gown brushed the dusty stone wall as she stood on tiptoe.

Chills prickled up her spine at the sight of Prince Gavrill Andreyev's retinue. Fear and anger stiffened her back.

The nerve of the marauding cad. Traveling back to Russia, he had decided to take his soldiers trekking through Sweden to Chalon-sur-Sônn where Cini's family had emigrated from England to join her father's people.

Prince Andreyev had made it clear he was sending word to his home in Russia to send more troops of soldiers to come and seize Chalon-sur-Sônn, where he would pronounce himself king and lay claim to Cini.

Cini's uncle had died and her father Garund was crowned king. Not only was Cini breathtakingly desirable, marrying her would solidify Prince Andreyev's desire to be king, although capturing and taking over the entire region would ensure that alone.

Yet, being king was not all Prince Gavrill Andreyev aspired to, his plan was to lay siege upon his own emperor, Boris Radisalvo, and take his sovereign royalty for his own.

"Cini," a hushed whisper drew her from her anxious viewing of the horses and men that rambled around the compound.

Cini spun around to see her best friend peeking out from behind a waist-high stone wall.

"Melisandra Maciel!" Cini scolded with her hand at her throat, "You scared the feathers off a goose." Her warm grin negating her scolding, she took a few steps from the edge of the edifice towards her friend.

The girls were night and day. Cini's palest of blonde curls twirling in fat ringlets down her back were a striking contradiction to Melisandra's raven black hair that hung straight as a whisk to her bottom.

Cini was petite and much on the thin side yet blessed with amazing curves, whereas Meli was tall and all willowy grace. Under sky blue eyes, Meli's generous mouth was full and always with a ready, if timid, smile, Cini's lips were tiny yet lush.

"Shh!" Meli warned, staying behind the pillar of rock. "Don't let anyone hear you. You don't want to draw that horrid prince here."

Quietly, Cini moved closer to her.

Her expression worried, Meli spoke hushed, "Do you think he meant what he said about sending his soldiers to occupy our town for good? They've already taken over."

Concern darkened her golden skin, she tugged the sleeves of her tangerine gown over her wrists. "And his crazy idea to marry you. The nerve! One kingdom isn't enough for him he has to have ours too?"

Cini petted Meli's arm in comfort. A steep serious tone roping through her words, she whispered, "Oh I believe every word he says. His countenance is too mean, severe, his smile twists cruelly when he strikes out at his men and our people."

Blonde curls bounced as she nodded hard and repeated, "Oh yes, I believe everything he says." A brow cocked, she asked Meli, "Why are you not at your lessons?"

"I was sent to look for you. Cook said you haven't finished the baking for tomorrow's dinner for the prince. She says you have the hand of a magical faerie when it comes to the lightness in your baked specials." Meli laughed then turned stern with suspicion. "You are not still planning your ridiculous escape?"

Cini took a step from her friend, fingers clutching her long skirt to lift it slightly from under foot.

"Meli, the prince has the village imprisoned, surrounded by soldiers, everyone who has tried to leave to go for help has been murdered. I know I can get out without being caught. I must go, I must get to the emperor and beg his aid."

"No, Cini, you can't-"

"There you are my summer blossom, my naughty Princeza Činnosti," Prince Gavrill Andreyev stepped out onto the stone landing. He didn't see Meli ducking down the second his voice barraged into the space.

The fifty-year-old king moved towards Cini, his barrel chest pumped up, he shook his dark brown head with a scold, "My dear, I've had my men looking everywhere for you."

He strode to her; the back of his dark red coat draped to his knees, the front was partially closed with gold buttons. Gold embroidery decorated the coat, his knee-length boots laced up the front also gilded, covered most of his black slacks.

Cini moved back from him, leading him away from where Meli was hiding.

At first he scowled, then with condescension oiling his tongue, Andreyev said, "It is time for you to stop being obdurate my child, embrace your destiny to marry me and combine our kingdoms."

"But you don't want to blend our clans together, Prince Andreyev, you want to raze our village to the ground, kill the native populace and take over completely." She discreetly motioned for Meli to leave while she could.

"Tis true." His hands clasped behind his broad back, he sauntered over to her. "Count yourself lucky you won't be a victim of my extermination. You will be safe as my wife."

He was physically fit and good-looking, but the mean bead in his brown eyes, and cruel curl of his heavy lips marred his classical features that were slightly thickened, squaring with middle age.

Hands slapped on her slender hips, small nose turned up in the air, Cini admonished him, "You are old enough to be my father, my grandfather," she could see Meli was creeping behind the prince and slipping down the staircase.

The prince huffed with irritation, "Stop whining. Many girls are married at your age and even much younger. I must return with my soldiers and make ready to gather more men to come and take this land over. In the meantime, I will leave a force to contain your people. Execution will be the only punishment for any who try to escape."

Cini tried again, begging, "Please, Prince Andreyev, you must reconsider your campaign!"

Coming closer to her, his smarmy smile unpleasant. Brooking no argument, eyes narrowed, he directed coldly, "We will be married. For now, I must have a little taste to hold me." He grabbed at her, she jerked to the side to avoid his grasp.

Off-balance, the prince staggered, tripped and toppled into the low wall.

Cini took her chance and bolted for the door. She rushed through it, slammed it shut and pulled down the plank that crossed over locking it.

The prince's roars were barely audible through the thick wood, and became less so as she streaked down the stairs.

Chapter Three

In the field, Kazak Adarken fenced and parried, then moved on to lance practice, and later to javelin throwing then onto hand-to-hand combat with his men.

In the cosseting warm day, knee-deep in grass, wheat fields wafting to the east, buffeted by pillars of glossy forest, the men, and a few women, sweated, grunted, groaned as they battled each other.

They worked hours upon hours of practice before Kazak allowed a break. Sweat pouring down his face, dragging his fingers through his long hair, he headed to a well.

Dipping a cloth in a bucket of water, he drew it over his wet face, scrubbing the thick dark beard, then rubbed it over the black mop that waved just past his shoulders.

Peeling off his chainmail and leather vest, he dipped the cloth in the bucket again, and wiped down his arms and bare chest, then pulled a dry shirt over his head. A shout drew his attention.

Two warriors on horseback clopped into the yard stirring the dirt into dust puffs.

"Liege," one laughed, "you should see. We were coming in from past the plum orchards when over the far hill we saw a…" His eyes darted back and forth with mirth and mischief,

12

and a bit of wonder. "You won't believe, but we saw a *zăna-a-a* bloody fairy-"

"Nay," the other warrior disagreed shaking his head, "it was an elfje, a *mica creatură*, a wee creature, Liege."

The first warrior argued, "Nay, could have been a *zburătoare-*"

"Nay, fool, it was not a damned flying bird-"

"*Basta!*" Kazak barked in a mixed guttural language. "Your bickering gives me a headache." He tossed the cloth on the mortared edge of the well.

Beside him, Bo said to the men, "Why do you care if there is a bird or a fairy or an elf, or whatever-the-fuck is out there?"

The first warrior responded, face aglow, "Because it was colorful, beautiful, a vibrant female on horseback, whisking over the hilltops with hair the color of the brightest sun waving behind her."

Frowning, Kazak said, "A stranger in the area our men did not detect?" Heading for his steed, voice of cold, rough iron, he barked, "And you let it go, and did *nu* ring the alarm?"

The second warrior watching his lord, more like an ireful bear stalking to the stable, he called out, his voice shaky with impending fear of future discipline, "There were others chasing after it, her, whatever it was. But," gulping nervously, "it suddenly disappeared, so we came to tell you about it-"

Kazak was already at the stables.

Soon he was racing as one with his stallion, **Falium**, across the farmland, and through the meadows filled with violet wildflowers then to the foothills.

Eyes as sharp as an eagle's, he scanned the hillside but saw nothing except villagers gathering berries, and a small crowd of men on foot and horseback meandering in and out of the thinly treed woods bordering part of the fields.

Kazak slowed his horse, gaze flicking from trees lavish with thick leaves to the softly rounded foothills. He saw nothing like the soldiers described. No elf, no fairy, no colorful bird on horseback.

He shook his head, crimson ire burned up the back of his neck at the foolish warriors. Wiping a hand across his thickly ridged brow, he cursed, "They will feel the lash of the whip, the bastards-"

Wait, one of the males traveling about on horseback in a group, a young boy, shot a nervous look at him under the bill of his cap, then quickly averted his gaze.

Too many battles burned under Kazak's weathered skin to not feel the tingle of suspicion trickle along his broad shoulders.

"Tck tck," his tongue clicked, spurring the horse to move. A slight knee to the side directed the horse in the direction of the boy. The stallion hardly took a few steps in that direction when the boy suddenly bolted from the loose group of men.

Kazak's heels jammed into the horse's belly and Falium took off like a flash of black lightening.

The boy had a good head start on Kazak, he was already over the first hill and bounding towards the cover of woods. But he was a piss-poor rider.

Falium streaked across the land as if he had wings.

The boy made it to the grove of trees.

Used to the pounding of Falium's hooves, Kazak finely-tuned his ears to the separate sound of the fleeing horse's galloping steps and easily followed the horse and rider.

Darting around trees, Kazak quickly caught sight of the boy.

He was clinging to his horse with a death grip, bouncing and jerking as the horse took off on its own, coming back out of the woods to run on the waves of flowing grass.

The reins snapping on his back, Falium turned sharply to follow the boy.

Within seconds, Kazak was riding alongside the boy. He caught a flash of huge, round, terrified orbs glowing green at him before the boy futilely tried to turn his steed away and rush back into the woods.

Falium's hooves pounded beside the boy. When their stirrups knocked together, the burst of terrified green surged as the boy struggled to maintain control of his mare.

Horseflesh battered against horseflesh, long tails stuck straight out with their speed, and Kazak reached out with long powerful arms and snatched the boy right off his horse, dropping him hard on the saddle in front of him.

The boy was so small and slender he fit between the butt of horn and Kazak's strong thighs.

Kazak's lips pursed at the scream the boy emitted, high and piercing as a girl's. Holding the young man against his hard chest, his broad hand clasping the panicked boy against him, he felt a weird softness.

Worse than weird, it caused his groin to suddenly burn. Even the most privileged of young men in their neck of the woods was taut and muscled with battle practice, but this boy was soft.

Pulling gently on the reins, Kazak slowed his horse. The shock of green glowing eyes and the delicateness of his captive confused him. He moved his arm around the lad to hold him tighter lest he attempt escape, and was astonished at the big lump he felt under his hard hand.

Before he could register it, the boy wrenched from his arms, and dropped hard to the ground.

He cried out, apparently injuring himself, but nonetheless was up and running, well, hobbling, towards the forest.

His bewilderment growing, Kazak slid off his steed and easily stalked after the lad.

The boy younger and smaller and obviously injured, Kazak quickly caught up with him.

When he grabbed his arm, the lad squealed and burst into a frenzy of punching, kicking, twisting, emitting a few English words said so frantically Kazak couldn't grasp them.

Grumbling a string of foul curses, Kazak had a mind to slam his fist into the lad's head, a good pop and as frail as he was, the kid would be out like a light, if he survived the blow.

Instead, he wrapped an arm around the boy's waist, hugged his back to his chest and lifted him up off his feet. He barely weighed a stone he was so light. Kazak could feel thin hands struggling to pull Kazak's arm off him.

"Calm the *føkk* down," Kazak commanded in his own language knowing it was unlikely the lad understood what he said.

The boy arched his back, tried to kick Kazak and attempted to slam his head into Kazak's.

But the lad was half Kazak's height and weight. Even if Kazak hadn't easily dodged and blocked his blows, the boy's attempts at strikes would have been like a fly swatting him.

"*Basta*," Kazak's deep voice a harsh rasp in the boy's ear, "enough." In thick mixed dialects he warned, "You fight me, I break you." Roping an arm around him and over his arms, Kazak gripped the boy's jaw and held it up, holding his chin hard in the air.

The lad kicked harder and screamed through his jaw clenched tight with Kazak's hand, "Let go of me!"

That weird feeling zinged up his spine, Kazak paused, then dropped to his knees laying the boy not gently on the ground on his back and straddled him.

The boy immediately tried to sit up and punched ineffectively at Kazak with gritted screams.

Kazak leaned over, staking the lad's wrists to the ground and glared at him. He ordered in heavily accented broken English, "Nay move."

His eyes drifted from the face blotched with dirt, so much it appeared to have been deliberately placed there, down the very slender neck, over the pulse pounding as the lad gulped hard and rapid, down to his waist-length jacket buttoned up tight.

Under the jacket, his chest rising and falling with his frantic breaths, looked funny, odd.

Kazak's gaze swept back up and was taken aback by the delicate bones of the boy's face. The high, round, childlike cheekbones, and he felt that peculiar tingle in his groin at the very small, perfect bow-shaped lush-as-hell lips.

Tearing his eyes away, he raised them to the lad's own terrified, crystalized sea-green orbs fringed in the longest lashes the warlord had ever seen, all the way to the curled ends that fluttered frantically over the frightened eyes.

With a grunt, Kazak sat up, gripped the lad's jacket with both hands and ripped it and the shirt beneath open. His pupils blazed at the linen breast-band that was wrapped so tight, full breasts mounded over the rim, Kazak wondered that he- she- could draw a breath.

He grabbed the stranger's hat, yanked it off and dropped it. Long, vivid yellow curls tumbled out. The boy-girl-squealed and thrashed anew.

Kazak could see why, and now understood those burning spikes to his manhood as he loomed over the obvious female who lay grunting, squealing, struggling to throw Kazak off her.

With every punch, and bucking writhe she made, the fair breasts bobbled even in the tight band, holding Kazak's attention.

Seeing the heat flaring in his ice-blue eyes, and the dark color spreading up his neck, under the layer of dirt her own cheeks flamed crimson. Kazak leaned over pinning her hands back to the ground over her head.

"Who you?" his guttural question ground out, aware he was barely intelligible to her.

He spoke many languages, but he hadn't been around a lot of English speaking people in his rough life and was well out of practice with that language.

At first, confusion laced through her fear. Then by the way her lashes lowered over those striking eyes, and the turn of her head, Kazak could see she grasped his question, and clearly had no intentions of answering him.

Kazak lowered his body over hers to partially cover her, holding her in place with his weight. Long, hard fingers gripped her jaw, holding it roughly, stiffly. His face already hard as chiseled granite didn't change, but his brilliant blue eyes darkened with impatient wrath.

"One time more," he muttered harshly, squeezing her tender flesh with the hard pads of his fingertips. Feeling her squirm beneath him, not a good move on her part as the friction heated his manhood, he demanded, "Name?"

If possible, the sea-green goblets grew wider with renewed fear at the harshness of his voice and the hard grip of his fingers.

Or maybe it was the other part of him that was growing bigger, longer, harder pressing against her thigh that made her struggle more frantically to push him off her.

He was like an ox, she couldn't budge him a hair. Except for the grunts from her struggles, the tiny, lush lips stayed firmly closed.

Kazak allowed himself a moment to lay his hard body on hers. She wasn't sturdy and strong like most of the women he dealt with.

He felt the fullness of her soft breasts frantically panting, pressing into the heaviness of his rock solid chest. The pure femininity of her flat belly, slender legs struggling, entwined in the musculature of his thighs.

Her girlish breathy gasps and whimpers as she fluttered desperately against him like the beautiful fairy they'd called her, the delicate scent of her soaked into his every pore.

The feel of her so heady, his body felt on fire, and heavy as lead, he couldn't, didn't want to move.

She paused in her struggles when he stuck a hand in a bunch of her curls. Feeling the silken tresses between his fingers, he crushed them in his fist and lifted them to his face and breathed in deeply.

Kazak was drowning in this girl. This exquisite, foreign fairy was encompassing all of his senses. The fire building inside of him threatened to quickly push him out of control. He was going blind and deaf with lust. He nudged a knee between her thighs and pushed them apart.

Falling into those frightened sea crystals, under lids heavy with arousal, he watched the flair of a new kind of terror strike her dirty face as his burgeoning manhood dug against her sex.

But, she was fighting so hard to get free she was harming herself.

Blinking back his lust, "*Bună*- ah, fine," Kazak grunted, rolling off her and to his feet. He jerked her up with him.

A cry of pain and her legs buckled.

19

Kazak struck his arm around her to steady her, and saw her face crease in pain as she favored her left leg.

"Serves right." He swung her up in his arms and trudged to his waiting horse, grumbling, "*Prost fată*, stupid girl jumps off moving horse, deserves hurt."

She continued to struggle as he carried her, but he ignored her as if she was just a pesky flea squirming in his big arms.

When he reached his steed, he threw her over his shoulder. With her squeal against his back, he mounted Falium then dropped her in front of him.

He wrapped a steel arm around her and over her arms roping them to her sides, this time she would not be jumping from the horse. His heels jabbed in, and Falium bolted for the compound.

Twisting side-to-side, "Let me go!" she screeched. "You have no right!" Her words were haughty and brave, but her back trembled against his chest.

Feeling him stiffen and his head bow, she peered a glance at him, he was staring down at her exposed breasts. "How dare you! Stop!" She jerked and tried to throw her body, which only made her full flesh bounce more.

If he kept her restrained as she was and her half-bared bosom joggling over his arm, Kazak would have her back off the horse, tossed flat on the ground and him impaled deep inside her.

Reluctantly, Kazak slowed the horse and moved his arm to her lower belly, freeing her hands.

She immediately buttoned the few buttons he hadn't torn off her blouse, and on the filthy jacket.

Chapter Four

Crushed against the fiend's powerful chest, Cini tried to quell her fear. She had done fairly well until now.

She had slipped through a secret passageway, and dressed as a male she was able to sneak away from her village and flee down the countryside using the woods as cover.

All she had to do, she figured, was get to the emperor and ask for his help in fighting Prince Andreyev.

Her mistake, she chastised herself ruefully, was stopping to bathe in the creek. She'd forgotten to put her cap back on and those horrible soldiers had seen her and chased her.

She thought she'd made it to safety when she blended in with the group of village men near the hills, then this- this-creature, saw her, captured her.

Cini didn't dare look at him. She didn't want to see the murderous glint in his uncanny blue eyes. Under the thick low ridge of his brow, they were so much brighter behind the foil of shaggy dark hair and thick beard.

He'd snarled and growled at her, spoke some sort of strange language like a barbaric heathen, and had shoved her on her back.

A blush warmed her face as she recalled his fearsomely hard warrior's body covering hers. The way he stared at her breasts like a rapacious gorilla all huge and strong and hirsute.

His harsh face was as expressionless as slate, but the wolfish sheen was clear in those freakish blue eyes, such a vivid color amidst the enveloping dark, cold, sheer hardness of him.

The blush deepened with anger at him taking her, and her violated modesty when he gaped unashamedly at her half-bared breasts. And fear, she feared the beast was going to bite her, chew on her, gobble her up like a troll under a bridge.

Even now she could still feel his…manhood, the blush darkened, pressing against her. She'd talked with other girls; she knew what it meant when a man's rod hardened. Then she had a new fear, that he would viciously rape her, likely kill her after.

But he had tossed her on his horse and was apparently bringing her to his home-base. Maybe he planned to share her with other apes in his cave then cook her up, skin her and eat her.

People tending to baskets of pulled vegetables, stoking fires, children playing, stopped what they were doing and stared at the woman on the horse with the massive, brutish animal crushing her with his heavy arm.

The beast dismounted. When he reached up for her, several men approached.

Instead of pulling her down, he took a length of rope from a saddlebag and tied her wrists together then handed the reins and the rope to a stableman speaking in Russian.

Cini only understood a few Russian words but the creature was obviously ordering the stableman to not let her flee. He stood between Cini on the horse and the soldiers. He wore but a plain linen shirt, breeches and boots, his big hands sat on lean hips.

The men clustered around him, blocking his way.

"We saw her first, we want her, Şef Adarken," one man spoke in Russian. His greedy gaze stroked over Cini from head to toe, lingering crudely on the swell of her bosom.

The beast had torn most of the buttons off the jacket and the shirt beneath she had worn so tightly to hide her breasts, and now they swelled out of the confines of the jacket.

The beast casually gazed from one man to the next, there were seven of them. Black hair hanging down his back ruffling in the wind, thick beard and low brow hiding his expression, his voice a deep burr, he ordered gruffly in Russian, "Get the *føkk* out of my way."

A crowd was gathering to watch the action. One of them translated in English to his friend beside him.

The men shuffled, glanced at one another.

The first man said roughly, "No Şef, you have the pick of women from coast to coast, go take another. This one is ours. I will take her from your horse."

Skewing a sly sneer at his men, he started towards the horse and said to the beast Adarken, "Make no waves, Şef, and we won't hurt you."

Strutting up to Adarken, the man started around him when the Şef, the chief, Adarken shot out his fist straight into the man's throat.

A gack sound, eyes bulged, his tongue stuck out and the man fell to the ground, dead.

"What the-" One of the other men yelled, "You killed Randall, you bastard! Get him, boys!" He and the other five men rushed Adarken.

High up on the huge horse, Cini clung to the short horn watching wide-eyed as the Şef slammed his boot into the first man's stomach. When he bent double with an *"Oof-"* Adarken swung and kicked him in the temple, he collapsed dead to the ground.

The remaining five jumped at Adarken swinging. The Şef elbowed one in the nose breaking it, bashed his fist into the next one's face, then grabbed him by the neck swung him around and slammed his head into the third man's head so hard the sound cracked through the air.

Kazak finished them off until all the men but one lay sprawled either dead or dazed on the hard earth.

The last man froze, standing on quivering legs, the smell of urine rose as his wet breeches darkened.

Calmly, the beast stood behind the first dazed man on the ground, bent, gripped his head and snapped it, then did the same to the second and the third, the fourth. As he turned to the fifth, the still standing man held up his quaking hands.

"Please, Lord Adarken, Şef, - prime *dominio* of Emperor Radisalvo's royal band of warriors. I beg you, mercy, please, I'm sorry, have mercy," tears streamed down his face.

Adarken steadily stomped to him, as the man cried out, "Mercy!"

Adarken twisted his head, snapping his neck. Releasing the man, he didn't watch as the corpse dropped to the ground.

Wiping his hands on his breeches, the beast tossed back his long mane, and apparently muttered to a guard to take care of the bodies. He strode to his steed and reached up, and untied Cini.

A sound escaped her contracted lungs, and she swooned from the horse into his murderous arms.

Chapter Five

$\mathbb{K}$azak carried her across the compound, ignoring the shocked looks the villagers gave him.

Reaching the castle, he strode up the ramp to enter through the huge open doors.

Everyone busy inside stopped what they were doing to stare.

The stone manor was five stories with numerous wings, turrets and chimneys. Soldiers swarmed about, eyes hard on the girl the lord carried, leaving it clear their desire for her even unconscious and as dirty as she was.

Kazak started for his chambers. As he hit the stone staircase, his friend, Bo, lurched alongside him.

Peering at the girl Kazak held, Bo spoke in their native tongue, "Kaz, you bringing the voman into the castle? You don't know who she is, she could be a *føkkunn* assassin or something."

Kazak glanced down at the delicate, soft, very young woman in his arms then up at blond haired Bo without comment.

"Gah, Kaz, killers can come in small gorgeous packages. Where are you taking her?" The staircase was wide enough for both massive men to walk together, their heavy boots clomping in unison on the stone steps.

"To my chambers."

"What? Why?"

Kazak lowered his eyes drily at his friend.

Chuckling, "*Da*, who wouldn't want to *føkk* something that beautiful, even as dirty as she is, she's ravishing. But, you don't know her." Bo hurried to keep up with Kazak's long quick stride.

"What if she refuses you? Unusual though it is for a warlord, you've never resorted to forcing a woman. You've never had to."

One broad shoulder shrugged, Kazak replied, "As you say, they've never said no before." He strode away from Bo as he grinned at Kazak, and headed down the opposite corridor.

Towards the end of the hall, a woman in a frilly white cap and apron bowed as Kazak approached.

"Sarah, come with me," he commanded.

Her lips pursed in instant nerves. She slid a quick glance at the unconscious woman in his arms, and stayed at his heels until he reached his rooms.

As another women in an apron and bonnet came down the hall, speaking in Mongolian, Kazak said to Sarah, "Get the door," and to the second maid, "come."

Both servants quickly, nervously complied.

Sarah opened the seven-foot tall, heavy wooden door.

"Come," the warlord commanded again as he entered the room. The women reluctantly followed him.

The large room was more round than square. Because like most castles there were two walls, both of stone, mortar and rubble core with a space between them and dug into the bedrock for stability, it was warm inside.

Cini and the Beast

The walls were covered with light colored lime and sand plaster making it feel cozier than the hard grey stone.

Inside, Kazak laid his prisoner on his bed. Staring down at the girl, he said to Sarah, "She should waken soon."

Studying the fatigue in the unconscious woman's face under the grime, and the dark circles under her eyes, he looked at one of her arms flung beside her head. Even in the jacket he could see her limbs were quite on the thin side.

In a mix of Romanian and Mongolian with some Turkish thrown in, he said, "When she wakes, you are to bathe her and find her something to wear. Something…light."

The two servants stared round-eyed at him and then looked to the sleeping girl and back to him. He started for the door. "Once she is dressed, put her in my bed."

Ignoring their duo of eyebrows arching in shock at the impropriety, and she's also a foreign stranger, and- he strode to the door and walked out, locking it behind him.

Chapter Six

Her lids flickered as Cini stirred. Realizing she was in bed, she smiled as her eyes cracked open slightly. Thank goodness, she was finally home- she gasped, her lashes flew wide.

She wasn't in her room. Without moving, her gaze traveled the dimmed room. It was not lavish, but luxurious nonetheless. A large room, all stone with tapestries on the plastered walls for decoration and warmth, and braided rugs on the stone floor.

Seeing the heavy furniture in dark wood, her brows drew down as her eyes opened further, it was obviously a male's room.

What in heaven? Afraid to, but she turned her head slowly and about fainted again. There was a man lying next to her. And not just any man. It was the heathen, the beast.

Cini shot up in the bed pulling the covers to her chin and gawked at him.

He was asleep. Under his shirt, she could see that massive chest rising and falling in a slow, deep rhythm. She looked down at herself and sucked in a breath of relief. She was dressed.

Then she frowned, but she wasn't wearing her clothes. Cini plucked at the gauzy material, the likes she'd never seen. The material was light, but although white, it was opaque, thank goodness.

As quickly as she could, making as little movement as possible, she swung her legs to the edge of the bed and carefully slid off and to her bare feet. Her heart hammering, she glanced at the gorilla lying there.

Although it was hard to tell under all that shaggy hair and beard, he still seemed to be asleep. As the curious thought moved through her mind as to why he would put her in his bed, clothed, a shiver ran up her spine, whatever the reason, she needed to get out of there.

She padded silently to the door, grabbed the big handle and pulled. It did not move. She tried again, pulling harder, then she yanked at it with a grunt. Nothing. It was locked.

Panic jangled in her belly as she frantically looked around the room. Huge dark wood furniture, obviously he needed it big, the beast was huge himself as all gorillas would be.

She saw an open door and scurried over and ducked into the room. It was a bathing room. An enormous tub was surrounded by soaps and large drying cloths, and a tiny fireplace to heat the water.

It had a modern garderobe, a seat built into the stone wall for personal waste that went directly down a chute to a deep stream that flowed to a fast river. What she wanted was a window or a door. Cini hurried back out.

She peeked over at him, he hadn't moved. Looking around, she saw a window. Hmm, the beast must be wealthy to have real glass. Normally, thin strips of horn or linens soaked in tallow or resin were used.

On the walls there were several lanterns with seed oil keeping them at a low, wavering orange glow.

She ran to the window and immediately tried to push the two copper-lined panes apart. But like the door, it was frozen. Stuffing her growing fright, she skimmed her hands all around the frame searching for a way to unlock them, but could find nothing.

Cini swung around quickly to make sure the heathen still slept. It appeared he did. The men he had slaughtered, she remembered with a shiver of grisly terror, had called him Şef, which seemed to mean Chief. How could that animal be head of those soldiers? Of the village?

Shaking her head in confusion, she scanned the dresser and saw long pieces of wood. Beside the bed the beast had set his sword to lean against the wall. Cini knew how heavy those were to lift. She'd have too hard of a time lifting it high enough to break it through the window.

She spotted a vase on a table. Again the thought that he was wealthy strummed through her buzzing brain. So few peasants these days had furniture, most had hay beds on the floor.

She hurried to the dresser and picked up the vase. "Oh yes," Cini murmured to herself. The piece of pottery was fairly heavy; she should be able to break the window with it.

She didn't even want to look out and see how high up she was, she'd cross that bridge on how to get down when she reached it. Right now, the window.

Tiptoeing to the window, she held the vase with both hands over her head, and swung- it halted in mid-bash.

Fear tingled and crept over Cini's skin, she could feel him behind her.

Even though he didn't touch her, his heat, energy, virile strength, enveloped her. She felt the vase plucked from her hands. She didn't want to turn around. She gripped the window ledge to steady her shaking legs, and then slowly turned.

He loomed larger, and more dangerous than she had remembered. He set the vase on a table.

The creature deliberately looked at the wood blocks on the dresser and his sword by the bedside with an arched brow, as if to ask why didn't she brain him with a board or stab his heart with the sword?

The terrified, innocent look on her face revealed none of that had ever entered her head. Only escaping, not harming.

Her body vibrating with fear, Cini crossed her arms to still the shaking.

The beast's feet were silent on the rugs as he moved to the bed. He looked pointedly at it then at her.

Cini's eyes darted around the room searching for any means of escape. She felt like the mouse trapped in a cage with the snake. There was nowhere to go. She stared at him without moving.

Adarken gestured to the bed, he grunted, "In, remove, ah," he struggled for the word, "gown." His deep, masculine voice gruff with stunted, heavily accented English, he regarded her under low lids.

Shaking her head, Cini edged to the door, keeping a wide berth between them. Her voice slightly trembling, she tried to sound cool, "No. I'll be leaving now." Reaching the door, she grabbed at the handle and again tugged uselessly on it, the door would not open.

Leaning her back against the door, her hands clinging to the handle, she demanded, "Open the door, right now."

His blue eyes now dark as midnight, leisurely strolled slowly from the top of her messy blonde curls, over her breasts and down her slender body, then made the trail back up. "In," he growled, nodding to the bed.

Scowling when she shook her head, he trod towards her.

Cini held a hand up, as if she could really stop him. "No. I insist you open this door and let me out!"

When he stalked nearer to her, she moved to the side hoping he would just unlatch the door and let her go. Instead, he slung out a hand and grabbed the back of her neck. She squealed and jumped.

He pulled her towards him, until she was almost pressed up against him. He bent and pushed his face into her hair. His iron fingers gripping her neck, he sniffed her hair, her neck. His hand shifted to her nape, moving her hair aside, he lowered his mouth.

His lips and fingers lingered on her nape as if he were going to sink his canines into her flesh, hold her down immobile, like a wild jungle cat would while he took her, rough, violent, savage.

"Stop!" Cini put her hands to his wide chest. Feeling the slabs of rock under her palms, she shivered with the utter strength of him and pushed as hard as she could. He didn't budge.

He stroked a hand down her back, and held her neck with the other while he licked her skin, sucked on her flesh as if actually, literally tasting her. He bit her jaw as he moved up to capture her mouth.

"No!" she shrieked shoving at him.

The behemoth stopped. A low growl rumbled in his chest. He lifted his big head, the dark eyes heavy and hooded perused her.

She was rigid with terror, eyes wide as green moons. Her tiny hands hit and pushed in vain at his huge chest.

His hands dropped. Taking a step back, behind strands of black hair, blue eyes glittered with menace. His voice deeply guttural, he growled, "We *førk*."

Blinking at him, it took her a second to interpret his filthy word. The crude pig said fuck. She took the opportunity to move away from him, shaking her head vehemently. "No, leave me alone." She peered up at him under those long yellow lashes, he looked confused.

"Nay?" His harsh eyes narrowed, apparently surprised she said no.

Wrapping her arms protectively around her body, she lowered her head and shook it again, curls bounced around her, "No," she whispered. Holding her breath, if he was the beast she thought he was, he would ignore her protests and leap on her.

His silence drew her covered gaze. She could see the lethality of him tightly leashed. It was apparent in the flexing of his biceps even under the shirt, and the working of his jaw that he struggled to restrain himself. His blue eyes darkened inscrutable.

An angry animal sound gnashing in his throat, he grabbed her upper arm and marched her to the door. The lock was way up, way over her head, even on a chair she would be hard pressed to reach it.

He slid it to the side, opened the door, and pulled her out and down the corridor. Positive he was now going to kill her, Cini tried to dig her feet into the braided rugs, pull her arm from his hold, but he had fingers of steel and she couldn't slow him down one iota.

He dragged her through the dark, vast castle, past anyone who paused to gawk at them. He took her down the stairs then along a long corridor to another chamber. Surprisingly, he knocked on the wood door. It took a minute before it opened.

The woman who answered appeared shocked to see him. She instantly bowed her head. "My Liege," she whispered.

Adarken pushed Cini inside and released her. In a mix of languages, he ordered, "Get her a bed, a cloak and shoes," and he pivoted and strode out the door slamming it behind him.

Her head spinning, Cini stood awkwardly, her eyes flipping around the room.

Dozens of women, lying, well, now sitting, on small beds lining both sides of the room, were staring wide-eyed at her. Even with a swift, uncomfortable scan of the room, she could tell she was in the female servants' quarters.

"Uh, Miss," Sarah said, just as awkward gestured to an empty bed. "You, ah, may have this one, and um, I will see to the master's other, uh, orders." Pink streaking her narrow cheeks, she tucked grey hair up in her bonnet and scurried off to get Cini a cloak and shoes.

When Sarah returned with the items, Cini was sitting on the edge of the goose-down mattress.

Everyone still stared; no one said a word to her. Sarah handed her the items, then said with a twitter in her voice, in English, "There is sage and salt tooth powder and other…needs, in the bath," she nodded to an archway.

"Uh, if you require anything else, that is, until morning, please don't worry to ask me." She shifted from one foot to the other pinching agitatedly at the long skirt of her nightgown.

Cini blinked at her, struggling to calm her swirling mind. "Uh, yes, thank you."

Sarah stood for a moment, when Cini said nothing else, she smiled, nodded, and went to her own bed.

Cini sat for a long time in the dark contemplating. Should she try to make a run for it now, in the dead, pitch black of the night, or wait and see what tomorrow brings?

Exhausted, she decided she needed sleep to plan what to do next.

After fitful sleep with terrible dreams of a big, furry, fierce grizzly with huge sharp teeth chasing her, feeling a shake of her arm, Cini finally pushed her weary eyes open.

Sarah was standing there. The look on her face showed she had been undecided how to wake the new woman. To not be at your station at the right time could mean lashings.

She handed Cini a thicker gown, underwear that tied on either side of the hips with strings, and socks. She said quietly, "The Master says to put you with the inside maids. Please, as soon as you complete your, uh, morning absolutions, come with me."

As soon as Cini cleaned and dressed, Sarah led her outside and down several halls to the main kitchen.

Along the way the older woman whispered in her ear, "Ignore the snipes you will hear. All of the servants must work their way up from the fields, mines, barns, everywhere outside work entails before being promoted to working inside the castle. It is the easiest, and of course, most comfortable place to work. The other girls will be infuriated that he, that is, the lord, has brought you in. I mean, a stranger and all…" she trailed off.

"Sarah, I am not a servant or a slave. I am a free women to come and go as I please."

Sarah cringed, "Please, shh, don't say that, it could cost you at the least, lashes to your back, and the most," her eyes winced, "your head."

Chapter Seven

Outside, Kazak was with his warriors practicing hand-to-hand combat, fencing, sword fighting, everything a warrior would need to survive in the most vicious of battles.

It was hard, grueling, endlessly painful work, and Kazak loved it. He was a physical being, he didn't like being in his head. He liked being outside, submitting his body to the hard work.

The pain of a sword slicing him or a kick at his head were only training to him, to keep him in optimum facility.

After midday, he led a troop of warriors south along the *Ită Cale,* the Spider Thread Trails. The trade route the emperor had sent him to protect from bandits.

Several days had passed since they'd taken out the last band of robbers. Now, not even five miles from the keep they came across a new gang of bandits attacking merchants on the trail.

With a battle cry, a roar that shook the branches on the trees and sent birds frantically soaring into the horizon, Kazak charged into the thick of the fray.

With only a dagger in one hand, within minutes, before the others even reached him, he had torn the bandits into bloody, pulpy, pieces

"Gods be damned, Kaz," Bo, Kazak's second in command and best friend since they met in military camp at age eight, bellowed.

Kazak had been at the camp since he was around four.

Bo, stolen from his family at six or so was hurled into the wretched existence. The only life actually, that Kazak had ever known. Bo had some recollection of his family, Kazak had none. He knew of no other life than the jungles and the military.

"You could have waited for the rest of us, you son of a bitch," Bo chastised his friend cheerfully.

Wiping the gushed blood of the dead from his face, Kazak started back to the trail, muttering, "Next time you fools will be quicker."

Following him with a grin, Bo winked at the other warriors that fell in line behind them.

Returning to the castle, weary from days of battle, the men trudged in for the large noonday meal. A lighter fare would come later in the eve.

Kazak was not a fan of seeing a mud-caked hand dipping into his trencher, or having to smell a hundred unwashed, sweaty bodies. As leader of the realm, he made the rules.

There were dozens of fresh water beds, hot springs and pools that streamed under the land where they could constantly draw clean water, and Kazak declared all must bathe daily, or face the consequences.

The soldiers griped and grumbled, complaining that washing was for girls, and that the caked on dirt protected them from disease. But no one dared deny the commander. He would just as soon take off a head as argue with it. So, basic cleanliness was the rule of the castle.

The men gathered at the long wooden tables, plunking down on benches and waited for the serving girls to bring the food.

Keeping his head down, Kazak only raised his eyes surreptitiously looked for...her. The girl he captured. His prisoner. He had fought the picture of those huge green eyes floating in front of his face the entire expedition of the last few days.

What had been going on with her while he'd been gone, stuck in his craw like a needling wasp. He'd had guards placed on her, and ordered Sarah to keep her in the kitchen or women's quarters at all times, away from Stelpha's clutches.

He'd worried Stelpha, the head of the female servants would get her hands on the little female and see her harmed, if not for her breathtaking beauty, then for the favoritism Kazak had shown her. First by bringing her into the castle, then to his bed, then to work inside when she had denied him.

The lines around his eyes sharpened in a squint as he realized he'd mentally used the word, worry. When had he ever, in his lifetime, used that word?

It was that bitch, his teeth grit. She had said no to him. A first. Normally he practically had to swat women away like pesky gnats to keep them off him.

He had finally put locks on his chamber door after coming back night after night of patrolling to find a female uninvited waiting for him, naked, in his bed.

He did not like women coming to him uninvited, and he sure as hell did not want them in his chambers, much less his bed. When he wanted sex, he sought it on his terms.

Sure, he needed the same release as other men, but he did not want more than the act. Last thing he wanted was a woman clinging to him, sleeping in his bed, nagging him.

His lip quirked. The girl, he still looked for her but hadn't yet seen her. He didn't fear she'd fled, he'd arranged guards on her.

When he captured her, he had put her in his bed when she was unconscious. For the life of him, he didn't know why.

Maybe the way she'd fought him like a little wildcat when he took her gave him a clue she might not be willing, and he figured if she was already half undressed and in his bed when she woke that she might just automatically...spread them.

But now, he was beyond livid that she had been pissed, and scared, and had ultimately refused him. Fine, the little bitch can make due in the servants' quarters. He didn't care.

"Hey, Kaz," Bo nudged him with his elbow as he slid in next to him, "where's your little catch? She still lounging in your bed?" He accepted a beor, a pungent beer, from a flirtatious serving girl.

She had most of the buttons of her peasant's top undone and the blouse spread wide open, and was bending so Bo could enjoy her wares, and he was.

The dark blond warrior kept the lethality of his essence tucked well behind dark blue eyes that always twinkled with mischief. Tall, with broad heavy shoulders like his Liege, his friend, Kazak, Bo was also usually deluged with the womankind of Salbaji Keep. The two men hadn't had a chance at private conversation for days.

They spoke in a blend of Romanian and Russian. "Nay. I put her with Sarah. She will be indoor *bwän*, servant." Kazak took a big swig of his own bowl of beor.

"Huh? What? I can't believe you could tear yourself from that unbelievable piece of feminine flesh. How-" Bo's eyes narrowed at his friend. "Ah, she denied you."

He watched Kazak and grinned at the dour turn of his full but relentlessly scowling mouth. "She did! I can't believe it!

39

That is sure a first, huh? A female turning down the big bad *dominio*. And one of the juiciest, most fetching women I have ever-" He broke off as Kazak's scowl deepened.

At that moment, Cini entered the room. Her spine was straight, but her head lowered as she shyly, anxiously scanned the room she was in for the first time.

The curly blonde hair was pulled back in a twist down her back with a bonnet on her head. She wore the brown gown and white apron of the female servants, and every eye, male and female alike, was on her.

She awkwardly carried a tray with bowls of food on it, keeping her eyes on the tray as she made her way to the first table.

"Aye, *da*, yes," Bo took a deep breath. "Hell, *mea frățe*, my brother, I wouldn't kick that out of my bed. And I sure the *føkk* wouldn't let her say no. But, since you don't want her," he made to stand up; Kazak grabbed his sleeve and yanked him back down.

Thumping back down with a humph and a grin, Bo said, "All right, I'll wait for her to get over here. But," his brows wriggled up and down, "she might not make it here before someone else claims her. Really, Kaz, as your friend, I really should keep the brawling down and take her myself now."

He moved to stand again, Kazak snarled, "Sit. Down. Keep your grubbing hands to yourself. No one-" he broke off.

Cini was removing the bowls from the tray to set them on the table when a soldier reached out and grabbed her wrist, pulled her to him, then yanked her on his lap.

Furious, Cini thrashed to get up.

The man laughed and held her down, she punched at him. Her futile struggles only made him laugh louder. He said,

"Come pretty one, I take you to my room," he pushed his hand up her skirt.

Panic in her slaps at him, Cini fought his leeching hands. One hand up her skirt, the other clutched her face, he put his lips on hers forcing his tongue in her mouth.

Then, his head suddenly lurched back, it was wrenched back so hard his neck arched on the edge of breaking.

"Release her," Kazak snarled, his fist twisted in the man's hair, he kept pulling even after a sickening snap sounded.

The man's arms fell away. Kazak snatched up Cini's wrist and jerked her off his lap. He hustled her to the kitchen.

When they reached the kitchen, the beast found Sarah and blew a streak of guttural curses at her.

His grip so hard, Cini pried at his fingers, trying to open them. His foul spiel done, he shoved Cini at Sarah then stalked from the room.

"Oh dear," Sarah murmured. "He said I am to keep you in here, only women are allowed in this section of the kitchen. I'm sorry my dear, I don't understand, but then," she shrugged narrow shoulders, "it isn't my place to. Come, let me set you to peeling the vegetables."

After the eve's later light dinner, many of the warriors sprawled around the great room. A fire flickered its heat and light in a wall-sized stone fireplace.

A container of ale in one hand, a plant rolled cigar in the other, Kazak sat quietly listening to the others tell their war stories.

With the background of male rumblings and the occasional shout of ribald laughter, although he fought it, his eyes constantly looked for her.

It wasn't until Sarah with a group of women, came into the great room to clean up after dinner, that Kazak saw her with them. He had earlier told Sarah she could bring the girl out of the kitchen only if he was present.

Sarah set her to cleaning the slates in the lower wooden shutters over the windows. Swilling his ale and sucking his cigar, his feet up, Kazak watched her work with Bo's snickering beside him.

A skinny young woman worked quietly with Cini. When the skinny girl went to move her bucket, the water sloshed onto the floor. Both women crouched at the same time to clean it up. But they weren't quick enough.

Stelpha, head of the female servants stormed over to them and walloped the skinny girl in the head. With a cry, the girl fell to the floor and Stelpha kicked her in her side.

Cursing the girl, Stelpha, with a heavy body like a bag of boulders and face to match, kicked her again spouting, "Useless whore, can't even clean a fucking window," and kicked her again. Kazak called out to Stelpha but she ignored him.

"Mistress!" Cini jumped up between the tough maidswoman and the girl crying on the floor with her arms wrapped around her body trying to block the savage kicks.

"Stop!" Cini shrieked, holding her hands up.

Stelpha hesitated, shocked that the girl would deign to speak to her much less try to stop her punishment of the clumsy girl. Her bulky face darkened with wrath, she reached for an iron pitcher on a table and lifted it to swing at Cini's head. Cini turned with an arm up to block the blow.

Already on his feet and halfway across the room, "Stelpha!" Kazak's shout instantly halted the furious woman's tirade.

She paused with the pitcher raised over Cini's head, turned her head slightly to look at Kazak in question.

He commanded in Russian, "You've been told not to beat the servants. Now, leave before I do to you what you did to the girl."

When Stelpha didn't move, he barked, "Now!"

Stelpha, with a ferocious sneer at Cini, and a promise of retribution in her eyes, spun and left the room.

Cini stood like a statue, blinking at the sudden violence that had erupted, and just as suddenly ended. Then she looked down at the skinny girl crying in a huddle on the floor, and bent to help her to her feet, whispering commiserating words to her.

With Bo's annoying chuckling in his ear, Kazak returned and plopped back down in his chair.

A woman with an extraordinarily huge bust and buttocks to match, sashayed into the great room from a hallway and seeing him, made her way straight to Kazak.

"Ah," Bo snickered, "here comes your future queen." His mocking grin widened at the irritated growl beside him.

The bodice of her pale pink gown scooped low to expose as much of her generous breasts that it could, the dress clung tightly all the way to her hips before it puffed to bell at her feet.

She strutted to Kazak, and when she reached him, sat down perching on his thighs. The woman had brunette hair that furled around her head and down over one shoulder.

She lifted a hand to stroke his face. "My Liege, Lord Kazak, when will you stop stalling and chose me to be your queen?"

"Huh," with a rude snort, Kazak turned his face from her caressing hand. Speaking in mixed languages he told the brazen woman, "I am not a king, Bonatella, so you cannot be a queen."

"Oh come now," Bonatella purred with a pout, "everyone knows when you have completed this assignment, the emperor has promised you a huge hunk of land over many territories and regions, and you will be titled king. Not a blood king," she sighed, not noticing the tightening of his brows, "but, a king is a king, right?"

Sliding a palm down over her ample bosom drawing his eyes to the exposed cleavage, she said, "And, you must admit, I would make a fine, a perfect queen. Don't you agree? I have the lineage to enhance yours, my lord."

Peripherally, Kazak could see the little woman he'd captured watching with disgust on her lovely face.

Before he could respond to Bonatella, the voluptuous woman grabbed his hand and set his palm on top of the huge swell of a breast.

"This," she cooed, wriggling under his hand, "could be yours, lord, every night, every day, you know you want me." Her other hand slid down to palm his manhood. "Ah, my lord, you are certainly huge all over, aren't you?"

Beside them, lounging in his large stuffed chair, Bo snickered, looking away with a grin when Bonatella shot a glare at him.

Half standing, Kazak roughly pushed Bonatella to get her off him. "Bonatella, I did not invite you to touch me, do not do so again," he growled in Romanian.

The abundantly curvy woman stumbled to her feet but caught her balance, pouted as if her feelings were hurt. "My Liege," she pretended to look around, whispered, "I know you don't want the other women to get jealous and into a snit so you can't...*yet*, claim you have chosen me."

She leaned over allowing the front of her gown to slip as low as it could go, a nipple was on the verge of popping out. "I am ready. Tis a wonder we women are drawn to your scarred, brooding, fiercely harsh face at all, but," she put a finger to her lower lip and let out a lusty moan.

"The violence of you, the sheer aggression that exudes from those masculine shoulders, those huge hands." She drew her palms from her breasts down her waist and over the big hips with a coo, "Gods I want to lie beneath you, let you pound-"

Bo made a gagging sound. He broke it off when Bonatella glared a threat at him again.

She wiggled her bust in Kazak's face and tugged his beard. "All right, sweetie, I'll see you later. Remember, my house is just down the street, you can pop in any time. Mam and Papi will be thrilled to welcome you!" She reached for his privates again.

Pushing at her before she could touch him, Kazak growled, "Bonatella, go."

She tottered off with a coy wave over her shoulder at him, and stuck her tongue out at Bo who laughed at her.

Kazak put his boots up on a hassock in front of his chair.

Bo groused, "Hell, *frăţe*, why do you let her climb all over you with that fat ass of hers? She's been pricked by so many men she's a damned pin cushion, she probably leaks!"

"*Yah, yah*, you try to keep her and the others off you, *føkkunn* vomen, like leeches." Kazak raked his sleeve across his face to erase the stench of her strong musk perfume while searching for the captive girl, but she had disappeared.

He made a move to get up to go look for her when she came out of the kitchen area and back into the main room.

Seeing Kazak no longer had that woman lying all over him with her hands grabbing at his privates, with a shudder, Cini set her cleaning rag down and approached Kazak.

Observing her coming towards him, his feet dropped to the floor and he sat up a bit straighter.

Bo's sly snickers grew louder.

Frowning at him, Kazak scowled at the girl. When she reached him, he grumbled a few words to Bo under his breath.

Nodding, Bo grinned cheerfully at Cini and said in English, "Lord Adarken wants to know if you have changed your mind about..." he looked a bit abashed. "Uh, his bedding you."

Kazak's face was completely blank as he impassively watched her response under hooded lids.

Her brows sprang to her hairline, then dropped in anger.

Glaring at Kazak, she said to Bo, "You tell your pig of a kidnapping chief, not for all the money in England, not if he were the last...*beast*, on earth. I would die before I let him put his filthy paws on me. And, I insist he let me go, let me leave this keep, right now."

Bo chuckled at the tightening of Kazak's jaw.

Kazak didn't speak English well but he understood it. He mumbled a few grunts with a scowl to Bo.

Bo started to translate, but Cini snapped angrily to him, "Can he not speak like a human?" She turned to Kazak, "Or are you the wild beast you portray?"

Black lashes lowered over darkening blue eyes that rolled slowly down the length of her, so slowly, Cini's stomach twitched.

When his gaze traveled back up to her face, with a slight smirk under the thick beard, he said blithely in Romanian, "*Da,* I speak, *fată,*" his tone insulting, "when I want to."

Bo interpreted with a mischievous grin.

Kazak's eyes skimmed back down her figure again then up, he said with a sneer, "Finding few uses for them, I have no reason to converse with *femelăs*. Fucking, and caring for the babes are the only two things I can think of that they can be good for, talking, not so much."

He waited with a smirk for Bo to translate. When he did, the corner of his harsh mouth lifted at her sharp, aghast inhale.

His nastiness infuriated Cini, but his intense perusal of her body, and the disparaging words disconcerted her into silence. Then she asked Bo, "Did he call me a bad name?"

Shaking his head, Bo replied, "Nay, he called you *fată,* a little girl."

Her lips pressed into a straight line.

His face impassive but the edge of his mouth quirked up, Kazak said, "Ah? No more questions, small bitch?"

Bo glared at him, Kazak glared back with a nod for him to tell her what he said.

Bo interpreted his words with a short smile of apology, added, "*Da*, now he called you a bad word."

Cini bit back a gasp at Kazak's crude insolence.

With a sneering snort at her dismay, sounding bored, Kazak added, "Oh, *yah*, of course, I forgot, there are other uses for *femelăs,"* he nodded at Bo.

Bo repeated his words.

Then Kazak continued, "When not bent over naked on all fours in front of a male, there is the cooking, sewing, cleaning."

"Kaz," Bo groaned.

"Say it," Kazak insisted.

When Bo repeated his words, lids lowered over snide eyes, Kazak watched Cini digest Bo's translation. When her face turned beet red, Kazak suddenly stood up.

Seeing her flinch and step back from him, his black brows slashed down in annoyance. He said to Bo, "Take her to the women's quarters."

Turning from them, he strode swiftly across the stone floor, his heavy boots clunking hard on the stone until he was out the main door.

Furious, Cini said, "He is a crude pig."

"*Da*, he can be. But listen sweet, you have to understand him. He's always lived in military surroundings. Practically from birth. Any kindness or politeness was long beaten out of him. It is hard to feel kindness when it has never been given to you."

"Don't make excuses for him, sir." She sighed wearily and said, "Please just take me to where I am to be housed."

"All right, little one, but only if you tell me your name. Mine is too hard to say, they just call me Bo." He held out his arm for her to take.

Cini looked at it warily, then gingerly slipped her hand around his arm. She considered if it was safe to tell him her name.

Then, she thought, she lived so far away, there would be no way anyone would recognize her name. "It is Činnosti, I was named after a grandmother. My family calls me Cini."

"Well then, Cini it is," Bo smiled, ushering her to the corridor that led to the women's quarters. He stopped at the door.

Dropping her hand from his arm, Cini faced him. "Bo, why has he taken me? Why is he keeping me prisoner? He has no right."

"Ah, well, he does have the right. Unescorted females on the trade road are violating the law, it is so vilely dangerous for a voman out there on her own. I don't know why he is keeping you prisoner," *although I have my ideas.*

"He could find out where you are from and return you, or take you to the local policing authorities, which of course are few and far between. Kazak Adarken is the only law around here really for hundreds, thousands, of miles."

Considering his words, Cini frowned, then gave Bo an appealing smile. "Please, sir, can you help me? I can't get outside, he's put guards on me, but if you were to take me, walk me outside, then, look the other way, I would never tell anyone you helped me. I would say I slipped away when you weren't aware. Please-"

"Nay," he shook his blond head with a sad frown. "I cannot, little one. First, I cannot go against the lord's rule, and second, I would never anyway, he is my friend as well as my Liege. And third," he chucked her chin lightly. "I would never allow a voman out there alone, law or not. So," he sighed, "for now, we will see what tomorrow brings. Go on in, things will look brighter in the morning, sweet."

Bo opened the door to the women's quarters and gave her a nudge inside, closing the door on her protests.

He nodded to a guard standing near the door, and wandered off to his own chambers.

Cini waited until she heard the snips and grunts and snores indicating everyone was asleep. She quickly donned a loaned blue gown and her ankle boots. Last night she had already opened the wooden shutters and peeked out the linen stiffened in resin that hung over the windows.

The back, lower floors had linen windows. She had seen only one soldier guarding their section of the castle. His routine was to turn at the elm tree and thirty seconds later stride back the other way.

Tonight, as soon as she watched him pass by on his rounds, she had thirty seconds.

She silently opened the shutters, then she carried a chair to the window. Climbing atop the chair, she pushed the linen out and slipped out the window.

Chapter Eight

Kazak stretched his limbs wide in his big bed. He had worked long and hard, nonstop the last days with little rest. He'd had a filling meal this eve, and his bed was amazingly comfortable, yet he couldn't sleep.

He knew why. The girl. When he had laid her on the ground and rolled on top of her, gods, she was so soft under him, plump breasts pressed against his chest.

Even covered with dirt, she smelled incredible, such a fresh, natural, *pretty* scent. Baby blonde tresses curling around her head, he had grown instantly hard feeling her slender yet sweetly curvy body squirming under him.

Later, after he'd put her in his bed, and she had woken and left the bed, he assumed she was just a bit shy. He thought, like any woman, all he had to do was nuzzle her and she'd be all over him.

But no. The little vixen, the tasty, fragrant, lush, vixen, pushed him away.

His nose in her hair, mouth on her neck, fingers stroking the silk of her nape, he had moved to kiss her. If he had, he wouldn't have stopped, no matter how much she protested, and his stomach turned at the thought.

He would have forced himself on the girl, something he's never done, has never had to do, and he has the right as lord under the emperor's rule to take what he wanted, anyone he wanted. And by all that's holy, gods he wanted her.

He had been so stunned that she denied him, surprise then frustration and finally anger filled him. He had needed to get away from her, quickly, before he either beat her, or *føkkend* her against her will.

Now, lying there in the dark, he couldn't stop the images of her face from penetrating his brain, so fresh, so ethereally beautiful it stunted a man's breath and hardened his cock. Eyes as big and green as a mermaid's of the sea, and her body, *yah*, so young yet made for sin.

He'd seen many *sâni*, tits, in his lifetime, but he craved to see hers, bared, ready for his man's hands to clutch and knead. With a groan, he palmed his erection that was hard as steel.

Cursing, he threw the blankets off and swung his legs to the side of the bed. Dragging his hands through his long hair, he pushed it off his forehead and scraped his fingers through his beard.

"*Føkk*," he cursed, why was he lying there suffering? He could go take any woman to relieve himself. Bonatella would be easy and quick, but his stomach flipped at the thought of her broad ass stuck up in front of his face.

Maybe Lucia, no, Bea, no, *føkk*, none of them appealed. And even if he sated himself on one, or more of them, he knew it wouldn't stifle the fire the little blonde had lit in him. The bitch. Huh. She dared to deny him.

With an angry snort of frustration Kazak got to his feet. He pulled on some breeches and jerked on a shirt, yanked his boots on, and headed for the door. He would show her, she had no right to refuse him, hell, he didn't even know her godsdamned name.

Regardless, he didn't need to know the name of the woman under him he was impaling. He would show her, no one said no to him, Lord Kazak Adarken. No one.

Slamming his door behind him, he stomped down the hall, down the stairs, through several corridors to the back of the castle where the servant women slept.

He nodded at the guard posted there to open the door.

The guard tried to hide his surprise, his Liege never came to the women's quarters in all the time he'd been at the castle.

Except when he'd brought the woman he'd captured and then ordered guards to stay to prevent her from leaving the castle. And from other warriors taking her for their own.

Quailing from the lord's wrath heating at his slowness to obey, the guard opened the door and pushed it aside.

Kazak stepped into the gloom of the darkened room of sleeping women. His eyes as sharp in night as they were in daylight searched the room. He didn't see anyone who looked like the blonde. He searched for Sarah.

Finding her asleep in her bed, he strode over and roughly shook her shoulder.

"What- what-" Sarah blinked heavily wondering what was pushing on her. Prying her glued eyes open, she looked up in shock at her lord glaring down at her. "Sire!" She gasped, one hand pulling her blanket up to her neck, the other went to her grey hair mottled up inside her night bonnet.

"Where is she?" he demanded in Russian.

"Huh?" Sarah struggled to wake, rubbing her eyes. "Who, my lord?"

His whisper a quiet roar, "The girl, the small *blondă* that I brought here, where is she?"

Around him, women started waking from the disturbance. Some squealed with fright, others moaned with desire. As scary as he looked and behaved, the women thought he'd be a rough and violent ride, and most were willing to chance him.

"Uh," working to wake her slumbering brain, Sarah glanced over to Cini's bed, and then blanched. It was empty. Frantically, her eyes bounced around the room at each bed, but to no avail, the girl was not in the room.

"I, uh, she," Sarah stammered, scratching her head. "The young girl, uh, I don't know where, uh," she sunk back from the ire that made the already harsh planes of Kazak's face harden, sharpen to axes.

"What do you mean you don't know where she is?" Rising impatience thickened his accent and roughened his already deep gravelly voice.

The women were now becoming rattled at the fierce warlord, so huge and menacing taking up space with his strong darkness. The lights seemed to dim, the air in the room thickened oppressive. He stood as a heaving bear on the precipice of a brutal attack.

"Uh," Sarah struggled to her feet, "her, there, I mean her bed there, is empty. Misha," she said to a woman near the far wall, "check the bathing area for Miss Cini."

The woman with dark skin nervously rose from her bed and disappeared into the arched doorway at the back of the room.

She appeared within seconds shaking her head. Seeing the dangerous master in their chambers, so huge and muscled, face darkening as he grew angrier by the second, she couldn't speak if she wanted to.

Kazak's skilled eyes flicked to the only window with the shutters open and a chair by it. He strode straight to it.

Placing his big palm on the linen resin window, he pushed and it moved freely. Cursing under his breath, without another word, he stalked out of the room.

Still holding her breath, Sarah reached out a shaking hand to close it behind him.

Grabbing a jacket then rushing out of the castle, Kazak hurried around to the outside of the women's quarters and to the open window.

He crouched, studied the ground beneath it. Small indentations indicated someone had stood there. Rising, he slowly scanned the area through narrowed eyes.

His attention drew to the woods. She would likely seek cover as soon as she could. His head twitched to a sound coming around the building. He stayed in the shadows, and waited.

In seconds, the one guard who patrolled the back where the few windows to the women's chambers were came stomping out.

The guard never looked around, never slowed, just marched on through. Kazak counted under his breath, 1, 2, 3, it was over 30 seconds before the guard returned.

Kazak made a mental note to meet with the guard in the morning. He would determine then whether or not the man would lose his head.

In the meantime, he saw the grass slightly smushed where the girl had gone. The space between the steps lengthened as she obviously started to run. Even so, there were several of her shorter steps between the long ones he made following them.

Making his way to the first line of trees to the forest, he started to steam. How stupid is a woman, a young woman at that, a *small* young woman, to leave the comfort and safety of the castle to go to the deeply dark, insanely dangerous woods? Either she was incredibly brain-addled, or she was desperate to get away.

As he entered the woods, he saw the trail she went to right away. Of course it was pitch black, he could barely see his hand in front of his face and he had nocturnal eyesight.

The girl would be stumbling, lucky if she didn't crash into a tree or fall in a ravine and break her legs before a wild animal got her.

Recalling her verbal bashing of him earlier in the great room, a tight quirk lifted the corner of his mouth at the girl furiously telling him off, it had been all he could do to bite off a grin at her fury. She was easy to stir up, like poking at a puppy and having it yap a tiny bark at you.

Nay, she wasn't addled, that meant she had a reason to flee. She didn't seem the criminal type, maybe it was man trouble. He felt a twinge in his ribs at the thought of the *blondă* having a man in her life. Even one she was running from.

She would tell him about it, he'd make her. Then he would eliminate whatever kind of *føkker* the man was to make this girl's life so hellish she fled across the most treacherous land in the world, alone, defenseless.

She hadn't had so much as a knife on her, even a big stick when he'd caught her. The bitch deserved a wicked paddling for being out on her own in the first place, and now, Kazak's hand tightened into a fist, daring to run from him.

Although the days were warm and balmy, the temperature dropped severely at night, especially in the murky shrouded forest dank with mud and ancient mossy trees.

A distant howl broke the black veil of night. The howl he could ignore, the growls ahead in the brush, he could not.

Kazak removed his dagger from the sheath at his hip and held it firm, low, a few inches from his thigh. Around him he heard green leaves rustling, dried leaves sweeping in the sudden chilly wind, and then the slightest sound of a leaf crunched.

Then he heard a female's sharp cry, and a whimper. Instantly the growls grew louder, there was more than one, how many, he couldn't tell.

"Voman!" Kazak called out.

All sound and movement ceased, except the wind blowing through the tops of the trees. He waited without moving.

Seconds passed, then the growls started again. "Voman," he struggled to pull the English words out of his brain, "vere...are...you? I nay can help *nu* ah, not, knowing vere," silently he cursed his lack of vocabulary.

The damned coarse, unintelligible grunts he made probably scared her more than the wolves. When she didn't respond, he moved silently towards where he thought the whimpers had come.

One of the wolves let out a short bark, advising his pack he'd cornered the prey. Cini's cry at the bark was wretched with fear.

"Dammit *femelă*, vere are you-" Kazak's own words ended in a dark loud growl to equal the wolf's.

At the sound of his rough voice, the wolf closest to him moved away in the brush, but Kazak could hear Cini crying.

Following the sound, he moved carefully off the trail slightly and almost tripped over the same rock she must have.

Peering carefully into the gloom, thank the gods for the full moon and cloudless night sky, he could see down a slight ravine. That color of her hair was so bright it was visible even in the lightless forest.

He could also see the white tufts of fur as a wolf crept towards her in the obscure duskiness. Kazak scooped up a rock off the ground and threw it at the wolf shouting, "*Yava-go!*"

The wolf, and a second behind him stopped and looked up at Kazak. Yellow eyes vicious, ready to attack gleamed menacingly in the dimness.

Not slowing down, Kazak grabbed up some more rocks, threw them at the canines while shouting in mixed Mongolian and Romanian, "*Yava lupesc, yava!*"

Kazak, a big man thick with a muscular chest, huge arms, broad shoulders, moving steadily with heavy steps in the dark, his voice a low roar and throwing stones, it didn't take long before he saw only the tails of at least four wolves disappear into the brush.

Sheathing his knife, he kept his boots almost sideways to get down the scrubby incline to where she laid huddled, dirt and rocks tumbling under his feet.

Her legs curled to the side, Cini clutched an ankle and held a branch in her hand apparently as a weapon. Large green eyes glowing with terror, tears streamed down her face, the plush lips shivered, her teeth chattered with fear and cold.

When Kazak neared her, she whimpered and tried to scuttle back, but cried out in pain.

"*Haltă!*" he barked sharper for her to stop than he meant to. It only made her flinch and shuffle further at the hill her back was already against.

Kazak forced himself to move more softly, making his steps shorter and slower.

She gaped at him like a trapped injured animal ready to fight or flee. The way she was curled up and wincing, she wasn't running anywhere. And she had even less a chance of fighting the infuriated warlord than the wolves.

Kazak stood in front of her and frowned as she put her arms up to cover her head, brandishing the branch like a weapon. With irritation, he bent and snatched the twig from her hand and threw it.

She turned her head with her arm up in defense waiting for him to strike her.

He crouched beside her. "Show Kazak," he said quietly, nodding at her leg.

Cini half turned her head to peer at him with tear-filled eyes through a curtain of flaxen hair, still expecting him to haul off and slam her.

Kazak let out a heavy breath. "Show," he repeated keeping his forearms resting harmlessly on his thighs.

Her head lowered, she looked up at him under a wave of hair and tried to straighten her leg. "*Uh,*" she gasped in pain.

Kazak knelt, sat back on his heels. He shrugged out of his coat and draped it over her muttering about stupid *femelăs* that didn't know better than to go out into the cold perilous night.

She stayed hunched over, curled around herself, shaking with cold and fright. He needed to get her back before she got hypothermia, or she went into shock from the fall and the scare of the wolves, he grunted, and of him.

He put a hand to her shoulder and gently pushed her to lean back against the hill.

She cringed from the angry heat radiating from the big man, his hard hand on her soft body.

Eyes huge and round took in the long black warrior's hair hanging over his shoulders, the beard that made him seem so bearlike, wide shoulders blocking out the rest of the woods, and his own blue orbs glittering fiercely so close to her.

A shudder rolled across her shoulders and down her arms and set her teeth to chattering faster.

Highly aware of the abject fear he was generating in her, he carefully grasped her leg and pulled it out. He felt around her leg and down to her ankle where she gasped with pain and tried to jerk her leg back.

"*Bine, bine,*" he growled, gently holding her leg and pressing softly around her ankle. His mouth twitched at her whimper, the girl sure had the weakest ankles he'd ever seen.

This was the second time she'd twisted one. The first when she'd fallen from his horse trying to run from him. Alas, and this second time she was again running from him. It didn't feel broken, and wasn't too swollen.

"*Bine*, uh, al-right," he said awkwardly, and moved closer to her with his hands out.

"No!" she yelped, shoving her back hard against the hill. Her face scrunched in pain when her back struck the rocky mound.

In an angry stream of Romanian words and curses, he told her to calm down, he wasn't going to hurt her. Seeing the fright in the big green eyes gaping wide at him, he took a deep breath and held his palms up in the sign of surrender, no harm.

But she clearly didn't know what he was meaning and continued to try to back away from him even as the jagged rocks dug into her body.

"Ah," he groaned, giving up. He had to get her out of there. He stood up then bent over and grabbed her around the waist. Hauling her up and over his shoulder, leaves flew, scattering everywhere.

Before she could catch her breath, he stomped back the way he came and made his way up the hill carrying her as if she was a sack of feathers.

"Please," her frightened voice muffled against his back, his jacket so big on her the collar fell upside down almost covering her entire head.

Kazak carried her through the dark forest and back to the castle.

As he strode past the guard at the back of women's quarters, he barked in Russian at him, "You be in my office at seven tomorrow morning," and marched on.

The color drained from the guard's face. He recognized the white blonde hair of the woman the lord had specifically told him to keep an eye on, and that she was over the lord's shoulder, and he was carrying her in the dead of night, from the woods.

It was obvious she'd tried to run and Kazak had recaptured her. *Skag-* shit, the guard was in big trouble.

Kazak carried Cini into the castle, ignored the few people wandering about that gawked at them, and hit the stairs.

At the top, he strode down the corridor to the end, to his chambers.

Shoving the door open, he carried her inside, kicked the door closed with his heel and dumped her on his bed.

Chapter Nine

Cini jumped to her feet clutching his coat around her.

Kazak dragged his hands down his face and over the thick beard, *the stubborn little…* at least her ankle was already better although she hobbled on it.

He searched for the words, said bluntly, "Sit. Girl, Kazak, talk."

Her eyes flicked back and forth to the door to him to the door. She favored her right foot but was able to put weight on it.

Furious that she did not do as he told her, he took a step to her, looming huge, hard and darkly foreboding over her.

Irritated at his own broken English, he barked angrily, "Kazak say sit. You obey Kazak. *Nu* more, uh, not obey."

He could feel the heat of exasperation flushing up his neck at her looking up at him, face white as a sheet, lips pulled in to still their trembling. Shaking her head no, she backed away.

How dare she not do as he commanded! "Ah, *basta*, enough," he spat and grabbed her arm jerking her to a stop. He gripped his coat and yanked it off her then he sat on the edge of the bed and pulled her over to lay belly down across his lap.

"Hey!" she protested.

"*Vă Føkkon asculta Kazak*," he snarled lifting her skirt. Repeating in garbled English, he said, "You fucking obey Kazak," and pushed the skirt up to her waist.

Realizing what he intended, she shrieked, "No! Don't you dare!" Cini tried to cover her bottom with her hand, but he had the strength of ten mules.

His big hand on her back, he gripped her wrists in one hand and held her motionless, then pushed down the small underwear that tied on the sides of her hips.

"No! Stop!" she screamed, kicking and twisting on his lap.

Whack!

He slapped his hand on her bare bottom and she shrieked. He spanked her several more times, her shrieks growing shriller.

Kazak struggled to keep his eyes on her back, her flopping head, her kicking legs, everywhere but the perfectly round, nude bottom splayed on his legs, quivering from his blows. In seconds, his erection was a hard bulge straining at his breeches. *Føkk.*

He's going to lay her on the bed, remove that ridiculous swath of undergarment, and shove inside her, thrusting furiously hard and savagely deep.

Then, the picture streamed in his mind of her at the bottom of the ravine, eyes huge with terror, nipping, slathering wolves surrounding her, her brandishing that useless twig at them.

He stopped smacking her and crunched his eyes closed tight, it was a fight with the devil to get control of himself.

Searing lust warred with his fury at her running away and defying him, and her obvious terror of him. It all instigated his lust to roar out of control, mucking his mind until he could barely gather his thoughts. In seconds he would be in her if he didn't get a grip.

His hand spread on her slim back holding her from moving, he opened his eyes.

His gaze glued to the perfect plump cheeks reddened from his hits. Gods he wanted to put his mouth on them, squeeze the firm meat while he licked her, bit her, felt every inch outside and inside her pleasing body with his long fingers. His erection swelled painfully.

She was crying silently, her back hitching with each sob.

He fixed her underwear, and snapped her dress down over her legs, then gripped her waist and lifted her to stand in front of him.

As scared as she was, she was equally outraged. The sodden green eyes pits of wrathful fire, her hands rubbing her butt she yelled, "How dare you! Who do you think you are? I will kill you for that, you will never touch me a-"

Kazak snaked his hand out, clinched her wrist, and pulled her back to him, between his legs. He wound his hand around her arm, with his other he netted long fingers under her jaw holding it rigid.

He ordered roughly, "*Vă*, ah…you- obey Kazak, or more paddle." His lips twitched at her eyes darkening to emerald in her fury.

She struggled, but he held her still with his hand wrapped around her wrist and her thighs cinched between his knees.

"No," she snarled through clenched teeth, "I will not-"

He swung her around and went to put her back over his lap.

She squealed, "All right, all right, all right!"

He turned her back around to face him, his knees still holding her legs.

Her lips pushed out in anger. "You are a horrid man," she declared. Squirming at the grip of his knees, she shoved at his hands, trying to dislodge the hand clutching her wrist, to no avail.

"Not a man, you're an- an animal," she disparaged, sniffing back her tears of frustration that he could so easily push her around the way he did.

Kazak was a bred warlord, skilled, ruthless, merciless and violent. Those that disobeyed his orders suffered the whip or worse, many he had beaten to death with his bare hands.

And this… *femelă*, half his size, he could snap her neck with his fingers if he chose, stood there bold as brass first escaping from him, and now fighting him.

Standing up, he gripped her jaw again holding her mutinous face up to his. Her face small, fine-boned, his thick fingers cupped it like a gorilla holding a child.

His voice cold, eyes colder, he said, "*Vă,* ah, you, obey Kazak. All time obey," his accent garbled his words, but it was clear what he said.

At her continued struggling, he threatened, "You not obey, Kazak paddle- more hard. *Bine?* Ah, al-right?"

His blue eyes speared into hers, mouth severe under the beard, a chunk of dark hair hung over his eyes. Cheeks and jaw even through the beard angular and hard as granite, he meant what he said, and Cini knew it, but she remained mute.

When she stayed silent, he snarled, "You say *da,* ah, yes," and gave her a snapped shake.

Her eyes dropped, but she said nothing.

Impatiently, he shook her jaw again and ordered, "You answer, or Kazak paddle. Now." His fingers dug into her soft skin until tears came to her eyes. Seeing them, and marks reddening on her skin, he hadn't realized his own strength.

Loosening his grip slightly, he pushed her chin up forcing her to look at him in his incensed eyes. "Answer Kazak."

"Yes," her whisper barely uttered.

Still restraining her but with a lighter grip, he apprised the soft woman he held.

Her lids lowered covering her eyes. A tear rolled out to pearl on her cheek that was red from her humiliating ordeal.

Kazak bent and touched the tear with the tip of his tongue, his breath a warm brush on her skin, beard a slightly rougher rasp. Her lashes flickered, but she didn't open her eyes.

His gaze lowered to her lips. Plush and pink and trembling, so angry, so stubborn, so afraid. His mouth was on hers before he could think.

She stiffened. He moved a hand to cradle the back of her head to hold her, and plundered her mouth with sudden crazed vehemence. The flavor, perfume, feel of her, hurled him into fanatical passion.

Unleashed heat roiled inside him in barraging waves so sudden, so shocking, like he'd never felt before. Stinging needles rushed up his legs to his groin so fierce and hot he almost doubled over from the intensity of it.

Steaming clouds of desire stuffed Kazak's head, blinding, deafening him to all but the sensation of devouring this spellbinding, heavenly tasting, scent of spring blooms, soft as liquid gold, female.

Forcing her mouth open, he thrust his tongue inside, sweeping every honeyed, sweet part of her. One hand still cradling her head, he released her jaw with the other to spread his strong fingers across her back to lift her, pull her up and tight against his chest.

The press of her breasts, firm yet womanly soft on his slabs of stone pectorals, drove his wanton heat up ten more notches of madness.

Cini and the Beast

At first stunned, Cini froze. Then, his demanding mouth, roving lips hard and rough, soft and seeking all at the same time, stirred something unfamiliar, deep inside her, between her legs heat and wetness mingled.

His masculine taste, manly smell of strength and power, faint cigar and ale, the vigor of his tremendous desire, his kiss made her knees weak.

The thick beard was surprisingly soft against her skin. The stiffness in Cini's lips diminished, they widened, allowing him deeper passage. A whimper fluttered at his bold strokes lathing her flesh, assailing the tender, untouched by any man, inside of her mouth.

She clutched his shirtsleeves and clung helplessly to his onslaught that was stirring fire and wetness in her.

He went after her tongue, sucking so hard, his own lunged halfway down her throat. His intensity, immense strength, the hard hand splayed across her back, holding her so tightly against his broad muscled chest unnerved her.

Unused to such a fierce man kissing her so fervently, started frightening Cini.

The fear was joined with anger at his treatment of her. The way he captured her, spanked her, even now, assaulting her as if she were a – a loose woman to do with as he chose. The young, innocent, furious girl tried to break from him.

Kazak's blood burned, his head spun, groin swelling to bursting, he was inured to her resistance. His hand, so large, his fingers encompassed the entire back of her head, and brushed the side of her face.

Her skin so soft, he opened his mouth further, he wanted more. If he could eat her mouth, her lips, her tongue, her teeth, climb down her throat, he would. Then he felt her little fists hitting at his chest, and he reluctantly leaned back, and peered half-dazed at her.

Her mouth firmed, hard, angry, she pressed her hands against his powerful chest. They were like miniature butterflies, he barely felt them.

"*Femeii…*" His eyes hooded, heavy with desire, he went for her mouth again, murmuring, "*Femelă*, ah female, Kazak take you, now." He moved his hands to slip under her, to lift her to put her on his bed.

"No," Cini declared. Twisting from his grip, wrenching from him she staggered back.

Panting, his hooded gaze through strands of dark hair on her, he palmed his engorged erection, making his intentions clear. "You stay…here," he motioned to the bed with a jerk of his jaw, the long dark hair flipping over his shoulder, "with Kazak."

Gripping the thick hard manhood over his breeches, his eyes burned so hot the blue blazed white.

Color fled her curved cheeks leaving her fair skin so pale it appeared pure cream. His tongue scraped across his teeth with the urge to lick her.

"No," she shook her head, backing away from him.

Kazak could not believe his entire body quivered and pulsated with his need for her. His shoulders hunched, abdomen rigid from holding himself back from jumping on her. Bicep bulging, he gripped his own sex hard in his raging hunger for his captive.

Dark brows lanced down in a fierce scowl at her objection. "*Fată*," timbre low, rough, "little girl, you… *føkk,* ah, fuck with Kazak, here," his brow bunched with the stress of pulling the English words from his brain.

"If you nay, *nu*, ah, refuse, you stay in… *väznic.*" Releasing his manhood he raked his hand through the loose black hair, he couldn't believe he was bartering with a woman.

Why didn't he just push her down, spread those shapely legs and plow into her? As *dominio*, prime warlord of *Împărat Radoslav's* army, he had the right to take any female in the village, with or without their consent.

He looked and sounded like an enraged feral animal. Her arms wrapped around her body, Cini took another step away from the huge, tough man who looked on the verge of exploding.

She recognized the word, *väznic*. "In- in, where? A prison?" she managed to choke out.

His hot gaze roamed her body, raised to her confused, terrified eyes, his narrowed, he said, "*Donjon.*"

Seeing her comprehending what he said, his lips pressed together. What he meant. It was fuck here in comfort with him, or stay in misery in a cold, dark, cell.

Her lips pulled in, Cini understood. She said stiffly, "Take me to the dungeon," and turned partially away from him.

Kazak didn't move. He was a warlord, a brutal warrior with enough blood on his hands to fill a lake, and this little, *femelă*, dared to say no to him? Chooses to be imprisoned in a goddamned dungeon rather than sleep with him?

Rage at her obduracy pumped through his body, expanding the massive chest. Dark color rushed his neck, his shoulders already cordons of iron, swelled.

Worse of all, clearly she was scared witless of him. Her small body shook with fear and trepidation. The trembling green eyes raised to stare levelly at him, still she defied him. *Føkk.*

An inhuman growl started low in his gut, rumbled up the muscled chest, he stalked to her. When she shrunk from him, he snatched up her arm and strode with her to the door.

Flinging it open, he stormed out.

Half dragging her with him, they went down the corridors, the stone steps, through the great room, across the grand hall mostly dark with lanterns strung along the walls for meager illumination, over the egress and out the door.

Outside the blast of icy wind, common in the late summer, slapped them both, stinging their skin. Kazak faltered, he was a strong, weathered soldier; she was small, delicate, almost frail.

But, he shook his head, he would not be denied in his own realm.

The night was pitch black, in the dark the trees and buildings looked unnatural and sinister. He marched her across the dewy grounds to a cluster of stones and mortar, partially covered with moss.

The mist surrounding it made it eerie, spooky, as if ghosts and spirits floated around the harsh, mean structure.

He felt her stiffen in his grip, her fear palpable. A twinge pinched in his gut. Ignoring it, he lifted the heavy iron handle and pushed open the thick wooden door, it scraped and squeaked, and he pulled her inside.

Normally dungeons were dug into the belly of the earth under castles, this one was constructed outside because the rocky ground was so difficult to excavate, simple buildings that didn't need fortification from raiders were built with quicker ease.

The dungeon was empty, most offenders committing grievous enough crimes were either immediately flogged, or executed.

The single guard, snoozing in a chair, his boots crossed and resting on the wall, snorted awake. He stumbled to his feet. It was his place to live there interchanging with another guard, one week on, one week off, even if the prison was empty.

"Sire," the middle-aged man coughed through husky sleep. He shoved back short greying hair with both hands and tugged at the helm of the midriff-length jacket of his uniform, the buttons stretched over a slight paunch.

Inside was almost as bad as the outside. Poorly lit, chilly and damp, cobwebs connected the corners, stains of blood and straw covered the cold stone floor. The guard's chair was placed beside a small fireplace.

Boots clomping, crushing crackling straw beneath them, Kazak stalked past him to a single cell, the door stood open. He pulled Cini to it.

She dug her feet in, tried to tug from his grasp. "No, please, don't," she cried.

He felt an odd pang in his chest, but he bucked up. He was lord, *dominio*, he had to have complete obeisance. She would learn to do as he said immediately without argument, never attempt escape again, and she would damned well come to his bed willingly. He abruptly pushed her inside and closed the cell door.

Cini looked around the stone room. Dirt and straw strewn on the floor, one dusty, tiny linen window leant little light, and the guard had only one lantern.

By the fireplace it was warm, everywhere else was dank, clammy cold.

Shivering, Cini stood, her hands at her throat, eyes huge, pleading, afraid. "Please, don't leave me here," she cried softly.

Kazak's gut revolted, it burned up his gullet to his throat. He stood less than a foot from the cell, blue eyes piercing the gloom.

The sight of the young woman, so small, standing in the pale blue gown, her hands now over her mouth, legs clearly trembling, he felt his heart pinch. His hand itched to reach through the bars to stroke her hair, her face.

A hard blink to clear the unfamiliar emotion, his voice a dark rasp, he growled in guttural English, "Here, or Kazak's bed," and waited. He held his breath, sure she would give in.

Then, at the shake of her head, his chest fell, eyes darkened, lids lowered hard over them. He spun from her, stalked to the door.

Her voice tiny, quivering, "You could at least know my name."

Kazak didn't stop, but his shoulders twitched. To the guard, in a low voice he said in Mongolian, "No one comes in, or goes out. You stay here, alert. You do not go near her, on penalty of death, yours. Unless she is in danger."

He drew a harsh breath, exhaled, then went on, "Give her a pallet, blankets, pillow, a lantern, see she is fed. Light a bigger fire. Any...problems," he paused, wanted to look at her but didn't dare, it would certainly break his reserve, "you summon me. Understand?"

The guard bowed. "Aye, my Liege."

Kazak hesitated only a few more seconds, then left the dungeon. An odd pain bit at his heart, gnawed at his belly, he hurried back to the castle to find something stronger than ale.

Chapter Ten

He left her there all night. He couldn't sleep. The picture of her little body all huddled up on the floor, cold and scared and alone kept pushing its way into his mind.

What happened to the compassionless warlord with ice in his veins?

At dawn, Kazak sought out Bo. His friend was in a room they used as a study and an office.

Bo looked up when he stepped into the room.

His grin mocking, he said, "Damn, Kaz, you look like *skag*, what the hell happened?" Bo was sitting at a thick block of wooden desk, papers spread out in front of him.

Ignoring him, Kazak went to a cupboard and pulled out a bottle with a cap on it. He picked up a pottery cup and poured several ounces of amber liquid in it, set the bottle down, and gulped down the fiery liquid.

"Ahh," he groaned at the burning in his throat. But it did nothing to relieve the knot in it. He stomped over and plopped down in a chair. Cradling the cup in his hand, he rested it on his thigh.

Blond brows arched, Bo pushed his chair back perusing his friend. "What the hell, Kaz?" This time his question was embraced in serious concern. "Did somebody die?" His dark blond hair was neatly tied back, sandy lashes circled the cobalt eyes.

"Huh," Kazak grunted and swilled half the cup.

Bo stood up, came around the desk and rested a lean hip against it, crossed his ankles, and his arms over his bulky chest. "What?"

Kazak stared at the liquid in his cup and grunted again.

Bo's dark blue gaze studied his friend, and lord, then, the dawning broke over him. His lips turned up in a grin,

"Tis the *blondă, a dulcet possunt,* the sweet pussy. What, she still turning you down?"

Seeing the wince on Kazak's dark face he knew he'd nailed it. "How dare the *jijig catea,* little bitch turn down the mighty Lord Kazak Adarken, the emperor's number one *dominio!*" he teased, laughing at the dark color that rose up past Kazak's beard to his sharp cheekbones.

"*Førk deg*, fuck you," Kazak growled at him and gulped the rest of his drink.

Bo's eyes tapered at Kazak. "You did something to her. You didn't *førk* her, or you wouldn't be so pissed, and you'd still be with her. One shot at that gorgeous *possunt* would not be enough," he laughed at Kazak's dark glower, then he sobered.

Brows lashed down in accusation, he said, "You didn't...hurt her?" He observed the guilty flush color on Kazak's cheeks deepen. "Kaz, nay, not a female, you would never harm a voman."

Kazak's head hung. "*Da*, nay," the black hair swung with the short shake. He got up and refilled his drink, stood with a hand in his pocket and threw down half the drink. "I have not hurt her. Last night, she ran. She escaped."

"Oh *yah*?" Bo's eyes lightened with mirth. "No kidding? How? I take it you being the great hunter you caught her?"

Kazak explained how she got out the window. His voice angry and worried when he told him how he'd found her, in the deep woods, freezing, injured, huddled against a hill, surrounded by wolves, a thin branch in her hand as a weapon. How he'd carried her back to his chambers.

Smiling proudly, "Enterprising, brave little *catea,* she is, eh?*"* Bo's brows drifted down. "So, what happened? Why are you here looking like the wrath of the gods, yet strangely bereft?"

"More like stupid and reckless instead of brave." Somewhat sheepish, Kazak told him, "I offered her a choice, my bed, or the dungeon."

"What? What the hell, Kaz," Bo's face creased. "Why don't you just godsdamned *take* her."

His face a rock of fury, Kazak snarled, "I am not the rutting beast she calls me. I will not force her, she will come to me of her own free will."

Bo rolled his eyes. "Gads, you making her choose between the luxury of the castle or the horror of the dungeon is the same as forcing her. Why put her through that? Most of the warriors that are married had to force their wives the first few times, tis the way it is out here. A male chooses, then takes."

Kazak said nothing, sipped his drink, lids low over the piercing blue.

"Hmm, judging by the blackness of your demeanor, she chose the dungeon."

When Kazak didn't respond, Bo rebuked him, "Gads, Kaz, she is too delicate for the cells! What the *føkk* are you thinking?"

Bo moved to his friend. "I've never seen you act like this, before, Kaz, this *chut,* cunt, has your stones clutched in her tiny hand. Either *føkk* her and get her out of your system, or go jab it to another. There are a million vomen out there wanting you. Bonatella practically falls on her back with her legs in the air every time you're near."

He ignored the sour face Kazak made. "Whatever. It's time you chose a queen anyway, Kaz, and you know it. So pick a willing one, and either let another warrior, me even, have the *blondă*," he smirked at Kazak's scowl, "or find out where she's from and send her back."

Kazak stood up and trod back to the bottle of spirits, poured another cupful.

"Kaz, *mea frățe*, my brother, you've always said one *chut* is the same as the other. Get over Činnosti, choose one of the females with the strongest lineage, Bonatella, Isabel, Margarite, they are as plentiful as sparrows in the trees.

"You're only marrying a voman to create heirs, it's not like you can't still *føkk* around as you want. Your wife will have no say, she will stay busy with running your castle, your keep, raising your babes."

His cup paused at his mouth, "Činnosti?" Kazak said, glancing at him with an arched brow.

"*Da*," Bo nodded. "That is your little *chut's* name." Bo dropped his hands to his svelte hips regarding his liege with a taunting smile. "You don't even know the *chut's* name that holds your ballocks twisting in her hand?"

Brows in a scowl, Kazak growled, "Stop calling her a cunt."

"Whatever, Kaz. Back to the point, you left that frail child in a dungeon cell?"

"Hmm," his lips pulled in, Kaz looked down at his drink. "I told Sarah to go with guards and get her, let her clean up and then work with the other women preparing the noonday meal." He got to his feet, plunked the cup on a table and walked to the door.

"Kaz, wait, if you don't claim her, some other warrior will. You can't just keep her as a servant, she's too beautiful. They will be sniffing after her the second you are not around and-" he was speaking to an empty doorway.

Hours later, the men came in for the noonday meal. Shuffling, talking, coughing, spitting, the warriors gathered around the benches waiting for the women to serve them.

Several village women were scattered amongst the men to share the food.

Bonatella, her friends Anya and Sasha, and a few others joined the warriors. They were titled women, yet it was well known most of them were free with their favors. The males fought over each other to sit next to them.

Bonatella had kept an eye peeled for Kazak. When he came in she hustled over to sit down beside him.

Seated on his other side, Bo smirked at her.

With her sniff and haughty chin raised at Bo, she fluffed her poufy brunette hair then smiled with her wide mouth at Kazak, who was staring at the entrance from where the servants would come from the kitchen.

The food was served, everyone dug in with scant interest, they were used to the normal fare of bland mutton and tasteless watery vegetables.

It suddenly grew quiet. One by one, each person stuck their knife in to pierce another piece of savory meat, or to use the serving spoon to fill their trenchers with perfectly roasted, seasoned vegetables, then pile creamy butter on toasty fragrant bread.

Murmurs of wonder and delight rolled up and down the benches.

In awe, instead of beor or wine, or cider juice, their bowls were filled with almond milk made from ground almonds soaked in water and sugar. The meat was tender and juicy, the vegetables spicy and tasty, even the bread was flakier, lighter than normal.

"Look," a man said, cutting a piece of huff pastry soaked with spiced meat. "This is not like the hard, disposable huff container for the stew meat, it's softer, it soaks up the juices and it is flaky, edible, try it!" he chirped gleefully to the person next to him.

After some time of moans and groans of delicious delight, many at the table were now eying desserts being brought in.

Dessert was usually a piece of fruit and cheese. But now, a fig and honey custard, cherry brie tart, and ginger-sugar candy brought tongues out.

Beside Bo, another friend, Liam, shoveled food quickly into his mouth expounding, "Kaz," he said over Bo, "*frăţe*, this food…" he gobbled more, "is amazing, delicious, unbelievable," he couldn't shovel the food in fast enough.

"Look," he pointed at his trencher with a hunk of bread. Speaking with his mouth full, "That is figs, apples, raisins, pears and fish, a wonderful fish stew like I've never had before, it has a light buttery crust atop it, damn." He scooped up a heaping of the stew with his bread and shoved it in his mouth, smacking his lips while he chewed.

As hugely muscled as Kazak and Bo, Liam had long, straight, shoulder-length light brown hair and eyes to match.

Unlike Kazak's brooding, hostile scarred mien, and Bo's equally harsh yet with a hint of mischief in his dark blue eyes, Liam was classically handsome. The girls constantly snuck into his rooms, scratching and clawing each other to gain his attentions.

Kazak was finding himself chowing as fast as everyone else. Between mouthfuls, he mumbled in Romanian, "Why is this so flavorsome?" He snagged several pieces of ginger-candy before it disappeared.

Sarah strolled by with a pitcher to refill almond milk, and a smaller container in her other hand. He stopped her. "Sarah, this food, it's…different?"

"Yes, my Liege," she replied. "Tis Cini, your…uh, prisoner. She knows how to use the bottles of colored dust the merchants brought that travel the Spider Thread Trails with trade. Along with dyes, fabric, ivory, horns, gems, fragrances, bronze, silk, sugar, all the merchandise they bring to sell and trade, they also bring these things called spices.

"Among the other items Stelpha purchased for the castle, and," Sarah made a face, "herself, she bought these spices, she, um, well, likes to be up on all the current things, but no one knew what they were.

"There is this cinnamon, ginger, pepper, uh oregano, and others, and also nuts like walnuts and almonds, so they were just sitting on shelves gathering dust."

Shoving bread in his mouth, Kazak grunted and reached for more.

Sarah dared a smile at her lord. "Delicious, huh? We can't keep the bowls and trenchers filled up fast enough. That girl has magic in her fingers. Here, try this," she poured a type of plum Brandewijn, brandy, into his empty mead bowl.

He picked it up immediately and took a sip. Without a word, he downed the entire lot and nodded for her to pour more.

She filled his bowl, but couldn't stop her frown. Bumping up her nerve, she said, "My Liege, she is so sweet, kind, not a bad person. And young, please, the girl doesn't belong in that stone cold cell. The drafts, the rats," she shivered. "Set her free. Please." She darted off before Kazak could order her head removed for her insolence.

"*Da*, Kaz," Liam muttered through a mouthful of food. "Bo told me about the *blondă*. I've seen her. I will take her off your hands. She's the marrying kind, I could get my babes on her so fast, just-"

A mumbled curse, Kazak abruptly stood up and strode from the great room out to the first kitchen.

When he reached the hearth area, he saw blonde curls on the ground. Cini was curled up trying to protect herself from Stelpha's vicious feet.

The older stocky woman was kicking Cini, then Stelpha bent over and slapped her, she lifted her fist to punch her-

Kazak caught her hand in midair then grabbed the housekeeper by her hair and jerked her to her feet.

"What is the meaning of this?" He didn't wait for her answer. He shoved her so hard she stumbled cursing into a hard wall.

"My Liege," Stelpha sputtered. "She," her arm out, she pointed a long thick finger at Cini. "She works too slow! Fools with those spice things, roasting too slowly, says it retains the juicy flavor. I've told her we don't have time for such *skag*.

"I've told her to just cook, *føkk* the spices, but she ignores me, Liege. She has the hearths filled with bread and tarts baking, wasting the wood. She is small and young, it will take me no time to beat the proper behavior into her-"

"Get out!" Kazak barked in Russian. "I have had enough of you and your abuse of the people. I don't care how you are related to the emperor, you are done here. Pack your *skag*, I will send a guard retinue with you to see you return home safely. Nay," he held up a hand when she went to speak, ordered, "go."

He turned from her and knelt beside Cini. Her lip was bleeding. In his halting, guttural English, he asked, "You *bine*, uh, all right?"

Swiping hard at her falling tears she turned her head from him. "Leave me alone, you- you beast."

Kazak twined his fingers around her upper arms and pulled her to her feet. Holding her in front of him, he brushed her hair from her shoulder.

Curling a finger under her chin then lifting it gently, he said softly in broken English, "Come to Kazak bed. Kazak treat like queen, no more cook, clean, no *donjon*."

She snatched her arm from his grip. "Don't touch me." Her cheeks were bright red with shame at Stelpha's treatment of her, and fury that he won't let her leave.

His face an inscrutable mask, he watched her wrap her arms around her thin body and turn from him.

A heavy hiss scraped from his chest. Kazak grabbed her arm again and walked her out the back of the kitchen and back to the dungeon. He felt her arm stiffen under his hard fingers when she realized where he was taking her.

Yanking at her arm in a futile attempt to get free of his iron grasp, Cini begged, "Sire, please, let me go. I will just go away, disappear. I am not a danger to you or your people. I must go, it is so important, please."

Kazak stopped so suddenly, she almost tripped. He stood more than a foot over her, the breadth of his shoulders under the linen shirt blocking most of the yard from her view.

He shoved a lock of hair back off his forehead. In his heavy accented, butchered English, he asked, "Why? Why important you leave?"

She looked up at him. His skin tanned from the outdoors, beard thick but neatly kept, the long dark hair pushed back behind his ears. The blue eyes so like a Siberian tiger's glittered at her from under the low masculine, ridged brow.

He was stalwart, amazingly strong, if only she could trust him, but, he was also a ruthless violent warlord. No, Mama had told her to trust no one. She lowered her eyes and said nothing.

Growling his frustration at her for closing herself off from him, he abruptly started walking her again to the dungeon. She had to take two or three steps to each one of his long strides. The guard stood up as they entered.

"Outside," Kazak snapped at him.

"Sire." The guard nodded and quickly left.

Kazak took Cini to the cell, opened the door, and stood still, waiting for her response, to change her mind. Beg him to take her to his bed.

Cini stared at the uncanny eyes, so brilliant under the low ridge of his thick masculine brow. The black hair flopping again over one eye, the beard made him look villainous, like a pirate, a brigand. She said nothing and took a step inside the cell.

Kazak's gaze rolled down her body and back up to those frightened green orbs. Frightened to be left in the nasty, wet hay smelling building, nonetheless, her chin lifted, she deliberately turned from him.

"*Fată*," he murmured, she kept her back to him.

"*Činnosti*," he said quietly.

Her shoulders shuddered, she turned to him, surprise on her face that he'd said her name.

Kazak stepped to her. He stood close enough he could smell her natural scent, it made his ballocks tingle. His breath heavy, he reached out and cupped her breast. His huge hand hot and hard over the thin dress, groped her plump flesh.

"No-" she swung from him and moved further inside the cell, away from his reach, all the way to the wall.

Kazak could feel the fury at her rejection burn up his neck, his jaw worked, fists clenched.

She moved into the shadows, only green eyes blurred with tears shimmered out of the gloom at the huge man so like a ferocious bear with his long dark hair, dark beard, the body of a brutal warrior, and eyes as cold and empty as a killer.

Furious, Kazak slammed the cell door closed, locked it, and stomped out.

Bo was waiting outside for him. The dark blond hair tied back, censure on his handsome face, he said, "Kaz, you can't treat a delicate voman like that. She will grow sick in that frigid cell. *Da*, you have a fire going, but it will only warm the dampness, the chill, so much."

At Kazak's mulish lifted jaw, Bo went on, "Trying to bend her to your will is not going to work. She's already shown you how stubborn she is. She is young and small and frail, yet she has a spine of steel and you will break her before she yields."

Kazak's voice low but harsh, "How about you mind your own business. She is my property to do with as I please. You are well aware I will not tolerate disobedience."

"Come on, Kaz. She is not one of your warriors. She is a free voman you captured, you can't-"

His dark hair swinging with his vehemence, Kazak said angrily, "*Da*, and that is it. *I* captured her, she is *my* prisoner. Prisoners are to obey, or they are punished until they do."

"Huh," Bo snorted. The two men started walking from the dungeon. "Are you punishing her for disobeying you, or because she refuses to *føkk* with you?"

His mouth set hard under the beard, Kazak stalked faster, not answering.

"Kaz, *mea frățe,* my brother, you can't make a voman like her submit by brute coercion. She is not a burro to be beaten to learn to mindlessly obey. And, she is not a man who will either cowardly submit or scheme to kill you. She will quietly revolt, and secretly plot to escape you."

"Men, like dogs, beaten and molded, become the best, the strongest of warriors," Kazak informed him gruffly, just look at him.

"Again, she is neither man nor beast. She is female, they are a whole different breed, Kaz. You've had your head stuck in warrior mode from birth and never learned about the fairer sex. They are much more malleable when romanced, seduced. Treat them as gentle and special as they are, and they will be eating out of your hand."

"I treat the *femelăs* here no differently and they climb on me like I'm a *føkkunn* tree."

"*Da*, sure, and look at the difference between the vomen here. The likes of Bonatella, Ivanka, Anna, and your little prisoner, Činnosti, Cini to her friends," he wiggled his brows mocking his liege.

"They are worlds apart. Cini is a lady, she is dainty in body and all grace in speech and movement. Yet with such femininity, she still has the backbone to run from you into the treacherous forest, for whatever reason, is serious enough to her to risk her life.

"Bonatella wouldn't leave the comfort of her home if her family was on fire. The harder you are with Cini, the more she will push back, mark my words. She is a true lady. You callously grab at her like she's a whore and she will shut down. Romance-"

Cini and the Beast

"Bah," Kazak spat. "I know nothing of romance. The only need for pairing of man and vomen is to *føkk,* or produce heirs. Vomen know their place, to do as the man says. She will comply, she will get tired of the hardness of the *donjon* and gladly come to my warm bed, you'll see."

Bo rolled his eyes at his friend's obstinacy. And Kazak thought the little chit was hard-headed, geesh.

Chapter Eleven

The warriors were training out in the south field. They wore cloth breeches and were shirtless.

A group dressed in leather breeches and chainmail gathered in a cluster off to the side.

Kazak and Bo joined them. Liam was there talking with another close friend of Kazak and Bo's, Thomas.

Thomas, also a trained warrior practically from birth had a strong face. Lines created from seriousness crinkled at the corners of his deeply tanned skin, lips continuously in a firm line like he was always on alert for an ambush.

The loss of his young fiancée to a tragic death haunted his brown eyes, he mostly ignored the females that swarmed him when he came in from the forests. Unlike the others, since he spent more time in the woods, he kept his hair short and beard trimmed short as well.

"Ah," Liam said when Kazak and Bo reached them, "they are beginning to come in." He nodded to the herd of reindeer and their *boazovazzi*, reindeer walkers or shepherds.

With skis strapped to their backs for use when up in the snow laden mountains, they were coming down the first hill to the keep.

The four warriors in leather observed the reindeer and their shepherds approaching, as well as other warriors assigned for guarding them.

"All is ready?" Kazak inquired, his voice and temperament dark.

Liam and Thomas glanced at Bo, who subtly shrugged.

Liam answered, "*Da*, Kaz, the men are getting their supplies ready to escort the natives, the Nanyets, and their *eallu*, their herds, while they continue their migration from the mountains to the forests.

"The first team," he nodded to a crowd of warriors warming their hands by a fire. Winter was heavy in the air already. "Have brought each caribou and calf in safely. We lost not a one."

"Aye," Thomas agreed. "Our regiment is ready to head out later tomorrow for the next leg of the journey. We will see them safe from hunters to the next encampment where they will then be ushered to their winter home."

The men watched the herd of reindeer coming towards them at a steady pace.

A few soldiers still surrounded the herders and the caribou as they made their approach. Even from a distance, the clicking of the reindeers' knees was audible.

Besides protecting the trade route from marauders, and training villagers along the way on how to protect themselves, Kazak had a duty to ensure the safe passage of the migrating reindeer and their herders from their spring home to the winter one.

Bandits and illegal hunters even hid on small islands ready to attack when the herd crossed shallow lakes and rivers.

"Their hooves are already changing," Thomas pointed to the ones that were the closest. "Their pads are between the soft, spongy pads for summer travel from the mountains and over this barren section of land, to the hoof rims shrinking and tightening in preparation for the cold snow travel to the forests."

"*Da*," his hands stuffed in the pockets of his breeches, Kazak nodded. "I see the *femelăs* are already losing their antlers."

"'Tis good to get them out of here, away from the close civilization before they enter into mating season, which is shortly upon us," Thomas said, as he left the group to go meet with the native herders, the Nanyets. He would be leading the troops that would be going with them on the next part of their journey.

Bo, Kazak and Liam stood in a huddle watching the life around them.

The reindeer were nearing, huffing and clomping they began blending with the men chopping wood.

Women chattered while doing laundry in the farther courtyard, young boys moved the cattle and hogs to a fenced pasture, and chickens clucked and pecked in the background. Children chasing each other spotted the caribou coming and ran off to see them.

Kazak and Bo mounted horses to travel a way up the trade route to the next juncture to check their soldiers hidden at posts before, at, and after the intersection.

They didn't return until the stars were twinkling in the crisp sky, their breaths puffing out in vapors. Then they went into the castle and joined the people still lingering from the lighter evening meal.

As soon as Kazak sat down, the people jumped on him complaining.

"Sire, the food, it is like dry grass in the field again! There are no desserts, no fruit punch or almond milk," they grumbled.

Kazak ignored them eating his own tough meat and tasteless vegetables. The bread, hard as a rock refused to sop of the little bit of gravy that was there.

He had considered letting Cini out to cook, but after the episode with Stelpha, he feared no one could guard her as well as he, and although it would be miserable in the dungeon, he felt she was safer there than out without him to protect her.

Again that night, he couldn't sleep. Finally, Kazak traipsed down to the library, the castle was lucky to continually procure books from all around.

Perusing the titles, he finally found the one he was looking for way on the top shelf. He had rifled through it in the past, but had tossed it aside in disgust deciding he knew enough English to get by.

Up on his toes, he used his long reach to grasp the English study book and took it down. Opening it, he flipped through a few pages, then with his nose in the book, he wandered over and settled down in a big chair by the dwindling fire.

A servant banging around in the predawn woke him.

"Ahh," he groused, stretching his back from sleeping crumpled up in the chair. The book he'd been studying fell to the floor with a clump.

Yawning, Kazak got to his feet, crouched down and picked the book up, then headed for his chambers to bathe and change his clothes.

He heated his own bath water over the fire.

He was bathed and dressed before the sun was up. Wearing breeches, a white shirt, leather jacket with fur collar, the leather provided by the cattle and the fur from the bear he'd killed himself, he left the castle.

When he reached the dungeon, the guard was half in motion with a bowl in his hand and a guilty look on his face.

"Guard? Explain what's going on," Kazak ordered, with a lift to his brow.

The grass in front of the dungeon was stomped down by heavy feet and the thick, weather-beaten door was slightly ajar. The sun just beginning to rise, lit pale yellow light on the grey stone of the dungeon.

Birds squawked, leaving their roosts, a cool wind ruffled drying leaves, some already turned autumn colors tore off in the snapping breeze.

"Uh, Sire, uh," the guard's head bowed, eyes on the bowl in his hand.

"Speak up, do not make me ask you again." Kazak glowered through a length of black hair hanging over his eyes. He smoothed it back out of his face.

"Sire, yes sir, the uh," the guard's voice had a slight shake. Keeping his grey head bowed, he peered up nervously at the warlord.

"The girl, Cini, the uh, prisoner, I just, well, I brought her porridge. She is so thin, and, even with the fire it is chilled and damp inside, I thought-"

"Kazak cursed, "*Føkkunn odit.*" Then he said in the guard's native Mongolian, "I said see that she is fed. Warm and fed, there is no need to hide from me that you are caring for her. As long as you do not touch her," he grumbled and shoved the door aside to enter.

Seeing the light from the opening door to the dungeon, with a smile, Cini rushed to the front of the cell and grabbed ahold of the bars.

"Alastair, have you found me a book as you said-" she broke off seeing the hulking darkness of Warlord Adarken in the doorway. The smile fled, she stepped back into the shadows of the cell.

Frowning at her obvious displeasure, and fear of seeing it was he, Kazak's jaw worked as he clomped across the stone floor, kicking aside loose straw.

Even with a fire blazing in the hearth, it did nothing to dispel the gloom and cold dampness of the roughly hewn building.

A weak ray of morning sun struggled to push past the dingy, tallow linen covered window. Strings of a spider web stretched across it glistened as the ray lit upon the strands.

He felt a jab of irritation that the prisoner, a stranger, knew his guard's name when he himself did not. He never let his people get close to him, no one but his closest longtime friends did he trust, yet, he should know every man that worked for him, and he would begin today to work on that.

Kazak strode to the chamber. Cini was as far away from the door as she could get trying to hide in the shadows of the clammy, fusty smelling cell.

He saw her pallet as close to the front by the bars as she could get it, a pillow and the blankets piled neatly atop it.

His voice deep and growly, Kazak said, "Voman, come here."

He waited, expecting her to come right to him. Glaring into the dim cell when she didn't, he said very quietly, "No come, Kazak paddle."

He could see her with her back against the jagged wall covered with cement of muck and limestone bricks. Her hands behind her back, her head lowered, the long blonde curls gleaming in the partial twilight, she didn't move.

With a quiet sigh he said, "Come now, uh, Činnosti." He unlocked and swung the barred door to the cell open.

She had no choice really. She could let him come and drag her out, likely hurting her in the process, or she could take a deep breath to steady her fluttering stomach, hold her head high and come out on her own steam. Which she did.

When she reached the door, Kazak stood back a few feet so she could exit without having to brush past him.

The ray of light through the window growing stronger lit her blond hair like a golden halo, and his dark hair like blackberries with its myriad of shades of shiny black, blue, purple.

When he said nothing, Cini raised her eyes gingerly, her head tilted slightly away, obviously expecting him to strike her.

Aware one punch from his huge fist hitting her delicate face would likely kill her, at the very least break every bone in her face, if not snap that slender little neck of hers, it pissed Kazak off that she would even think he, a godsdamned warrior, would deign to hit a *femelă*.

Even a husky bully like Stelpha, *da*, he had shoved her in his fury, but he would never cuff her like he would a male.

"Činnosti."

When he said her name, she looked warily at him.

His gaze went from her luminous eyes to the sumptuous lips. His ears tinged red at the remembrance of how they felt under his fevered onslaught, how they had briefly responded. His mouth twitched as he recalled how her silken skin tasted.

Then he made the mistake of looking lower, just the very top swells of her breasts rounded slightly from the bodice. It was enough to make his manhood stir to attention, and the skin of his sharp cheeks darken.

Cini made a tiny indignant, fearful sound when she saw him staring, she dipped her head to make her hair fall over the front of her and crossed her arms.

She turned again from him and moved a few steps away. Not that putting a slight distance between them would stop him if he decided to take her.

Kazak leaned to her, unconsciously raised his hand to reach for her breast like he had before…Bo's words about grabbing at her like she was a whore came to his mind, he let his hand fall back to his side.

When he said her name, "Ah, Činnosti," she lifted her head to him.

"You, ah," *skag,* he cursed under his breath, where was all that *føkkunn* English he'd studied all night? "Come, uh," he dragged his hand over his hair, trying to gentle his voice, "fresh air for you."

He went inside the cell and picked up the cloak he'd had Sarah give her.

When she flinched as he walked past her, he said quietly, "Kazak nay hit Činnosti, just come, *bine*?" He held the cloak up for her to put on.

She watched him suspiciously. Again, if he wanted to harm her, assault her, he could with no effort.

Her steps slow, Cini moved carefully to him, then nervously turned her back, holding her breath, waiting for him to suddenly stab her in the back or strangle her with his burly arm. But, he only helped her into the cloak.

She was more bewildered when he gently lifted her hair out from under the collar with his big thick fingers and settled the curly locks to spiral down her back.

"Come." Kazak gingerly set a hand on the small of her back and led her up the couple steps to the door, then out.

To the guard, Kazak said in Mongolian, "Guard, ah, Alistair," he coughed, ignoring the guard's surprised look.

"Get the miss a hat from Sarah, tell her it is for the prisoner," so she wouldn't give him something too big she couldn't wear it.

He walked Cini down a small cobbled path.

Her eyes widened when she saw the caribou scattered like moving brown and beige fuzzy hills with antlers and legs meandering in the east pasture.

"Oh my gosh, what are those? Horses with horns?"

Kazak bit back a smile at her naiveté. She had obviously grown up in a very sheltered homestead. His hand on her back, he moved her in the direction of the caribou.

They stopped near a few villagers wearing sheep's wool hats and embroidered wool coats, some had wool-topped boots.

Kazak told Cini, "*Renilor.*"

At her quizzical look, one of the villagers, a round jolly man with a red nose offered, "In English they are called reindeer. And those are antlers, honey," he smiled with good-natured humor, "not horns."

"Oh! They are so funny looking!" Cini moved from Kazak's hand at her back and hurried over to where the herd gathered. Cini's energy and childlike delight was engaging.

Covering his smile, Kazak tucked his hands in his jacket pockets and strolled behind her. When she started onto the pasture, he strode up and grabbed her arm.

"Nay, stay back."

Cini's eyes on the animals, she asked, "What do they eat?"

The villagers had followed them. The cheerful man bowed to Kazak, "Sire," he greeted him with a bow then filled her in, "They eat lichen, a kind of moss, conifers, ferns, horsetails, things like that."

Cini asked, "What about fruit? Like apples?"

"Yah," the man nodded, his wife chuckled beside him. "They like fruit, and some will eat vegetables from your hand."

"Oh!" Cini turned to Kazak. "Sir, uh, *Dominio*, could we please get some apples to feed the reindeer? There's a ton in the larder."

The big harsh man looked down at the young woman, so fresh and pretty, the cool air reddened her round cheeks and tiny nose.

She begged him, her smile eager, forgetting how cruel he'd been to her. It was the first time he'd seen her smile. It was…enchanting.

He found it hard to say no to her. "Apples Kazak favorite," his mouth turned up in a rare smile, then firmed. "But, nay, too many, you small, *renilor* crush *fată.*"

The villager's wife laughed. "The lord is right, honey, they would crush a little girl like you. They wouldn't mean to hurt you, but they would crowd you in their excitement to get to the apples, and you would get squished between those big furry bodies."

Her lips pushed out, Cini frowned at Kazak. "I am not a little girl, please stop calling me that." Her attention back on the reindeer, she made to move towards them again, but Kazak slipped his hand around her waist holding her back.

He said, "Sorry, small *miera*, *renilor* dangerous."

Disappointed she couldn't get closer to the unique animals, Cini was still pleased to be outside under clear blue skies and bright sun, in the fresh albeit cold air.

She didn't notice that when Kazak held her back, he kept his hand on her waist and nudged her against him. She leaned into the warmth of his broad chest without realizing it.

Alistair, the guard, brought a fur hat. Kazak took it from him then dismissed him and set the hat on Cini's head. She turned her red-tipped nose up with a soft smile as he tied the strings with fur balls on the ends under her chin.

"How is that?" he asked in stunted English.

She rubbed the fur around her face and smiled. "Nice, it's really nice, soft, what kind of fur is it, *Dominio*?"

Kazak brushed his fingertips along the fur brim of the hat, slightly stroking her face as well. Then he tucked a few stray hairs behind the ties. "Tis mink," he answered.

"It's very beautiful," the woman with her husband said with a friendly smile, "but not as beautiful as you. Right, Sire?"

Cini blushed at the attention.

"Mmm," Kazak murmured. His hands clasped behind his back, he bowed his head towards Cini, and said seriously, "*Da*, Činnosti verra beautiful."

Cini ducked her head, embarrassed. "Please, don't be ridiculous. My mother always told me I was lucky I was so plain I wouldn't need to worry about men chasing-" She broke off, confused, Kazak clearly desired her.

Blinking rapidly, she told herself the harsh warlord merely desired what was new to the village. He'd probably tasted every woman in the area and wanted new meat, and his ego was bruised when she refused him.

She moved away from him not noticing his frown.

Cini and the Beast

The villager, who introduced himself as John, and his wife, Marie, chattered almost nonstop to them.

John rambled on about the natural predators to the reindeer, eagles, bear, wolves, wolverines. And the worst of them, human hunters. He clearly loved his village and was grateful to Kazak and his warriors for their protection while they patrolled and cleared out the bandits along the trade routes.

The message Kazak sent out to the outlaws and marauders was that no one traveling, the Spider Thread Trails would ever be threatened. Those that took the chance to try to rob anyone would not survive.

The warriors would mercilessly hunt them down and kill them, most of them. Occasionally they left a thief alive, barely, to go back and warn the others, spread the word that the merchants traveling the trade route were untouchable.

Seeing Cini stifle a shiver, Kazak told the couple in Romanian that it was time for Cini and him to go.

Everyone said parting pleasantries, and Kazak put his hand on Cini's back to guide her across the field to the castle.

When they started over the field, he lowered his hand to span her waist. She stiffened and attempted to move from his clasp, but he held her firmly all the way back.

When they reached the castle and went inside, Kazak nodded to the guard he'd tasked with watching over Cini. His voice brusque, he said to her, "Go to kitchen now."

Cini said with seriousness, "*Dominio* Adarken, thank you for showing me the reindeer and letting me enjoy the outdoors. It was chilly but so refreshing," her voice held a gentle wistfulness that tugged at Kazak's heart.

He'd kept her locked up one way or the other since he'd brought her there. She smiled so prettily at him it made his mouth water.

"*Da, bine.*" Without thinking about it, he touched her arm then untied the strings to the fur hat. Removing it, he handed it to her and combed his fingers through her curly hair.

"There you are, Cini," coming out of the kitchen Sarah's anxious voice reached the pair, her sturdy shoes clopping across the stone.

Keeping the amazement out of her voice at seeing the rough warlord petting his prisoner so gently, "My Liege," she said quietly to Kazak, "the people are asking for her. They are crazy for her cooking. Can she please," she looked towards the kitchen.

Lifting Cini's hair and sliding it off her shoulders to tumble down her back, Kazak stroked his hands down her arms. His gaze direct on her, he said, "*Bine*, go to kitchen."

Leaving her infectious grin reeling in his head, Cini danced off with Sarah to the kitchens.

"Liege," one of Kazak's warriors came up beside him.

Kazak was still staring at the hallway to the kitchen.

"My Liege," the soldier repeated.

"*Da.*" Kazak half turned to nod at the soldier.

"The woman," he said, then cleared his throat at Kazak's puzzled look. In Romanian he said, "The uh, prisoner, the blonde girl that was just here," he took a short breath at Kazak's frown.

"What about her?"

"I uh, the men, soldiers as well as villagers, are preparing to submit their requests to you, and I wanted to get my bid in first."

Kazak's voice darkened, "What requests? What the hell are you babbling about?"

The warrior bumbled on quickly, "Yes Liege, I request to have the girl in marriage."

Brows rose then sliced down hard. "Marriage? You want to marry *my* prisoner?"

At the soldier's eager nod, Kazak said, "You don't even know her. You've never even spoken to her. Why would you want to-" He stopped, frowned. "You would marry the *femelă* without having yet met her?"

"*Da*, sire, she is extraordinarily beautiful, sexy as *skag*, it doesn't matter what kind of woman she is, I want her. What do you say?" The warrior's brown eyes lit up with expectation.

Really, he figured, why wouldn't the sire want him to take the beauty off his hands? The lord is a lusty red-blooded man, there's no doubt that he's fucked her, that would have been like putting the bunny in with the hungry wolverine and expecting him not to make rabbit stew.

The sire would have had his fill of her by now, and wouldn't care if he, Stanislau, took her for his bride.

"*Pučipišpa-*" Kazak spat a vulgar curse, spun on his heel, and left the soldier standing there with his mouth open, and unsure if that was a yes or a no?

Chapter Twelve

𝔇inner was roasted pork. The meat juicy with a crisp casing, fresh baked bread layered with sweet creamy butter, seasoned vegetables introducing a new one, the potato that the merchants brought. Fried in oil and butter with green seasonings, the men asked for more until every spud was gone.

There was also seafood soup, and fried battered apple rings powdered with sugar that according to Sarah, Cini made especially for Kazak as a thank you for taking her to see the reindeer.

He had mentioned apples were his favorite as he held her back from wandering into the midst of the herd. Kazak ate his fill then left the dining area.

After stuffing himself, Bo went to find Kazak. He came across him in the study.

Kazak was sitting in a big chair, his feet up, cigar in one hand, new pear Brandewijn that Cini had made in a pewter cup, and a brooding look on his face as he stared blankly at the fire dancing in the fireplace.

"*Mea frăţe.*" Bo grinned at him, bent and swiped a cigar off the table, lit it in the fire, then tossed his strapping body into another chair. He puffed the cigar and regarded his friend.

Kazak chewed on the end of his cigar, still staring blankly.

Bo spoke in a dialect only they, and Liam and Thomas knew from their early years in the warrior camp, "What is troubling you? I heard the emperor sent down commendations for the job you are doing cleaning up the outlaws on the trade roads and ensuring the villagers that lived along the way were kept safe. The word is that you will have your own kingdom before new spring."

"Hmm," Kazak muttered, tugging contemplatively on the dark hair on his jaw. The cigar had gone out, he set it on a tin on the table, sipped some brandy while stroking his fingers through the thick beard.

"Uh huh, then what is the problem? Why are you so pensive? Everything is perfect. You have the respect of the emperor, you have riches and are free to do as you please, bed any voman you desire, you-" his grin became knowing. "That's it. It's the little one. She still denies you?"

Bo sighed, "Again, Kaz, just take her. You are lord, she has no family or authorities to complain to, and you are the law here, what is the problem? Is it just your ego that needs for her to bend to your will?" His cobalt eyes twinkled, the edge of his lip nicked up at Kazak's frown.

"Or is that you truly want her to come to you, to want you as much as you want her? Damn, Kaz, I tell you again, you catch more flies with luxurious fur than cold, dark dungeons."

Dark hair tied back with a strip of leather, Kazak leaned forward resting his forearms on his thighs and leveled his gaze at his friend. "I have made a decision. I need for you to interpret."

Bo's bottom lip pushed out. "I'm not sure I like the sound of this. Interpret for who, what?"

An hour later, Bo retrieved Cini from the kitchens and brought her to the study.

It appeared Sarah had given her an opportunity to clean off the grease and spatter of cooking and gave her a gown to change into. The blonde hair curled in damp ringlets down her back.

Lounging back in his chair, under hooded lids, Kazak's gaze scrolled down Cini in the cream colored gown. It hugged the curves of her breasts and bottom yet was loose on her tiny waist, the lacey bodice exposed just a bit of her lush cleavage.

His pupils enlarged so much the blue eyes darkened to onyx discs. He rose slowly to his feet, mouth bunching when she took a step away from him and nearer to Bo.

Realizing she'd sought the protection of one warrior from the other, neither man she knew, or trusted, Cini backed away from both.

Her head tilted up towards Bo, the question of why she had been brought there clear in her wary gaze.

Both men stared so intently at her, Kazak with undisguised heat in his eyes, and in Bo's, an apology along with the bit of mirth that was always present.

When neither man said anything, Cini felt the uncomfortable aura in the room. Perhaps they were going to attack her at the same time? She inched to the door.

Keeping her eyes on both men, she saw Kazak nod slightly to Bo.

Nonchalantly, Bo drifted unhurriedly to stand between her and the door.

Cini's nervousness increased, her fear tangible to both men. She anxiously wrapped her arms around her upper body, and prepared to run.

"Ah, Cini, would you like something to drink? Kaz," Bo nodded with a grin at his friend, "has appropriated the container of pear **Brandewijn** you made." His brows wiggled at the table next to the chair Kazak had been sitting on.

"As well as those fried apple rings you made. People were disappointed when they went back for seconds and found their lord had made off with the last of them."

He smirked at Kazak's warning growl and continued amiably, "Or would you like mead, fruit water? We also have Chinese tea if you'd like."

She pulled a long lock of hair around and fidgeted with the curl while still inching to the door. Carefully maneuvering around Bo, she shook her head. "No. Tell me why you've brought me here."

She felt like a doll between the two tall warriors with powerful shoulders and massive chests. Hips and legs muscled yet lean enough they could race as fast as jaguars after prey.

"Ah," Bo gave her a supportive smile that twisted at Kazak's grunt for him to get a move on. "*Bine*, uh, all right."

Cini paused in her inching to the door and looked with curious wariness up at his friendly face, then over to Kazak's dark glower.

Both men had their long hair tied back. Kazak's black as midnight, Bo's dark blond. Bo's cobalt eyes lay lightly, friendly on her, Kazak's face, partially covered with the dark beard, was an implacable, unreadable mask.

His piercing blues were half hidden under hooded lids. He tried to conceal his overwhelming desire for her, but it flamed out at her nevertheless, making the air constrict in her lungs, it was suddenly hard to breathe.

Bo said kindly, "Cini, my lord, and friend, Kazak," he nodded in Kazak's direction, Kazak ignored him, his gaze unwavering on Cini.

Bo went on, "He has asked me," his mouth tugged up at that, everyone was aware Kazak never asked, he just instructed. "To tell you what…he wants, um, of you."

The more confused she became, the more Cini fidgeted with her hair and continued inching to the door. She didn't know what she'd do when she got there. Bo made a solid wall of blockage, there was no way she was moving him.

She'd have to wait for a distraction then she could try to flee. "Listen," her voice weak, she coughed to start again stronger. "I've said before, you have no right to keep me here. I insist you let me go, right now."

She glared at Bo as if she expected him to immediately step aside. He didn't.

"Sir, please move out of my way."

But Bo's lip curled ruefully. "Sorry, sweet, we've told you before, we have every right to take you and keep you. Certainly leading to trouble, the law states a single woman is not allowed on the trade roads alone, it's a wonder you haven't already been…hurt."

"Yes, well, I've done just fine so far. I don't need any stupid men to protect me, I can take care of myself." Looking up at Bo, she set her hand on the door handle.

The men regarded the petite young woman, all dainty and feminine, Bo almost laughed out loud.

But Kazak wasn't amused.

Bo reminded her with a droll smile, "Honey, you forget that Lord Adarken rescued you from wolves, and initially captured you. It easily could have been some other less scrupulous man."

Her blonde brows arched, her eyes flicked from Kazak to Bo. She said with slight sarcasm, "Really? He has taken me by force, pushed his unwanted advances on me, and kept me prisoner in a dungeon. What part of scrupulous am I missing?"

Both warriors studied her. Bo with humor, his grin widened at Kazak's growl at her words.

Frowning his annoyance, Kazak grumbled something to Bo.

Bo's eyes flit to him and back to Cini. "Lord Adarken wants to know what you were doing out there alone, where were you coming from, and where were you going?"

Her brow furrowed in an irritated frown, she replied, "I don't have to tell you anything."

Bo bit back a chuckle at her mettle. Then his mouth firmed, his tone more serious. "Cini, if you tell us, we can help you either get to where you're going, or take you home. Safely. And if you ran from something there, we will eliminate whatever it was."

She pulled her lips in and crossed her arms defiantly. Cini was trusting no one.

Seeing her mute determination to keep her secrets to herself, Bo sighed. "Ah." He glanced at Kazak who nodded.

Bo said to Cini, "You won't tell us. Maybe in time you will allow us to help you. In the meantime, I will tell you why I've brought you here now. You are going to marry Lord Adarken. Tomorrow."

Chapter Thirteen

Cini started, eyes popped and bounced from one man to the other. She sputtered, "You're joking!"

Both stared gravely at her, Bo clearly meant what he said.

"You two are crazy," she choked out. "I most certainly am not! I am leaving." She jerked the door handle to open the door, but Bo leaned against it with an apologetic smile.

Green eyes wide as bowls, she spat out, "But you can't! He can't make me do that."

Cocking his head at her, Bo said simply, "Ah, well, yes he can. He has the blessing of the emperor to do whatever he pleases. Trust me, with his value as a superior warlord, what he does with the vomen of the land is of so little trivial concern to the emperor. He wouldn't even blink if someone complained."

Her lashes flapped in dazed confusion at them. Stammering, "I- still, no, you can't, you have to let me go," she tugged vehemently but in vain at the door. There was no way she could move the hulking blond.

Her fists clenched at her side she scowled up at Bo insisting, "Step aside, I said I am leaving."

Bo wiped at the hair that fell in his eyes and glanced at Kazak.

Kazak's expression was rigid, implacable, eyes steely and narrowed at Cini, he nodded again to Bo.

Sighing, Bo said, "Honey," he spoke with weary kindness, apology in his deep voice. "You're wasting your breath and your energy," *and pissing off Kazak more every second you balk.*

"You have no say, you will marry him. Make it easy on yourself and just," his sigh heavy, "acquiesce. Give in gracefully and let the course go as it will."

Her head swung in consternation from one to the other.

Bo still carried an apologetic kind smile, Kazak's face was unreadable iron.

Wringing her hands, she cried in disbelief, "But- but, I don't understand? Marry him? Why?"

His small smile lopsided, Bo explained, "The lord requires a queen to strengthen the fiefdom the emperor is giving to him. Kazak will want, need, heirs." He shifted away from the door, moving a bit into the room to face her.

Flabbergast splattered all over her face, still not believing what he was saying, she blurted in agitation, "But- there are millions of women out there to choose from. They throw themselves at him."

"*Da,*" Bo nodded, "tis true. He could *føkk* ten vomen a day in this region for a lifetime and still not have them all."

His ears tinged pink seeing her embarrassment at his crudity, and Kazak's growl of displeasure. "Ah, sorry." Bo shrugged a big shoulder, "He wants you as his queen."

Cini glanced briefly at Kazak with a furious glare then back to Bo. "Huh. Well, you tell him I don't want him. He can have that- that woman that he had on his lap and his hands all over the other night, she would jump at the chance. All the women talk about how much you men like her big-big, uh, assets," she turned redder.

"Anyway, she is apparently quite desiring of him as are several others I've seen in the castle. They throw themselves at him, he doesn't even have to ask them. Tell him to go marry one of them." Her chin up in the air, she jerked her head to the side with a noble sniff.

Kazak's mouth thinned and turned down at her reference to Bonatella dumping herself on his lap and before he could react, grabbing his hand and setting it on her fat tit.

He had seen Cini's look of disgust at him. Obviously she thought he hopped from female to female with no discernment, having no class.

If he had no deportment he would have dumped Bonatella on the floor and fucked her right then and there in front of a room full of people. Bonatella would have been thrilled, as long as he claimed her as his afterwards.

But, he wasn't the mindless, crass animal that Cini called him. Angry, he opened his mouth to spout furiously at her, but Bo cut him off.

Lifting his hands up, palms out, Bo said, "Cini, there is no point in arguing about it, he wants *you*."

Stamping her foot, Cini clenched her fists tighter and professed furiously, "Well he can't have me. This is ridiculous, you can't make me. I'm leaving." She pulled at the door, but with a few long steps, Kazak was in front of it.

He said nothing, just glowered down at her, scowling darkly at her when she cringed from him. He grunted at Bo.

Nodding at Kazak, Bo said to Cini, "*Da,* yes he can. Lord Adarken has the right and the ability to marry you. Vomen have very few rights here, that's why you need protection."

Practically spitting in her exasperated fury, she screeched, "I don't need protection!" Yelling shrilly at Kazak, she gestured fervently at him, "Get out of my way! I am leaving!"

He didn't even blink as she tried to shove him, he was a big wall of rock. Tears of frustration and growing fear that he could, and would do what Bo said, gathered in her eyes blurring her vision. Trap her, bind her to him and the keep.

Kazak was like an ill-bred colossal bear, grunting and growling, intent on devouring her. Her breath hitched shallow and fast as panic was setting in.

The beast just stood there, he didn't touch her, or push her or say a word to her, he just blocked her from leaving.

Terrified and infuriated, Cini swung around to face Bo, it was easier to look at his kind face than Kazak's darkness.

She ground out, "You want to force me to marry this brute? The heathen can't even speak like a human, can't ask me himself to marry him, he just grunts and scowls like the beast he is, he has you talk for him."

She could literally feel Kazak's heat and masculine energy radiating at her back, his flagrant desire for her wrapping insidiously around her like an erotic blanket.

Even without looking at him she could feel such potent carnal hunger emanating from him, she knew if Bo wasn't present, he'd likely have her up against the wall, or flat on her back on the wool rug, snarling and spitting his animal lust and ripping at her clothes.

Bo said matter-of-factly, "Cini, Lord Adarken is not asking you to marry him, I am just here to tell you that you will."

She shouted at him, "No, Bo, tell him he can't-"

Kazak opened the door and stepped over the threshold, Bo walked around Cini.

"Honey, he understands English perfectly well, he's just rusty with speaking it. That's why I'm speaking for him, he doesn't want any misunderstandings."

Plus he knew Kazak felt he sounded like an inbred barbarian with his guttural English, and Cini already had a low opinion of him.

The anger descended into helpless, indignant fear. "But Bo, I refuse, I will not agree, it will all be a waste of time."

Lips pulled down at her distress, Bo said kindly, "He doesn't need for you to agree, or even say anything at all. Again, he is not asking you, but telling you. All the words will be verbalized by the priest. Your consent is not necessary."

Her eyes rounded at Kazak. For the first time she spoke directly to him with disbelief, "You are Christian?"

His mouth remained hard closed, he just stared at her. The inscrutable blue eyes cold behind a field of unwavering harsh darkness.

Bo answered for him, "Nay, he has no affiliation to any higher being. He was treated so viciously, without mercy, violently beaten and whipped, terrorized, knifed, worse-since a toddler found in the forest by soldiers. No one cared for him, treated him with any nurturing, or kindness, no one came to his rescue, ever-"

"Bo," Kazak grunted with a lowering of his brow.

Bo glanced at him with a shrug, then said to Cini, "There is a chapel if you desire any time to use it. You would have to of course attend under guard, but you only need to ask to go and you may. The wedding will of course be held there." His gaze skewed momentarily to Kazak and back to Cini.

Seeing her raised brow, he said, "All marriages have to be conducted by a priest to be legal. I am sure it tis the same in your village?"

At her brief nod he cleared his throat. "Uh, anyway, Sarah will bring you sustenance and something to wear. You will stay here tonight," he motioned to the room with his head.

"Of course the door will be locked and a guard posted. I will come for you tomorrow at five."

Kazak's impatient heavy breaths behind him, Bo held a hand up at her shaking head. "If you are not ready, the lord will come and dress you himself and you will attend your own wedding over his shoulder."

"Bo, I refuse-"

"Cini," stepping out the door, Bo said sternly, "don't test him. He will strip you, dress you, and carry you ignominiously to your wedding. You can't fight him, honey."

"No, Bo, stop, wait-" Cini tried to follow them out.

Bo held up a hand. He said gently yet firmly, "Cini, don't waste your energy fighting this. You will be married. When he is given his land and title, you will be his queen.

"Every girl in the land would give anything to be in your shoes, try to accept your great luck in capturing the emperor's highest lieutenant, and a future king. A very wealthy king."

He closed the door on her shouting at them, "No! Tell him I will not marry him!"

Cini paced half the night unable to sleep. She avoided the bed, it gave her the willies, it was *his* bed and he wanted her in it.

Stalking back and forth, she groused out loud, "Big hairy heathen. Can't even speak the Queen's English. Just grunts and growls like some caveman."

Why did he lock her in here instead of the dungeon? Must think it was more secure in his chambers than a steel cell. Shows how stupid he is.

She paused in front of the bed. He was a goliath, she would be unable to fight him off. He would probably rip her

111

clothes off her, put his hard nasty hands all over her naked body. Force his lubricious kisses on her and then rut like a savage dog, and would likely get her with his child as soon as he could.

She ignored the heat that percolated between her legs at the thought of his hands on her, those full yet wholly masculine lips sucking at hers, him lying atop- gah.

Cini shook her head to dispel her thoughts. She had no desire to be with the fierce, crude, warlord. Even if she did, she wasn't going to let anything or anyone keep her there.

She could not allow herself to have any feelings for him, she needed to get to the emperor to obtain his help. She would have to keep her eyes open all day tomorrow for an opportunity to escape.

Exhausted, she finally lay on his bed, curled up and slept until the dawn's soft light crept through the windows.

Chapter Fourteen

There was a quiet knock and the door opened carefully. Sarah stuck her head in. Seeing Cini sitting rubbing her eyes, she smiled and entered the room. She carried a gown and a straw basket.

"Miss Cini, good morning!" Sarah greeted her cheerfully.

"This is an exciting day for you! Who would have thought, the lord would capture you, and you would capture his heart? Oh," she flitted around the room hanging the dress on a hook and taking things out of the basket and setting them on the table.

"Tis so romantic, Miss." In her gay movements she didn't notice Cini's furious scowl.

With a heavy reluctant sigh, Cini decided it would be best to keep her dissenting anger to herself. Her complaints would only upset Sarah who was obviously loyal to the heathen lord.

It was still beyond her deepest fathoming why the barbarian wanted to marry her. What on earth could he think he would get out of it?

If he only wanted sex, her cheeks blushed, he could have just taken her when he felt like it. But marrying her? It made no sense.

She asked Sarah, "Why are you here so early? Bo said he would be coming at five."

"I know, dear." Sarah couldn't contain her glee, her face beamed with a wide grin. "But we have much to do. You need to soak in a perfumed bath. I need to oil and scent your body, wash and set your hair, make sure the dress fits, oh, yes," she nodded happily, "we will be lucky if you are ready by five!"

She hurried to the bathing room calling out, "Come child, we have no time to waste!"

When Sarah had opened the door, Cini saw the guard stationed there and knew she would not be able to attempt an escape until she was brought out of the room.

She reluctantly followed the maid into the bathing room, it already smelled of bath salts.

Exactly at five, Bo came for her. When he passed over the threshold, he halted, his eyes popped, mouth dropped.

"Gads, Cini, you look...unbelievable. If only I'd gotten to you first..."

Coming towards him, Cini complained morosely, "I wish it had been you, Bo. You are sweeter, kinder, gentler, you are light while he is dark-"

"Oh hell no, Cini," he spurted aghast. "I am a warrior, you can't describe me like that! Bite your tongue!"

Looking miserable she murmured, "But you wouldn't force me to marry you, would you?"

His lips pulled in, he didn't answer her. He walked a circle around her taking in every aspect of her gown.

"Damn, honey, for sure the gods only made one of you." He gave Sarah a quick wink of hello before his attention lit back on Cini.

"You think I look all right?" Cini might be furious Kazak was forcing her into marriage, but she was still a girl, and she wanted to look presentable.

Bo nodded, his gaze traveling all over the dress. "Oh, *yah*, breathtaking."

The crimson gown was embroidered with gold. Gold threaded through the draping sleeves and across the deeply cut diamond shaped bodice. The dress fit her like a glove, a silk belt hung from her slim hips, and she was to wear a matching cloak.

"Bo, where on earth did he get this dress from?" She went to the looking glass and studied her reflection. The long blonde curls were pinned around her crown and tumbled down one shoulder.

Bo answered, "Every merchant passes through here. We are stationed here because it is the intersection of many crossing trails of the trading route. Uh, I guess as soon as he made up his mind to…marry you, Kaz hit up all the merchants for a gown. He bought it and had Sarah alter it. I must admit he has damned fine taste."

"Well," she smiled bleakly. "I have to say you look pretty good yourself."

She admired his puffy long-sleeved, pale blue shirt with black tunic with silver braiding. He wore black breeches and boots, sword at his hip in a breasted silver belt. The dark blond hair was tied up in a knot at the top back of his head, per regal warrior status.

"Thank you, Cini." He moved towards the door. "We need to get going." His cheerful grin fell at her despondent demeanor.

Turning to face her, he scrubbed his fingertips down his face.

"Cini," he said gently, "please accept this. He can be a…brutal man in battles, but he has never harmed a voman. He won't hurt you, trust me, he is insane about you, he will treat you as the queen you will become."

"Bo, he locked me a cell in the dungeon because I wouldn't sleep with him."

Her voice dropped with embarrassment and fury, "He," she blushed at saying it. "He *spanked* me, Bo. Just because I escaped and refused to- to obey him. He is a tyrant, a bully. He will beat me as soon as look at me, I know it."

Surprised that Kazak had spanked her, that was something his friend hadn't shared with him, Bo shook his head.

Kazak was inordinately strong, but Bo doubted he had really hurt the girl. He was likely frustrated at her escape attempt and refusing to let him bed her, and had no other way to demonstrate and relieve his anger and frustration.

He explained, "Nay, sweet, he, uh," trying not to picture the beauty over his friend's knee, "spanked you because he is…lord, *dominio* - he can't have you disobeying him. It would cause terrible dissent within the troops.

"All must obey without question, without hesitation. He had no other way to…punish you, show you he was serious without truly harming you. Seriously, did he really hurt you?"

The color deepened over her fair skin. It was more the humiliation, and the helplessness against his powerful strength than the pain.

"No, not really. But still, I refuse to have a husband who- who pushes me around, punishes me, spanks me, forces me to do things, to do as he says, to- For heaven's sake, Bo, he is forcing me to marry him! We don't even know each other, and it is against my will!"

Bo looked sheepish. "*Da*, well, I never said he wasn't a bull-headed, domineering jerk with a bad temper."

His mouth curved up in a gentle smile. "Cini, it tis more not the norm, than it is normal for a marriage to be equally desired between a couple. Usually it is determined through the parents, the father.

"Or, in our case, we are basically nomadic warriors. We aren't usually in one place long enough to develop a relationship with a voman. So when we see what we want," he shrugged with faint apology, "we take it. It is legal, it is our right."

Her lids lowered, Cini turned from him. Her whisper bleeding with fright, "Bo, he is like an animal. He is…huge…and tough…and too- too strong, he even has," the color rose to cover her face, "sharp teeth, canines, like a- a savage-"

"Siberian tiger?" Bo put in quietly. "*Da*, Cini, you have heard the legends. That he was dumped in the jungle, the deep forest as a small child, left apparently to die. But he did not. Somehow he survived. There are marks, like, birthmarks, like tattoos, of Russian symbols on his back that indicate," he paused.

She turned to him.

He took a breath and said, "His royalty. As well as what looks like a tiger's paw, claw marks, over his shoulder, the sign the tiger beasts claimed him as their own. So, your impression of him as a savage beast, ah," the side of his mouth nicked up, "is pretty much true.

"The legend claims he lived with the Siberian tigers and they raised him. *Da*," he grinned at her lips curled in disbelief. "Tis hard to believe. But, when you get to know him, it will be clearer to you. He may be part man part beast, but I swear, he will never hurt you."

"Oh Bo, please-" her hands covered her mouth in despair.

"Shh, shh, Cini," he soothed her, patting her shoulder. "I speak the truth. I have known him my whole life, at least from six or seven years old, he has never harmed a voman. Even those that are to be punished for crimes, they are incarcerated but never whipped or beaten or, ah, beheaded. I promise."

He trod to the bed. "Come." He picked up her cloak and said, "We need to go. Any longer, and," he gave her an abashed smile, "he will come for you. Unless while hunting, patience is not one of his virtues."

As the pair trod down the corridor, Bo took Cini's hand and strung it through his arm.

She had put on the scarlet wedding cloak, pulled the hood up to cover most of her face per tradition, and Bo carried the long train of her skirt over his arm.

He led her out of the castle and down the length of the keep. Most of the keep was empty of the regular village residents, only shepherds, the reindeer herders, a few villagers caring for animals, merchants taking respite at the compound, and soldiers guarding the village were scattered about.

Under the hood of the cloak, Cini peered around nervously. She had been mostly unconscious when Kazak had brought her to the castle, and he had kept her virtually a prisoner since, so she has seen none of the compound.

It was a basic village. Clusters of huts, wooden and stone, knotted in groups of mostly one and two rooms covered the area. A few two-story buildings were scattered amongst the smaller huts.

The village was wealthy enough that most homes had chimneys and separate kitchens and hearths for safety from fire. Goats and chickens, and a few loose pigs wandered around the grass, hard-packed dirt and some stone paths.

Even though it was chilly, the lowering sun was warm, lazy dogs slept under the shade of maple trees.

Cedar trees and birches surrounded the village, fowl hung drying from branches. Leather and furs laid out stretching and drying in the sun.

In the pens surrounding the pastures, horses nibbled the tall grass occasionally whinnying or stomping a hoof.

Bo walked Cini to a huge building constructed of connected logs, sand and muck. It was the town chapel.

Huge double doors stood open. Soft stringed music trickled out to meet them.

He tried to hide the fact that he was literally dragging her inside the grand chamber.

They stood in the threshold. Bo tugged the partial bit of train of the skirt from her stranglehold on it and let it drift to the floor behind her.

He smiled down at her as Cini, keeping her head lowered, her face shadowed under the hood, stared wide eyed around at the high arched ceiling, polished wood gleamed from floor to wall to ceiling.

Fresh colorful flowers sprung from lovely vases, and white ribbons draped everywhere. The building was packed with villagers that hushed the second she stood in the doorway.

Her stomach tightened, throat constricted. Cini didn't want to look up to the front of the chapel. Except for the soft music in the background, the room was in utter silence, all attention was on her.

Her head still lowered, she peeked up, her legs turned to liquid, she felt a panicking scream rush through her head, she could hardly think.

The heathen bear, Lord Kazak Adarken stood at the head of the room, his eyes on her.

She could see, feel, his sheer power pulsating, affecting everyone in the room. The air left her lungs in a suffocating vacuum.

The potent bestiality speared through the crowd from his eyes arrowed at her like lancing blue lights.

Lord Kazak stood tall and confident, huge muscles bulged under his uniform. His black breeches were tucked into black knee-high boots.

He wore a sapphire blue shirt with long puffy sleeves under a silver tunic, the left breast layered with colorful studs of military medals.

A scarlet mantle that matched her gown hung from his shoulders to his heels. A silver chain strung from shoulder to shoulder across his front, and a silver, elaborately carved sword hung in a baldric that crossed his chest to hang at his hip.

The long dark hair was pulled back tied in a knot at the top back of his head, as was all his warriors. His full beard trimmed around his square jaw, he still looked like a savage warlord to Cini, which he was.

He waited arrogantly with his hands clasped behind his back, as if they were the only two people in the room, his gaze never wavered from her.

Cini's heart clenched in anxiety, he was truly going to make her go through with this. Take her freedom from her, trample her rights. She couldn't believe he was doing this, why?

Any woman he wanted in the world could be his, and he was forcing her to marry him. The same as Prince Andreyev wanted, except Kazak Adarken wasn't also razing her village and killing her people.

But the *dominio* was going to continue to keep her prisoner, as his wife. The way he looked at her, he was definitely going to force her to…

Oh, my, God. Cini's skin quivered with fury, fear, and contrarily, as frightening as the heathenish beast appeared to her, heat stirred between her legs. The burning intensity in his gaze brought that unfamiliar tingle, a warm sensation serrated her core.

She felt inexplicably drawn to him. The heat in his eyes pulled her like a wave to shore, her body craved to be wrapped up in his- no- a hard gulp squeezed down her throat, she closed her eyes to his lure.

She could feel nothing for him, her captor. Nothing was going to keep her here, nothing. Especially not a wild animal dressed in men's clothing.

Bo squeezed her hand with his arm to bring her to focus. Everyone was waiting on her.

What was she to do? Should she cause a big scene and fight it? Bo told her if she did the creature would come and get her and carry her to the altar, and make her do it hanging over his broad shoulder.

He said they didn't need her acquiescence, that she didn't need to verbalize any agreement, well, we'll see about that.

Angrily, she moved one step forward, then faltered. Her rubber knees turned positively weak, she couldn't move her feet.

Bo strengthened his arm around her hand and discreetly pulled her forward. Propelling her to take one step after another, almost carrying her to her destiny, her future, like a lamb being led to slaughter.

Cini took a huge shaky breath. If the wedding was inescapable, she would do it with as much dignity as she could.

She straightened her spine, lifted her head, and proceeded forward without Bo having to drag her, the long, wide, crimson train trailed behind them.

Cini was amazed when as she passed villagers, they all smiled joyfully, like they were happy for her. Many nodded, genial murmurs of good will and how beautiful she was surrounded her journey up the aisle.

Suddenly, a hand snaked out and snagged her wrist, jerking her to a stop. The people closest to her gasped.

Bonatella held Cini fast. She pulled Cini down and sneered in a nasty whisper to her, "You may be getting his name, but it will be my bed he sleeps in at night, missy, you remember that."

Her brunet hair was in an intricate twist on her head sprinkled with ornate gems. Her green gown, unseemly low-cut for the homespun village, revealed much of her ample bosom. Livid hazel eyes turned gold with animosity, glared malicious hate at Cini.

At first, Bo was stunned at the audacity of Bonatella grabbing ahold of Cini. Glancing up, he saw Kazak, his face livid, start down from the podium.

Bo shook his head at him to wait, and reached over and gripped Bonatella's wrist, and squeezed, hard. Until, with a sharp huff of pain, she released Cini.

Mortified, Cini reeled back against Bo, rubbing her wrist.

Bo bent and whispered in her ear, "Tis *bine*, tis all right, sweet, the hag is just a jealous bitch, come on, forget about her." He wound his arm around her waist, urging her forward.

Even more rattled now than before, Cini's body shook with shocked reaction of the assault.

Bo brought her to the podium.

Kazak came down the steps, his anger at Bonatella's behavior darkened the electric blue orbs.

Seeing Cini's green eyes huge and round with apprehension, he rolled his arm around her back, supporting her. He nodded at Bo who released her, and Kazak walked her up to where the priest waited.

Bo trod up to stand beside Kazak, and, surprised yet pleased, Cini saw that Sarah would be standing for her. The servant's broad smile showing how happy she was for Cini.

In that day and age, mostly men stood in as witnesses. Cini was surprised at Kazak having Sarah as her witness, bucking societal dictates that she was female and a servant, to help ease her. That touch of kindness relieved some of her tension.

They stood facing the priest as he prattled on, and on in Latin. Kazak kept his arm around Cini even when she moved to part from him.

True to Bo's words, Cini was not required to say anything. She recognized very few words, but she did hear her name, the priest said, "*Printesă Činnosti, y, Lord Kazak Adarken,*" with a string of words she didn't understand. He had called her Princess.

Cini glanced up quickly at Kazak who never looked away from the priest. How did he know? He couldn't, if he knew who she was he would have sent her back home.

He either took a wild guess due to her higher class elegant bearing, or was trying to lift her to a more equal level with him. The man was ever confounding.

Her lips bunched as she turned her attention back to the priest, and realized her last name wasn't said, so they didn't know who she was. How legal was that? Marrying her without knowing her full name?

But, in the area they were in, except for nobility, most people had no last names, they went by their father's. If the boy's name was Joseph and his father's was John, the boy's name was Joseph John, or, Joseph of John.

Her thoughts running a mile a minute, Cini didn't realize the priest had stopped talking and was looking at her, as was Kazak. She looked up at Kazak in question.

His face a harsh inscrutable mask as always, he said nothing as he lifted her hood and removed the cloak, and handed it to Sarah.

Cini shivered, suddenly feeling exposed.

He lifted the long tumbling ringlets and gently let them fall behind her back like fat springs, then, he took her hand, and before she could object, pushed a ring on her finger.

Gawking down at the ruby and gold twined band, Cini uttered, "No," and went to pull it off. Kazak put his big hand over hers, curling it over her hand so she couldn't remove the ring, and frowned at her.

Bo handed a ring to Cini, she just stared at it like it was a viper about to bite her. Kazak took the gold band from him and pushed it on his own finger then clasped her hand with the ring on it again.

Still stunned that he had put a ring on her, basically putting his brand of ownership on her, Cini didn't hear the rest of the priest's speech until he boomed out a few words ending with, "*Bărbat y Soția.*"

Sarah leaned over and whispered, "He has proclaimed you husband and wife, you are married!" Her excitement for Cini glowed in her voice, but her words clanged heavy on Cini's numb ears.

The priest said a few more words, and with both hands, Kazak seized her face and held her while he brought his head down to kiss her.

Cini and the Beast

Surprised, Cini started, but Kazak held her while gently covering her mouth with his. The kiss chaste at first, then as he tasted her, he pushed her lips apart and the kiss grew rampant, deep, turning wild like the animal he was as he consumed her.

The priest cleared his throat and the congregation twittered.

Grudgingly pulling from her, Kazak kept her face cradled in his hands, looked down at her, connecting their eyes, they had yet to speak a word to each other.

The crowd started chattering. Kazak grabbed her hand, raised it in the air, and turned them to face the congregation's cheers.

They paused, then he led her down the steps.

As they promenaded along the aisle, Kazak moved his hand under the ringlets that twirled down her back to settle on her bare nape, and austerely nodded to people along the way.

Cini couldn't breathe. His hard fingers stroking the sensitive skin exposed by the dip in the back of the bodice, he ushered her to a huge chamber behind the first room.

It was decorated with red ribbons and flowers, chairs and tables, music and food filled the room.

The crowd followed them in, the building was suddenly loud and boisterous.

After one brief dance, Cini and Kazak were separated by the exuberant crowd.

Cini found herself bounced around, congratulated in so many different languages, she barely understood what anyone said to her.

Eventually, Bo and Liam came and got her and brought her to a table where she gratefully sat down. They helped themselves to bowls of food placed on the table.

Not that she wanted to see him, but when she didn't spot the tyrannical lord anywhere, she asked Bo, "Where is he, my, uh," she was not going to call him her husband.

He could spank her, incarcerate her, beat her, torture her, but she will refuse to acknowledge this marriage forced on her against her will.

"Unfortunately, sweet," Bo lifted a clay cup and drank its contents, "there was some trouble between the reindeer herders and the silk merchants, arguments about territory or whatnot."

Not that she cared, but was curious, after all, her groom left her already? She asked, "Why couldn't you or," her gaze flicked to Liam and now Thomas who had joined them at the table, "anyone else go?"

"*Yah*, well, the silk merchants speak Chinese and Kaz is pretty much the only one around here that speaks it relatively fluently. If he didn't go smooth things over there would likely be some deaths by morning. We," he shot a glance at the other two men, "have orders to bring you to his...ah, your chambers upon the conclusion of the feasting. He will join you there when he's gotten things settled down."

The side of Bo's mouth pulled in at the color flooding her face. The awareness hit her that now she would now be sharing Kazak's quarters, with him. Unless he would be returning her to the dungeon, but that would look odd to the people if he put his bride in there.

But, she shrugged, then again, Bo had told her Kazak didn't care what people thought of him or what he did.

She asked him, "Why do you all have to take me?"

Liam answered her, "Some of the traditions that the villagers do to the newly married couple can be a little on the," he glanced at his friends, "rambunctious, uh, ribald side."

"*Da.*" Thomas added, "Plus, there have been rumblings of some of the men that were…let's say, a bit put out, that Kazak married you without giving them the opportunity to press their suit. Apparently, there were threats voiced that some of them would try to come and take you from him, then they would fight over who would keep you. That was one reason why he rushed this wedding."

Cini sat in crazed disbelief. She was in a darn jungle with irrational animals that had no laws, no morals, no integrity.

She said quietly to Bo, "Can we go now? I'm…tired." She had no desire to rush things to be alone with Kazak, but she felt like such a fraud.

All the people and their best wishes and happiness for her, and she had married under duress.

"Sure." Bo stood up, and Liam and Thomas followed suit.

Bo pulled Cini's chair back to help her up.

Sarah hurried over. "Boys, mind her skirt, the train, you will have to help her carry it." She grinned at the men's flustered dismay.

The three males stared at the long crimson train.

Bo grinned. "I had my turn earlier."

Sighing, Liam and Thomas gathered up the material. Thomas held it in his arms, and Liam and Bo walked on either side of her.

They slipped out the back way to save Cini having to endure more well wishes and raunchy chatter of the marriage bed and what to expect. Or worse, the crowd picking her up and carrying her with bawdy singing and lewd chants to her and Kazak's chamber.

Then, there was the likelihood of the people undressing her, and putting her naked into the bed to await Kazak, and, there was an even more likelihood of people climbing in with her.

The four traveled without incident until they had just about reached the castle.

When- out from a hammock of trees, more than a dozen men emerged and swarmed around the group.

Instantly, Bo, Liam, and Thomas turned their backs to each other with Cini in the middle.

Bo called out, "What's this about, Caine?" He addressed the huge, barrel-chested man with an enormous club in his hand that appeared to be the leader. In fact, all of the men were armed with clubs, or swords out and ready.

A smirk on his filthy face, Caine stepped forward. "We want the girl. The *dominio* had no right to claim her like that. There were plenty of others that let him know of their interest, I was one of them. Since he ignored our wishes, we will be taking our taste of her now."

"Yes," another man said, raising his club and moved beside Caine. He told them, "You boys don't want to be hurt, just step aside and let us at her."

Chapter Fifteen

With a chuckle and a shake of his blond head, Bo said, "Nay, not a chance. Now, you fellows move along peacefully and we will let you live."

"Ha!" The group of attackers laughed crudely. "There are three of you and a big bunch of us, son. Do yourself a favor and move away from the girl, let us take her with no trouble."

"Bo," Cini's voice tiny and scared, "do what he says. I don't want you guys hurt. I'm sure they won't…harm…me." She tried to push out between Bo and Liam. The two men moved closer together.

"Nay, sweet," Bo said with a chuckle, "you will be fine. Just stay right where you are."

"Your last chance, warrior," Caine barked, moving closer. His club in both hands raised over his head ready to strike.

"Do your best, Caine," Bo's voice lost all its mirth, it had turned cold as vicious steel.

With a roar, Caine and his men charged the warriors, rushing them from all sides.

Bo gave Cini a push against a wall out of the way and the men went at it.

Punches and shouts, Bo went for Caine first. Dodging the club swung at his head, he jammed his fist into his gullet and then bashed his other fist into his face, knocking Caine out cold.

The huge man slammed to the ground. Bo stomped on his neck with his heavy boot. Caine drew his last breath and Bo went for the next one.

The men battled; Bo, Liam, and Thomas were making quick and easy mincemeat out of the attackers. Bodies lay sprawled, blood and sweat sprayed and spattered everywhere.

Cini huddled against the wall unsure what to do. She'd be a fool to rush in and try to help, not that they needed help, but she felt helpless and useless just standing there cowering. She eased back from the spot Bo had pushed her to.

"Eee!" she screamed as another man dashed from behind the trees and grabbed her.

"Hush, little bitch and I won't hurt you. I just want a quick piece of you." He slapped his hand over her mouth and cinched his arm around her waist lifting her in the air.

"Put voman down," the deep, gravelly voice demanded in guttural English, "or I kill you." Kazak stood twenty feet from them.

His warriors had bested the assailants, all lay dead or critically injured. The three friends came to stand beside Kazak.

Panting from the fight, Bo told him, "*Frăţe*, we have this, no need for you to get your hands dirty."

His eyes on the man that held Cini, Kazak's head cocked to Bo. In Mongolian, he said with heavy sarcasm, "*Da*? You have it handled? Then why does that *føkkeh* have his hands on my wife?"

He didn't wait for Bo's reply, he strode straight at the man holding Cini.

Cini was kicking and struggling for all she was worth, but the thug outweighed her by more than a hundred pounds, and he held her right up off her feet.

The man shouted at Kazak, "Don't come closer, Lord! I mean no offense, but I am taking a piece of this woman. I'll give her back when I'm done. I told you I wanted her but you married the bitch out from under me."

He let go of her mouth to wield his sword. Slashing it in Kazak's direction, he taunted, "Many of your warriors share their whores, just relax, and-"

Announcing, "You die for hurt Činnosti," Kazak kept coming. His steps hard and enraged, he moved so fast-before the man could open his mouth for another threat, or flourish his sword, Kazak was upon him.

The enraged warlord jammed both hands on his head and slammed it against the stone wall, blood gushed onto the stone.

His hands still on the man's head, Kazak snapped it to one side. The man made a cackle sound, dropped Cini, and crumpled to the ground.

Bo was there, he caught Cini and moved her out of the way.

Kazak crouched beside the man. The thug's eyes were staring blankly at the night's sky. Standing, Kazak strode over to Bo and Cini.

Snatching her arm, he grabbed a fistful of the train and ripped it completely around and off, then holding her arm he walked hard and quickly to the castle.

Bo, Liam and Thomas shared a grin. Then Liam said, "I guess we have cleanup duty, eh?" They went to the task of disposing of the attackers.

Kazak didn't say a word as he walked Cini through the grand hall, the great room, up the stairs, down the corridor, to his, their, room.

He threw the door open so hard it banged into the wall, he blocked it with his arm on the rebound and ushered Cini inside.

Chapter Sixteen

Enraged, shaking with fury over the attack, villagers daring to try to take his woman, his wife! Fuming, Kazak stomped over, grabbed a cup, poured a drink, threw it down, poured another.

Watching him, Cini wormed her way back towards the door, tugging at the band on her finger. The now short red skirt twirled above her knees.

Kazak turned to see her moving to the door and pulling the ring off her finger.

Incensed all over again, he stomped over to her, grabbed her hand. Twisting her wrist, holding it up to show the ring, he snarled, "You *nu* take off ring, Kazak break finger, husband and wife bound."

He threw her hand down, and tossed back the drink. Returning to the bottle he refilled the cup, then slugged down every drop.

Rubbing her wrist, her voice trembling, how dare he threaten her! Her nose in the air she stated, "I refuse to be your wife."

Kazak stared down at the cup in his hand, his eyes turned up to glower at her through a lock of hair that escaped the knot. His gaze of ire rolled down her body, then back up to

133

see her face pale, nervous, yet angry herself, and still moving to the door.

Slamming the cup down, he removed the baldric and laid it and his sword aside. Unchaining the mantle, he pulled it off and tossed it on a chair. Then he removed the silver tunic and dropped it on the mantle, and stalked to her in the sapphire blue shirt, black breeches and boots.

She hovered against the door, fluttering delicately like the colorful ethereal fairy the warriors had first described.

Lust warring with his fury blasted white flames in the blue eyes that dropped to the low bodice of her red gown. He wiped the back of his hand across his mouth, over the beard, pupils radiating raw hunger.

"St- stay away from me," she demanded. Cini was annoyed that her voice shook betraying her fear of him, but he was so aggressive and formidable.

The heat scorching his eyes, his lips curled back in a hiss exposing his canines. Cini felt a chill bolt up her spine.

Growl cave-deep, he stepped to within inches from her, and stated harshly, "You *nu* tell Kazak *nu* touch wife."

His gaze fierce on hers, lowered again to her bosom. Without more preamble, he lifted his strong warrior's hands and roughly palmed her full breasts.

"No!" she shouted and turned to the door. Grabbing the handle she jerked hard, then harder on it. Frustration and fear threatened to strangle her as she realized he had locked it.

It didn't matter, because he slammed his hand on the door over her head, then caught her arm and swung her around.

"*Basta*," he barked, "enough you say nay to Kazak, enough." He gripped the front of her gown with both hands and ripped it apart.

Cini screamed and threw a flurry of slaps at him.

Ignoring her puny strikes, Kazak moved his hand behind her and clinched her neck. Dragging her in, he jammed his mouth hard on hers, at the same time he shoved his hand in her torn gown and seized her breast over the tight band that bound them.

His body immense with muscles, hard and pumped up with anger and seething with desire, Kazak overpowered her with his strength and vigor.

Hugging her tight against his brawny chest, he roughly squeezed her breast with his strong hand. His thumb rubbing her mounded flesh, fingers gripping, trying to feel her soft curves over the binding while bruising her lips with his punishing kiss.

Putting both hands to his chest, Cini shoved him as hard as she could, it took him off guard and he took a step back, she ran-

For three steps, then he scooped her up and carried her screaming to his bed. After laying her on it, he dropped down with her, throwing a leg over her to secure her.

"Leave me alone!" she cried, twisting to get away from him. Kazak grabbed her flailing wrists and staked them to the bed. He tried to kiss her but she tossed her head back and forth.

He let go of her wrists, pushed aside the torn sides of her gown, shoved the band down past her ribs then tore it completely off and put his mouth on her bare breast. Restraining her hands again, he sucked so hard she cried out.

To Kazak's ears her exclamation was part pain, part ecstasy. He saw goose bumps pop and run up her arms, her nipples hardened like pink buds. His lips and teeth enclosed over one, his beard ruffled over her flushing chest.

The shiver that wrought her body was not missed, his tongue lashed a peaked nipple.

Louise Furley

Thrashing under him, Cini bucked and screamed, "No! Get off of me, let me go! Let me go!"

Kazak lifted his head, eyes already glazed. Eviscerated with desire, he said forcefully with gutted English, "Činnosti, you *nu* say *nu*, ah no, to Kazak, you are *soția, Kazak's wife.*" His eyes fell to her bare breasts, he lowered his mouth to her flesh again.

Holding her arms over her head with one hand, he reached down pulling her skirt up, and reached for her underwear. His erection hard and bulging strained against her thigh; she squirmed, struggling to get away.

Cini felt his weight on her, his heavy, strong body pressing against her feminine curves. His mouth on her breasts, somehow she could feel it on her private parts, below.

He was rough, sucking hard, it hurt, but, it tugged dampness between her legs, and lit an odd yearning so enflaming her head boggled.

She felt his hand on her thigh, the heat of his rugged palm sizzled her skin, making her crave for more. But she couldn't. She couldn't be his wife, she can't stay here, she has to get to the emperor.

"No," she jerked at his hands. Bending her knees, she lifted her legs to block him. And was surprised when he stiffened, and moved off her.

His brow low, masculine ridged, under it his eyes burned confused. Face tense with desire, he stared at her in frustration.

She moved away from him.

Kazak scrubbed his hands down his face, dragged his blunt fingers through his beard, then his gaze went to her bare breasts, his cheeks singed dark red.

"Činnosti," came out in a growl steeped in want, excruciating hunger for her, and fury that she continued to deny him.

She rolled off the bed pulling her torn dress together and went to the door. Her head down, she murmured, "Dungeon."

Kazak moved to sit on the edge of the bed. His expression inscrutable, so hard to read with the thick beard, much of his black hair loose from their struggles hung over his face.

Locks draping over his darkly enigmatic eyes, he regarded his bride under the thick brow. His new wife preferred the dismal cell to sex with him?

Lids weighted with surging desire tapered over his heated gaze in rumination. She had reacted to his mouth, his hands, she couldn't hide it, or the hot blush that covered her face before she ducked it down. She was clearly turned on, but resisting.

Was she that afraid of him? Or was it something else?

"You have…" his mind filtered through his rusty English, "want, for other man?" He had never considered she left a suitor behind, or, maybe that was whom she was running to?

His skin darkened with possessive fury as the thoughts crossed his face. He observed her mannerisms carefully for the truth. But she kept her head lowered and turned from him.

Kazak slid to his feet, adjusted his pants over his hard-on that fought against his breeches to get at her.

Seeing her back go rigid, he didn't move to her. Like a belligerent bear, his thick shoulders bunched. Voice hard, he told her, "You Kazak's *soția,* wife, now."

The fierce command brusque and angry, "You *nu føkk* other man, men, *nu* more, only Kazak, *bărba.*" Jabbing his thumb at his chest, he searched for the English word. Then he said roughly, "Husband. Only *føkk* husband, Kazak." His halting guttural English only made him sound more the crude barbarian.

Keeping her head down and turned, hands pressed against the door behind her, she mumbled, "Dungeon."

Letting out a heavy breath, Kazak trod, still in his sturdy boots to a trunk. On the trunk was a stack of clothes. He gathered them up then went to Cini and handed them to her. "Put on dress, Kazak take to dungeon."

Cini stared wordlessly at the clothes, then took them. There was a dress, clean stringed underwear, shoes. She noticed no breast band. Was that his doing or Sarah's who had plainly provided the clothes?

Kazak obviously knew only about men, he knew nothing about females other than to fornicate with them.

She waited, hoping Kazak would leave while she changed, but clearly he was not budging. He just stood there with those cold, impassive eyes, watching her.

With a sigh, she went into the bathing room to change.

When she came out dressed in a soft, cream-colored frilly gown, too light for the coolness of the outdoors, she nervously held the shoes in her hand.

Last thing she wanted was to go to the dungeon, but, she thought she had a better chance of escaping when he hopefully had her brought to the kitchens to cook.

A tiny quirk lifted the corner of her lip, he clearly loved her cooking. He always ate every bite like a voracious pig. He gathered up as many ginger-candies and desserts he could carry, and with a container of her pear or apple brandy under his arm before he'd disappear from the dining table.

His hooded eyes stroked down Cini's body like hot hands. He was unaware how prehistoric, how lusting his gaze was. How he looked at her like he wanted to strip her and wolf her down. He acted like he'd never seen, or had, a woman before. She moved gingerly to the door, expecting him to pounce on her any second.

Kazak did move then. He strode to the chair he'd laid his mantle over, picked it up and came to her. Ignoring her shrinking from him, he draped it over her shoulders, then stepped back, muttering, "Cold outside."

Bo's words of romancing, seducing a woman came to his mind. Bo had told him Cini was a sweet, honorable, innocent woman. That just grabbing at her would only cause her to run faster from him.

Kazak was used to not having to pursue a woman, be gentle with her, seduce her, but, under low lids he observed Cini.

She was young, and scared, on the run from or to- hell knows what. The cold blue eyes softened, and she was now his wife. He chose her. He had no thought of, no desire for any other woman, and he knew he never would again.

She had crawled under his skin and into his head and heart before he could get defense walls up. He'd been too extraordinarily attracted to her from moment one.

Kazak felt no guilt whatsoever for forcing her into marrying him. He was a warlord, a lord, and a *dominio,* one of the emperor's top lieutenants. He was within the law, he had every right to make her marry him. And, he knew he had to do it if he wanted to keep her.

She was on the run, his only ways to keep her were to incarcerate her in his dungeon… forever, or make her his wife.

He'd known when he had straddled her on the ground that day he captured her, when he at first thought she was a boy, when he looked into those gorgeous, cock-pounding eyes, he was lost. He had to have her. He had never felt the way he felt in that moment for any other woman, he knew that very day she would be his. Forever.

The other men were coming after her, wanting her. He had to marry her quickly, get her under his claim and protection to stop them.

He had been shocked when those soldiers had tried to take her earlier. It was the last mistake they ever made. Their brutal deaths will be a deterrent to any others thinking they can just up and take what's his. His wife.

Kazak was plenty experienced, she obviously was not. It was time to teach his young wife to desire him, get her to the point where she was asking him, begging him to take her. Without grabbing at her, without forcing her to spread her legs and just shoving himself inside her beautiful body.

He wanted her to want him, and that was a new, totally unfamiliar feeling. And, for the first time in his life, he wanted a woman's trust. He wanted her to trust him, to tell him what she was running from so he could help her, protect her, eliminate whatever the threat was. So she would stay.

Swallowing hard, Cini bent to slip on a shoe, and said, "I...just need to put on my shoes and I'll be ready to go-"

That's when he sprang. Like a slingshot held taut then the rock let loose- He jumped at her, shoving her against the door.

Surprised, she dropped her shoes, her mouth fell open, he slapped his lips over hers forcing her lips to stay apart for his assault on them. Her startled gasp puffed into his mouth, down his throat. He swallowed it as if it were substantial, a physical part of her.

Kazak pushed the mantle from her shoulders, her hands instinctually went to his chest to stop him. He grasped her wrists, secured them over her head, and pinned her roughly against the heavy wood door with his hips.

Belatedly the thought flickered in that he wasn't going to attack her, he was going to seduce her, but he wanted her, needed to take her, so badly.

Having to control himself had never been something he'd had to undertake before, it was a new thing he needed to learn.

He must put aside the ruthless, aggressive warlord that he was, and using his own skills of experience teach Cini to come to him.

Yet, he clinched her wrists, holding her prone against the door, bearing his body into hers.

Chapter Seventeen

His sudden assault stunned Cini, knocking the sense, her resolve right out of her brain, blowing it completely blank.

Kazak's broad shoulders blocked any escape she could attempt. His powerful chest pressed against her bosom. It was hard, unyielding, warm and strong.

His heated breath tousled her hair, the side of her face before he seized her mouth again. Through the thin dress she could feel the contours of the slabs of muscles beneath his shirt rocking into her chest making her breasts swell, nipples beading. All thought of not getting involved with him fled like the wind.

His erection had not gone soft since he was all over her on the bed, it was already an iron club straining against his breeches. His mouth still besieging hers, Kazak moved his hips between her legs, and nudged them apart.

Bending his knees, he positioned his shaft directly on her womanhood.

Cini was unprepared for the feel of it, his thick hardness pressing right on her sex. She couldn't hide the shudder that ran through her body, or that she unconsciously clenched his legs with hers. When he moved his shaft very slightly with increased pressure, Cini's core burst on fire.

Suddenly dizzy, her head swimming with the rush of burning fever, her arms restrained over her head, Kazak's big body pinioning into hers, his hips forcing her legs apart, Cini forgot to fight him, to struggle.

His mouth ransacking hers, his hot torso covering her, the hard length of his cock pressing, moving against her pulsing cleft was all she could feel.

The rush of blistering heat chasing up her body obliterated all thought, she was a disembodied being with no conscious thought, just pure radiating sensation.

Feeling her surrender, her body clinching around his, Kazak's own brain reeled. His burgeoning phallus throbbed against her. Through their clothing, he forced it hard into the folds of her cleft.

Rubbing it wantonly, vigorously over her core, he was shocked when he felt her breathy moan slipping from her lips into his mouth, misting his tongue swirling inside her mouth.

He lodged the length and breadth of his rigid manhood as hard against her woman's sex through her light gown as he could, and was rewarded with another moan. And her pelvis writhing against his, her breasts wedged, rubbing fiercely against his chest.

"*Miera*, precious," he groaned against her lips. "*Mea* Činnosti, *mea* wife." Holding her wrists over her head with one hand, Kazak moved the other to slide along her jaw.

Cradling her face, he slanted his to seal their mouths tighter. His tongue painting his abandoned desire, slashing over her teeth, the roof of her mouth, her tongue. When his tongue stroked hers, Cini made tiny tentative lashes against his, then sucked on it like he had done to her.

Kazak groaned out loud, his shaft shoved into her. So big and hard he abraded her woman's cleft through their clothes, dry-humping her. He lifted his thigh between their legs to tighten their closeness, pressed it into her so she could ride it.

A searing whine hissed from Cini. Her cheeks bright red, she thrust her sex against his erection feeling the hard, thick ridge throbbing over her sex.

He could feel her sheer inexperience, which only excited him more, the blood pounded in his head deafening him. And now she was writhing even more wildly against him.

Her writhing ground her breasts on his chest loosening the ties on front of her gown.

Cini's chest heaved at his. Kazak pulled from her mouth to watch her ride his thigh, practically masturbate his shaft with her body.

Her eyes rolled back in her head, cries whimpered out as her body undulated and flayed at him, in frenzied arousal she didn't know what to do about it.

Gods, Kazak thrilled at her reaction, her virgin body's assault on his. Her face flushed, neck arched, her head dropped back as her eyes scrunched closed in passion, he could watch her like that forever.

The ties on her gown came completely undone. With one hand Kazak pushed the parts of the bodice apart, baring her breasts. His groin burned, cock jumped, every part of him wanted every part of her.

Her eyes opened, glassy, unseeing. Lips parted damp from his kisses, unaware the bodice was splayed open, fully exposing her breasts. His mouth was drawn to them, but he didn't want to pull her attention from precisely what she was feeling at the moment.

Didn't mean he couldn't drink in his fill of her plump succulent *sâni,* her breathtaking tits, the most beautiful he'd ever laid his eyes on.

His hands itched to crush them in his big fingers, to suck them until there wasn't an inch of her creamy skin not blemished red from his mouth.

But he resisted the overwhelming temptation, not wanting anything to stop her momentum. Not wanting to grab at her, not force her, he wanted her to be the leader, ask, or show him what she wanted.

Wincing with the torrid sensations blitzing her sex, Cini wriggled, needing, wanting, something, more, she didn't know what. Dazed, feeling out of control but she didn't know why.

Her delirious blind eyes beseeched him as she wailed, "Kazak, help me," her hitching breaths nicked up her throat. She tugged at her wrists, struggling for him to release them. Her pupils overcame the green irises until they were huge, black erotic discs of fear and scalding heat.

Her rasping plea stabbed Kazak in the groin, skyrocketing his desire. And it knifed him in the heart, it was the first time she has said his name. His ballocks ached, cock screamed to be let out and get its release inside his beautiful bride.

Releasing her wrists, he spread a hand across her back and the other cupping her bottom he lifted her up, murmured, "Legs around waist."

In her urgent delirium, she wrapped her legs around his waist, her hands clutched at his big shoulders.

He couldn't help himself, Kazak shoved his face into her cleavage, scrubbing his bearded jaw against her supple breasts, he sucked one until a red mark grew. Then he lifted her and brought her down chafing hard over his manhood that was bulging out of his breeches.

Her hands moved to twine around his neck. Keening sounds deep in her chest, Cini's neck arched, head lolled back. Reveling in his mouth on her bare skin as he kissed and chewed her flesh, bit and suckled her nipples.

He lifted her up then slammed her back down, grinding her against his clothed cock with every move.

Her aching breaths tight and squeaking in his ear grew rougher, rushing, legs squeezing his waist, her body quivering.

Kazak knew she was at the top, ready to soar off, but it was unfamiliar ground for her and as frenzied as she was, he could feel her starting to panic from the radical, piercing sensations she was experiencing for the very first time.

His forearm holding her bottom, he pulled her skirt from beneath her and over his arm so he could touch her intimately.

Eyes heavy lidded, her voice a befuddled rasp, whisper a slur of delirium, "Lord, what…"

"Kazak, *mea miera*, my precious Činnosti, say Kazak." He needed to know she was aware of who was loving her, her husband, not her Liege.

Slowly, so she wouldn't feel he was grabbing at her, Kazak stroked his hand up her side and cupped a breast. At her moan, he kneaded it, she felt amazing, full and soft, firm and ripe. His hard fingers squeezed it as he lowered his mouth to suckle it briefly.

He then skimmed his hand down her ribs, over her tiny waist, he felt so strong and masculine, hot and protective, with her so petite and dainty and curvy in his arms.

Letting go of his neck, Cini stroked her palms down then up his chest, her brain buzzing with sensual overload. She enjoyed the differences between her soft body and his toughness, her hands moved up and she tangled her fingers in his hair.

Kazak could have come right then and there. But, he wanted his wife to truly learn to desire him, so he garnered his self-control and did not crouch, lay her right down on the floor and take her.

He slid his hand down her hip, under her dress, along her thigh, and gently cupped her sex over the underwear. He paused, judging her feelings, she stiffened, fingers tightened in his hair.

But her legs stayed wrapped around him, her bosom pressed against his chest. Kazak pulled one string then the other, the underwear undone he pulled it off and dropped it.

His arm still under her butt, he stroked his fingers up the folds of her sex and felt her quiver with a husky moan.

Encouraged, he dipped his fingers along her entrance and shivered, gods she was soaking wet, for him. He got her silk on his fingers and slid them up her slit and lightly touched her bud. Everything about her was so tiny and sweet and perfect.

Cini about exploded when he touched her so intimately. She wriggled against his hand, a choked whisper, "*More*."

"Ah, *mea* wife," just what he wanted to hear. He fingered her slit, brushing and circling her bud with her own silk until she was squirming, and moaning gasps came faster, shallower. Soon she was breathless, gasping, trembling.

Kazak couldn't take his eyes off her. Her lids were heavy, and puffy and low over the green glimmer barely visible. Her lips parted with frantic breaths, he wanted badly to kiss her but he wanted more to watch her come.

She was squirming so hard against his hand now he had to hold her tight or she'd wriggle right out of his arms. Her whimpers were aching pleas.

Kazak twirled and plucked at her bud and when he just barely inserted his thick finger into her sex, her entire body went rigid, her spine arched and her head fell back with a cry. His hand splayed across her back, he lifted her to watch her.

Cini's face scrunched as if in terrible pain. A pearly pink blush and shiny perspiration sheened her face, her lashes flit up and down, her breath gushed out.

Kazak pushed his finger in just a little more, even there she was tiny. He rubbed his palm hard on her bud and she cried his name, "*Kazak!*"

Holding her, he felt her shudder and her body bucked and shimmied. He murmured, "Kazak has you, *mea* wife, *mea* Činnosti."

Then she came like a firecracker. Her channel clenched his finger, pelvis grinded at his hand. Her convulsing body an exploding volcano, she threw her arms around his neck holding her body tight against his, and screamed into his neck.

Kazak tried to move his finger deeper inside her, but she churned and tossed so much he lost contact with her channel. He just held her until she gave one last shudder and then lay pulsating, gasping against him.

He moved his arm to support her butt and wrapped the other around her, holding her tightly while whispering words of mixed languages in her ear.

Then he felt her stiffen in his arms. Lifting his head, he looked down at her. Her lids heavy, her eyes were glazed and unfocused, but they were rapidly coming into focus as she was becoming aware of where she was, and what just happened.

Her hands went to this chest. "Let me down," her voice hoarsely rough with her orgasm and now her mortification.

"Činnosti, Wife," Kazak murmured, petting her hair, trying to keep their closeness from disintegrating.

Her voice now tight and clearly upset, Cini insisted, "Let me down, right now."

Grumbling curse words, Kazak let her slip down his body to her feet.

As soon as she was standing, she ran to the door pulling her bodice closed. Of course the door was still locked but she pulled at the handle maniacally, the enormity of what they'd just done hitting her, when she had sworn to keep a distance between them.

She looked down, her dress was wide open. He'd had his hands on her breasts, on, in- her most private parts. Cini frantically pounded on the door. "Let me out!" she screamed desperately.

Kazak went to her, tried to put his hands on her shoulders, his arms around her, quietly saying soothing words to calm her, but she shook him off and kept pounding on the door.

He said, "Činnosti, *haltă*, stop, we did *nu*, ah, no bad, tis *bine*, all right."

She swung around, desperation and flowing tears marring her face. "Don't touch me, leave me alone, you- you- took advantage of me." Turning back to the door she resumed pounding on it.

Not wanting any guards or soldiers to come, he rolled his arm around the front of her and pulled her away from the door.

"No!" she cried, twisting and wrenching from him. Feeling the burn in her core, already her body was craving his, she needed to get the hell out of there!

"Shh," Kazak said quietly. "Kazak leave, Činnosti stay." Letting go of her, he stepped back.

Her face white as snow, teeth chattering, her arms were wrapped tightly around her body to try to still the trembling.

He didn't get it. What happened? Seconds ago she was writhing in his hands and screaming his name, and now?

But she was in such a panic he couldn't bear to see her like that. Dragging his hands through his hair, he went to the door and unlocked it, opened it. Took a last look at her.

Tears streaked down her face. The urge to go to her, hold her, was overwhelming. But, she was obviously distraught over what they'd done, he needed to leave her alone. He stepped out the door and shut it.

Out in the corridor, Kazak leaned against the door and let out a long breath. He palmed his raging erection, well aware he would be reliving all night the way she came apart in his arms.

Combing his fingers through his hair, he looked for a guard to watch his chamber, and headed towards Bo's rooms. He would bunk with him like he had been.

He didn't get it. He and Cini had just had an amazing moment together, what he hoped would lead to wildfire catching inside her and she'd come to him from now on, or at least welcome him with open arms, wanting more.

Like when she was in his arms and she'd whispered with agonized rapture in her hoarse voice, "*More*."

Hell, he sighed, he would never understand women. He'd have to talk with Bo about it.

Bo spent time actually talking to females, he might know what happened and be able to explain it to him. **Tell him what to do next.**

Chapter Eighteen

Cini, stood looking out the window the next morning. She was up too high to climb out and down even if no one heard her break the window, which would be highly unlikely as there always seemed to be someone out and about in the keep.

The warriors were on horseback wending their way down the main road out of the keep. She recognized Kazak's strong, confident bearing in the lead.

When Sarah had brought her more clothes at dawn, she'd told Cini the men were going out to quell an uprising between outlaw rebels and a small village a few miles outside of the trade route into the forest.

They would likely be gone a few days.

Cini rubbed the ache in her stomach as the picture of a dead Kazak lay bleeding on the dirt road sifted into her mind. She shook her head, he was the ablest of all the warriors, which was why he led, she didn't need to worry about him returning alive.

Why was she even worried about him dying?

Heavens, Cini thought of all the times he's rescued her. She scrubbed her eyes with a pained sigh. It was too late to protect herself from him.

When she should have hoped he'd be killed and not return to her and she could go on to complete her mission, instead, a dread filled her of never seeing the big, crude lummox again.

Rough masculine face of hard ridges and sharp planes, his brilliant blue eyes such a contrast to the darkness of the rest of him filled her mind.

The way those piercing eyes bloomed with desire whenever he looked in her direction. The way his muscled body pumped, and his biceps bulged when he clenched his fists to keep from touching her.

The way his hands felt when he did touch her…the way his manhood grew so frightening big and powerfully hard-no, she had to stop. They were not meant to be. She needed to go.

There was a knock at the door before it opened. It was Sarah.

"Good morning, Miss, I mean Mistress, Madam Adarken, uh, Lady Adarken," Sarah's face filled with the red of uncertainty.

"Sarah, please, call me Cini like you were. I don't want to hear-" she stopped, smiled bleakly. She didn't want to be reminded that she was now a married woman. "Uh, have you come to take me to the kitchens?"

Rubbing her reddened cheeks, Sarah nodded. "Yes. Lord Adarken left me orders to see that you do as you please in the kitchens and everyone is to follow your orders." A smile grew on her pleasant wrinkled face. "You are in charge now, the lady of the castle."

Rolling her eyes, Cini slipped her shoes on and grabbed her cloak, "Please, Sarah, don't-"

"No, Mistress Cini," her brows down in sudden anger. Sarah said seriously, "You are the mistress of the castle, you are Lord Adarken's wife. No," shaking her head at Cini's disputing expression, "there is no denying it or undoing it. For all the gods' sake, why you would want to deny something so glorious, something every maid in every village for thousands of miles would die to be, Lord Kazak Adarken's bride, tsk," she shook her head again.

Sarah continued before Cini could speak, "I understand how…scary he is. But," her bottom lip pushed out, "in the time that he has had you here, he has not harmed you, has he? I see no bruises, no welts. As far as your sex life I-"

"Sarah please!" Cini shouted with her hands out, enough was enough. She exhaled quietly, "Just take me to the kitchens."

Embarrassed that she had made the new missus uncomfortable, Sarah nodded. "Yes, of course." She opened the door, saw Cini frown at the guard posted outside.

"Sorry Miss Cini, but the lord's instructions were that you were to not leave the safety of the castle, or the kitchens, and you are to be under guard at all times."

Her lips pulled tight in chagrin, Cini followed the servant out the door. Of course, she was still his prisoner.

Seeing her black look, Sarah said stiffly, "Yes, of course he is still worried you will flee from…the castle, but more importantly he fears for your safety. Especially after what happened last night with those men," she closed the door not seeing Cini's look of quick fright recalling the episode.

Men had tried to take her…to…rape her…and Kazak's men had murdered them. All. Cini's body rolled in a terrible shiver. She was living amongst animalistic bloodletting killers.

As they headed down the stairs with the guard trailing, Sarah said, "Lord Adarken also instructed me that you were not to get over tired, not to work too hard. That we others were to do the heavy lifting, the hard work. And if I thought you looked at all peaked, that I was to immediately remove you and bring you upstairs to his...uh, that is your, chambers."

Cini let Sarah's rambling voice wander in and out of her ears as they went to the kitchens.

Once she reached the lovely, vast rooms, her breath expelled dissipating some of her bottled-up tension. She inhaled a deep tranquil breath.

She loved to cook, and at home she'd never had such luxurious kitchens or such free rein to work in them. If only, her shoulders slumped, things could be different.

If only her family and village could be safe and happy, and she could stay with Kazak, be his wife and- no, she shook her head vehemently. She could not let her mind go in that direction.

Things are as they are, she must remember her...husband, is a savage, murderous beast, and it was her duty to get to the emperor to secure the help her village needed to fight off Prince Andreyev....

The women had been preparing and cooking for several hours.

Cini watched one of the women, and older female with grey hair, dusky brown eyes, a substantial nose and full, lumpy figure, stripping leaves from the stem of a plant she was unfamiliar with. She wandered over to watch her.

"Elsa," Cini asked with interest, "what is that? Why are you peeling the leaves from it? Is it a new spice?"

Elsa smiled shaking her head. "Nay, Milady, tis cresentail, a delicious plant to add to flavor the stews, but the stems are...well," she cocked her head at the plant she held in her hands over a bowl. "Tis not poisonous, but they can render a person, um, unconscious for many hours."

"Oh dear," Cini exclaimed, watching her continue to peel the plant. "That sounds sort of dangerous. Should we have it around then?"

Elsa gave her a kind smile. "Tis perfectly safe, Mistress, as long as you know what you are doing."

"Uh huh. Has it ever been used deliberately, say for medicinal purposes?"

One lumbering shoulder shrugged, Elsa replied, "Aye, of course. The doctors use it when a patient they are trying to sew a sword wound or such is in terrible pain that it would be better if they were not conscious. Even if a lot is used, it does not cause death, only sleep."

Watching her pluck the leaves and set the stems aside, Cini's lips pulled in as she thought. "Um, what would be the difference in a dosage, uh, say for a woman, or a child, or a man?"

Pleased that the new mistress of the castle was interested in what she had to teach her, Elsa spoke eagerly, showing her how much would be necessary to knock out an adult or a child.

"This," she indicated two stalks in one hand, "is enough to put out a woman for several hours, and this," she picked up six stems, and winked, "if you have a man, like my husband," she rolled her eyes with an aggravated sigh.

"One who likes the gaming and the drinking and the whor- uh, anyway," she held out the handful of stems, "this would knock him out cold for almost an entire day, or," she winked, "night as it were. To keep him home thus, you understand?"

Cini reached over and picked up a stem, twirled it slightly while pondering the yellow stalk with yellow and green striped leaves. She asked, "So, how long does it take to work? What do you do, put it in his stew?"

Elsa sniggered. "Aye, you can, but it works faster in his drink. My husband, Hans," she picked up a huge handful of leaves, "he is a big man, it takes about this much to put him out for the night.

"I grind it up into a powder and put it in his mead and add a lot of sugar. He drinks it right down, and voila- out like a light!" The older woman laughed. Wiping her hands on her apron, she excused herself to retrieve a stew pot heating over the fire.

As soon as Elsa's back was turned, Cini grabbed up handfuls of the plants, took off her bonnet, stuffed them in it and popped it on her head just as Sarah came in.

"Oh, there, then, Mistress, you have been here too long on your feet. I don't want the, uh, your husband to be angry with me for letting you become over tired."

Returning with her apron wrapped around the metal handle of a pot, Elsa snorted, "Oh no, wouldn't want that *fiară brută-*"

Sarah suddenly squawked in a loud warning whisper, "Elsa! You can't call Mistress Cini's husband, our *dominio,* a ferocious brute!"

Her skin paling, Elsa gulped hard, her smile shaky, she quickly apologized. "Um, yes, so sorry, Mistress, uh, please, it just slipped out, don't tell your husband, the *dominio,* he would have me whipped for calling him that in front of you. In front of the others, eh," the edge of her mouth pinched in, "he would not care.

"The warriors call him that to his face but you, he's so careful and gentle with you that, well, anyway, what I was saying before I stuck my shoe in my mouth, if I allow you to tire out and get sick, he will have my... uh, he will be furious. So, please, it is time for you to return to your rooms, Sarah will take you."

Cini glanced over at the guard. He stood just inside by the doorway, bored out of his mind, but at constant attendance. He wasn't watching the women, he was continuously scanning the area for any danger that could be coming at Cini from any direction.

To allow something to happen to the lord's wife would mean an instant beheading, it was enough to keep his eyes open. Wide.

Two other guards were posted outside the doorway and another in hall.

"Oh," Cini demurred with a frown. "I thought I would help serve tonight, get a bit of exercise and meet some of the townsfolk?"

Shaking her head adamantly, Sarah said, "No, no, Miss, the lord said it is too dangerous for you to be out of the kitchens or your rooms. Besides," she grinned at Cini, "you're lucky he lets you cook. Most ladies of the castles do not lower themselves to do any of that kind of menial work. But," she sighed, "Lord Adarken said you love it so he allows you to do it."

"Huh," Cini grumped under her breath, "he *allows* me to do it, how nice of the tyrant." Untying the apron, she folded it and set it on the counter.

Wiping her hands on a cloth she said, "Fine. Let's go, we have been working for hours, I could use a cleanup and a change of clothes."

Several days passed, after the noonday meal, up in their chambers, as she did every time she was back in the rooms, Cini stood looking out the window.

Warrior horses were coming up the road, many villagers ran up to them with cheerful welcomes. She pressed her hand on her stomach, her pulse sped up, finally, the men were back from their mission.

Craning her neck, she studied each of them, looking for- There, the big warrior, even covered with chain mail and dirt, there was no mistaking Kazak's powerful warlord's authoritarian figure on the massive black stallion.

Even the horse seemed to strut and swagger as if knowing he carried a king. Torn between the twittering in her heart that Kazak was back safe, and the gnashing nerves of her plan, Cini felt sick.

Butterflies fluttered in her stomach at the relief that he was home safe and well. Relief? That signified that she had been worried about him. No, she shook her head, she did not care for him. He was a tyrannical beast, she could not-

At the soft knock at the door, Cini rushed over and opened it. As she hoped, Sarah was there to take her to the kitchens.

Sighing with relief, she was grateful she wouldn't be in the rooms when Kazak came up to bathe and change out of his armor.

"Mistress," Sarah greeted Cini with an unsure smile. "I've come to take you to the kitchens, but I see that Lord Adar- um, I mean your husband has returned. I assume you would rather stay here and…" her cheeks blushed, "welcome him home?"

Cini hurried past her out the door. "No, I want to make sure that the evening's meal is perfect. Let's go."

She moved quickly down the corridor letting Sarah close the chambers' door. Cini moved so quickly she even took the guard unaware and was yards down the hall before he realized she'd swept right past him.

He scurried after her.

Chapter Nineteen

Kazak scanned the grounds searching for brilliant blonde hair. His impassive face and bearing didn't reveal the disappointment he felt seeing that Cini was not out there to welcome him home.

He observed many women running up to their men and welcoming them enthusiastically.

"Ah, *mea frățe*, don't be so woeful that she's not out here to meet you," Bo chided him with a roguish grin. "You're the one that gave the strict orders she was not to leave your chambers or the kitchen, much less the castle itself."

The two men rode closely together, same as they fought. Caked in mud and muck, they headed to the stables to care for their horses.

"*Da*, sure," Kazak said with a dour expression, then perked, maybe Cini was upstairs in their rooms waiting for him. Naked. No, he bit off a smile, his shy little bride wouldn't do that, not yet, not until he got her used to him, trusted him, desired him.

Plus, he sighed, the way they had parted before he left, they'd had a fantastic intimate time together, then she suddenly became upset and wanted to flee as fast as she could.

Kazak had pondered her reaction the entire time he was gone. She'd been into it, their sexual encounter, her first orgasm. He could tell by her responses he was the first man to ever touch her like that, feel her amazing tits, her sweet woman's *possunt*, gah, his pants tightened.

He decided to hurry and get his horse taken care of so he could go find her.

Judging by her wildcat response to his ministrations when he had her up against the door, she was damned seducible, and he wasn't wasting another second away from her.

He'd get her settled, comfortable, then make her tell him what she was afraid of. Why she wanted to run from him when it had been so good between them.

Other warriors grooming their own horses chattered at him and each other, congratulating themselves on the job they'd done conquering one of the biggest outlaw gangs on the route.

They left two men barely alive, so their stories would be the same, and believable. To go back and spread the tales of the warriors who killed their comrades and will kill anyone else foolish enough to come on the *Iţă Cale*, the Spider Thread Trails, the trade road again and try to rob people.

Only one of Kazak's men incurred an injury. Jes the Bull, the largest of all the warriors had caught a sword blade across his arm, but he will recover.

The mission was a huge success. Soon, the roads would be completely cleaned up, and the emperor would give him his title and his lands, and he and Cini could build their own castle and raise their family.

Kazak shook his head with a chuckle. A few months ago, he would have choked himself laughing if anyone had said he would be married and desiring children as soon as possible with his beautiful wife.

Brushing down his horse, he kept thinking about their time together, and finally came to the conclusion that she'd left him right after her climax because she hadn't planned on letting him get that close, and he had managed to seduce her and now she was distraught about it.

She didn't want them to become intimate because she still planned to leave, him, the castle. That thought made his hair stand on end.

He hurried and finished grooming the steed, put him in his pen and made sure he had feed and water.

Taking the stairs two at a time, Kazak ignored greetings people called out from the great room. His long legs ate up the corridor in his haste to get to his chambers. Their chambers.

He threw open the door, and was met with crushing disappointment, again. It was so quiet, he knew she wasn't there.

Kazak checked the other rooms and the bathing room, but he already knew, he would have sensed her presence if Cini was in the room.

"Føkk," he cursed, dragging his grimy hands through his filthy hair. Hell, he was starving. He'd get cleaned up, she was undoubtedly in the kitchen. If she wasn't, heads would *føkkunn* roll.

Washed, beard trimmed, hair tied back, wearing fresh black breeches, boots and a black shirt, Kazak thumped down the stairs.

If he chose to, he could tread as silently as a jungle cat, but right now, he was too eager to find his bride, and fill his belly.

In the dining area, he slid onto a bench between Bo and Thomas.

"Frăţe," Thomas greeted him through a mouthful of food, "dig in brother, this is incredible." He shoveled in another mouthful of roasted beef on an au-jus sodden hunk of bread.

Bo said nothing, just grunted as he scraped a ton of mashed root vegetables slathered with butter on his trencher.

"Heya there, Şef," Bonatella cooed in Kazak's ear, her hand on his shoulder. "You have returned triumphant and alive."

Kazak cranked his head away from her, both hands were full, one held his cup of ale, the other a chunk of bread soaked in gravy.

He was still livid at her behavior during his wedding, grabbing Cini and frightening her. He had the whore banished from the castle and on home arrest, and he had locked down her spending money through her parents.

He wanted her thrashed, but Bo had talked him down. Voman was damned lucky to still have her head and no welts on her back. Kazak never physically had vomen punished but when he saw danger to Cini, and her fear, he'd gone manic with rage.

"Bonatella, I told you-"

"My handsome warrior, you are so brave," she cooed, running a hand over his hair loosening the tie, then she stroked her palm down the front of his chest and under his shirt.

"Let me show you how much I appreciate your valor, take me upstairs, that *sluţit* you married is busy in the kitchens, we will be alone, we can lock the door."

Her hand still down the front of his shirt pawing his muscular chest, she leaned around his shoulder so he could look down her dangerously low-scooped blouse.

"I understand the chit tricked you into marrying her to…oh, keep her safe until you could return her to her family, that your marriage is in name only-"

"Yes," a voice throttled with hurt cracked from the doorway to the kitchen. "Please tell us, Lord Adarken, how you married the stupid girl because she tricked you-" Her green eyes huge with humiliation and pain, Cini was standing there.

Blanching, then turning red with discomfiture at Cini seeing him in such a compromising position, and fury at Bonatella for causing it, Kazak threw down his food and cup and shoved to his feet. He barked, "Činnosti!"

But Bonatella clung to him like an octopus. Her hand clutching the hair on his chest, her other arm wrapped around him, she even tried to lasso him with an ankle, holding him back.

Cini choked down a sob and rushed back into the kitchen.

Cursing a blue streak that made even Bo's ears tingle, Kazak grabbed Bonatella's hands and wrenched them off him. When she was off balance, he shoved her at Bo and Thomas.

Both men, surprised, caught her, then chortled at Kazak's furious crimson face as he hurried to the kitchens.

He ran through the doorway and looked around, he didn't see her. He did see her guard jogging to the back door.

"Alistair." Kazak strode up to him and demanded, "Where is she?"

His face colored with guilt, Alistair said, "Şef, I- I- didn't expect, I mean she- she-"

Kazak grabbed the guard's collar and jerked him up on his toes. Crushing his shirt in his fist, Kazak shoved his hand under his jaw forcing the guard's face to painfully cock up with his fist, he shouted, "Answer me! Now!"

"Sir- sir-" Alistair coughed. "She ran out the door," he pointed to the back exit. "She ran past me, I- I was going after her when you-"

Kazak released him, sprinted to the heavy stock door, shoved it open, and raced outside.

The chilly air blasted him in the face. Muttering in Romanian, "Stupid girl, again she flees into the cold without a cloak."

He spotted her right away, and with legs twice as long as hers, quickly caught up with her.

"Dammit, Činnosti," he snared her arm bringing her to a hard halt. So hard, she spun and fell against him.

Kazak accepted the excuse to hold her. Wrapping his arms around her, he clutched her to his chest. "*Miera*," he soothed, his mouth in her hair, he inhaled her fresh scent.

It went straight to his groin, never mind that her full breasts were plastered against his chest. His breath whooshed into her hair. He stroked his palm down her tresses, then sifted his hand under her hair to cradle her neck. Lifting her head, he sealed his mouth over hers.

The kiss was hungry and greedy and aching, Kazak was instantly on fire, his manhood sprang like a thick bolt of lightning.

Cini pushed at him, her face flushed with anger. "You, you were with that woman, Bonatella. She told me you married me but she would be the one to warm your bed every night. You don't want me, you want-"

Kazak fisted his hand in her hair, dragging it back until her face tilted up and he crushed her lips with a savage kiss.

After a long moment, he moved his mouth an inch from hers, their breaths mingled, eyes linked, rich and aching, smoky with hungering desire.

His thumb caressing her delicate jaw, he said, "Bonatella is whore, liar, always. Kazak want Činnosti, want no voman but wife, beautiful wife," and his mouth descended on hers.

He consumed her with his passion until neither could speak, or think, only feel.

Chapter Twenty

As much as she told herself she hated him and feared him, Cini melted right into Kazak's big hard body, her hands glided up and around his neck and into his hair.

The tie holding his locks back in the ponytail gone, Cini tangled her fingers in the long loose strands, surprised how soft and thick they were.

Kazak slid his lips from hers to kiss along her jaw, behind her ear, down her neck where he paused to suck her skin until it was red, then he kissed back up to her mouth. "*Miera*," he whispered.

He'd studied the language book while they were on their way to take out the outlaws and on the way back, refreshing his English. "Come to bedroom, be wife of Kazak," his accent distorted the words but Cini understood them.

She was good with going to their chambers, she had everything set up. Nodding shyly, she said, "All right," and saw his face relax and the blue eyes light up.

Not waiting for her to change her mind, he rolled his arm around her shoulder as if to hold her in case she ran again. It was freezing, Cini shivered, but huddled against him with his big arm around her she was soon warmed.

Kazak barely nodded to people they passed through the grand hall and the great room, he had only one thought in his head and that didn't involve anyone but him and his wife.

They didn't see anyone else as they trod up the stone stairs and down the corridor strewn with sturdy rugs.

So eager and impatient, and turned on, his hand shook as he unlocked the heavy door and pushed it open. As soon as Cini went through, he followed her, quickly closing and locking the door.

When he turned around, Cini had crossed the room and picked up a decanter and poured some liquid into two cups.

She said, "Um, I thought we could-" His arms wrapped around her from behind.

"Činnosti," desire flamed so brilliantly in him his growl was a rasp. "Kazak miss *soţia,* ah, wife, miss you." One brawny arm holding her against his strapping chest, he lifted her hair, the rough pads of his thick fingers skimming over her skin.

Lightly brushing the tresses back, his breath on her flesh drove a shiver down her neck to her breasts, her nipples pebbled into hard beads.

He put his mouth on the back of her neck. His lips firm yet soft, warm and damp on her skin, he kissed her quivering flesh then lowered to where her neck met her shoulder.

"Uh, wait, *Dominio,* I thought we could-"

"Kazak, not *dominio,*" he muttered while licking his way down her neck. His large hands stroked her waist then thick needful fingers came up to cover her full breasts.

He squeezed her rounded flesh, so plump they molded over his greedy fingers, he gripped harder to hold more of her in his strong netting grasp.

"Kazak," Cini tried to get out of his embrace but he had no intentions of letting her go.

He kneaded and groped her breasts while murmuring foreign words in her ear.

She caught some English mixed in as he crooned, "Sweet *sâni,* tits, Kazak's tits." His grip grew rougher as his desire rose so high she could feel the heat pouring off him.

He released her breasts to reach for the ties on her gown giving her the chance to step away from him.

She grabbed up a cup and thrust it into his hand as he reached for her.

Frowning at the cup, he said, "Kazak nay drink, want wife, bed, now." His broiling gaze scored down her body leaving rivets of what felt like strips of burning flesh to Cini.

His eyes rose to hers, the desire blared out of them, striking the blue so intensely they flashed to a searing white.

"Please, Kazak." Cini picked up the other cup and took a sip. "You've been gone, we hardly know each other, can't we go a little…slow?" She took another sip and motioned with her head for him to drink.

He frowned at the cup again, then smiled at her. "*Da, bine* wife," and he took a swig. Swallowing, he prowled towards her, she backed away.

He kept stalking her, huge and hulking, desire burning from his entire being, Cini stepped back until her legs bumped the bed.

Kazak's eyes glowed brightly, sizzling so hot. He growled, "Want wife now," he reached a hand out for the tie at the top of her dress.

Dancing out of his reach, Cini said, "Um, all right, let me, just have another drink, Kazak, let's relax."

He gulped the drink down and set the cup on a table. "Kazak verra relaxed, nay need drink." Stepping to her, he plucked at the dress tie, yanking it, it came untied and the top of her dress started to fall. His eyes gleamed as her bare breasts came into view.

"Oh!" Cini caught at the bodice to hold it up with one hand.

Smiling, Kazak took the cup from her trembling hand and set it next to his on the table. "Kazak," he frowned, thinking of his English lessons, "*I* want wife, Činnosti, I want see wife." He grasped her wrists and pulled her hands aside letting the bodice fall.

Her breasts bared, he licked his lips, and just stared at her creamy flesh like perfect round pillows made for a man's hands to relish.

Pupils dilated a raging black, he muttered, "Kazak, ah, *I* love wife's beautiful *sâni,*" He covered them with his long fingers, lowered his face to them. "I love wife's beautiful tits," and rubbed his face over her mounds with a groan.

Gripping them tightly, he kissed and sucked both, growls rolling in his chest. Pinching her nipples between his fingertips he licked then suckled the hard buds.

Cini pressed her arms together to force his hands and face away, it made her breasts swell more. Kazak licked his lips again and reached for them.

Trying to stall him to get him to take in more of the sedative plant, Cini said quickly, "No, wait, Kazak, another drink, I would like another-"

He shoved his hands under her legs and back and lifted her in his arms.

Anxiously she cried, "No, Kazak, wait-" her breasts rubbed against his shirt with her struggles, his eyes were on them as he carried her to the bed.

"Nay drink, love now." He laid her down and started to undo his shirt.

Cini rolled to the side to get off the bed but he bent and pushed her back into a bunch of pillows and moved his knee between her legs to prevent her from leaving.

His eyes on her exposed bosom, Kazak undid his shirt, shrugged it off and dropped it.

His smile lengthened at the way Cini's eyes grew wide at his chest. "Wife like Kazak body?" He grinned and rubbed a palm on his muscled pectorals over a patch of dark hair.

Cini lay on her back surrounded by fluffy pillows and sheets. His knee kept her from being able to move her legs, she stared at his naked chest.

She hadn't seen many men's bared chests, but she doubted many looked like Kazak's. Huge, buffed with rock-hard muscles, covered with manly hair like the wild bear that he was, when he rubbed his chest his huge bicep flexed and bulged.

She had to admit, he was a strapping man with a handsome body, strong and powerful, her eyes drifted down to his lean hips, and muscular legs.

Getting off the bed, he crouched, undid his boots and kicked them off.

Her eyes still on his hips, she could see his heavy erection ramrod straight up his breeches. It was long, seemingly as thick as her arm. Swallowing hard, Cini squirmed in the pillows to get away.

Kazak knelt on the bed. "Nay, wife, *nu* more run from Kazak." When they were outside a few minutes ago, she had responded with heady shaky breaths at their kiss, he knew she wanted him but was still afraid.

He was not going to let her go this time. He bent and grasped the waist of her gown and pulled it down before she could object.

Cini and the Beast

Enveloped in a cloud of pillows, bare to Kazak except for her underwear, Cini looked soft and pretty and fresh as his mystical fairy in a palm of fluffy cotton.

Embarrassed, she pulled her knees up and her hands covered her breasts.

"Nay, *miera*, wife beautiful, Kazak...*I* want to see," he pushed her legs back down and pulled the strings on her underwear.

Slipping them off, he tossed them on the floor. Kneeling beside her, Kazak clasped her wrists and pulled her hands from covering her nudity.

His tongue wetting his lips, Kazak's heated glower scrolled up and down Cini. His skin darkened, glittering eyes shadowed blue and enigmatic under hooded lids.

"Wife *nu* move," he instructed, holding a hand out then got off the bed.

His eyes never leaving her, he unbuckled his belt, removed weapons stashed around his body, then pushed his breeches down, and watched Cini's skin pale but her cheeks reddened while her eyes rounded wide at his huge, erect manhood.

He took a step to the bed and stumbled. Catching his balance, he laughed, "Wife so beautiful make Kazak dizzy."

He fisted his shaft, swayed slightly, and moved back to the bed. Climbing on, he nestled down beside her and cradled a breast. Bending his head, he kissed her, then lowered his hand to titillate her sex.

Cini pulled from his mouth, pushed at his hand and said, "Just do it, Kazak, just put it in," she ordered nervously.

"Nay, hurt Činnosti," he protested. His fingers stroked her soft folds of womanhood, but his eyes were now blurry. Soon, his head lolled, the long hair flopped down the sides of his tanned face.

"Now, Kazak, do it now," Cini urged in a hard whisper. She grabbed his arms and tried to pull him over on top of her.

Although becoming disoriented, with pure instinct, he moved between her legs and nudged her thighs apart. Clutching a breast, he rubbed his thumb over a nipple and grinned at the shiver it brought Cini.

Kazak blinked to clear his vision and keep his head up. "Kazak feel strange," he slurred, not realizing he was crushing her breast with his hard fingers.

"You're just tired," Cini cooed. She murmured urgently, "Do it, make love to me, Kazak, Husband, put it in," and wriggled under him hoping the more he moved the faster he'd pass out.

His head drooped, his hair drifted over her face. Cini inhaled the scent of him, pure man, strong, earthy.

Kazak struggled to lift his head, braced on his elbows his biceps flexed and pumped to hold his weight up. He slurred, "Need slow, wife too young, nay ready…"

"No," Cini said angrily. "Do it, just do it," she insisted.

Barely able to hold his head up, Kazak fisted his phallus again and put it to her opening, then hesitated, protesting again, "Wife too small, need make ready-"

"Do it, Kazak," Cini ordered.

Her voice sounded like it was underwater to his ears. Kazak couldn't think, all he could fathom was he was between his nude wife's legs and she was begging him for it, and he wanted her so badly.

But something was wrong, yet she kept urging him to do it. Dizzier by the second, he held his shaft against her, moved to his knees and in one thrust shoved inside her.

Cini's back arched, she jerked up and screamed. The pain- he was too big-

He wasn't even halfway in, his mind was clouded, but he knew he'd broken her hymen and hurt her. She knifed forward gasping and crying.

"Činnosti," Kazak mumbled, pulling out, and she gasped back a scream at the pain of his huge erection scraping out of her tiny passage.

The big warrior was so dizzy he could not make a coherent thought other than he'd hurt her. He knew something was wrong.

He fell down to brace on one elbow. Looking down at her with hazed eyes draped over with strings of hair, he finally started to realize why he was so delirious.

"Why? What Činnosti do to Kazak? Make Kazak hurt wife? I not prepare young wife…" Kazak's face screwed up in confusion and dizziness.

In the back of his mind, he knew he shouldn't have just plunged into her. She was a virgin, he needed to make her ready, but he felt so strange, and she had kept urging him.

His voice a gruff rasp, "Why? Why let Kazak hurt Činnosti?"

"Because I thought you would pass out before you got in me," she wept.

His big body heavy over her, he struggled to keep his weight from crushing her. Blinking confused, hair falling over his face, over his blurred eyes, he asked, "Why? What wife do to Kazak?"

"I drugged you." Seeing his confusion Cini said, "I'm sorry. I need to go. I have to leave. This was the only way, you would not release me."

She dragged in a heavy rough breath, her voice shook with pain and despair for what she did, and what she still needed to do, get to the emperor. "Please forgive me, I had to do it."

"Činnosti, nay leave Kazak," his growl broke off as he slumped to the bed.

Cini waited a minute, then struggled to push him to roll on his back, then wriggled out from under his leg. She looked at him.

He was sound asleep. He looked just as dangerous asleep as awake. The shaggy dark hair, beard covering his strong jaw, lids shrouding the intense blue of his eyes.

She laid a hand on his face and whispered, "I'm so sorry. If only things could be different." She leaned over, kissed him gently, then climbed off the bed.

Then she saw the blood on the sheets, on his manhood that was still semi-hard, and she looked down, there was blood on her thigh.

Cini cleaned up and went to the trunk that held his clothes. She took out the shirt and pants she knew she could roll up, adjust so she could wear them, took a hat, grabbed her hooded cloak, and silently let herself out of the room.

There was no guard posted outside since she was with Kazak. She trod quickly down the hall, and down the back stairs.

Outside, she hurried to the stables. Since the men had returned and all the horses were taken care of, brushed and fed, everyone was inside eating, drinking, celebrating their victory, there was no one in sight.

Cini ran in and found her horse and the saddle she'd had.

It was hard, took great effort, but she got the saddle on, mounted the horse, and rode out of the keep without looking back.

Chapter Twenty-One

Cini kept to the trade road but far inside the woods so she wouldn't come across anyone.

At some point, she knew Kazak would come looking for her.

And he did. Hearing the pounding of hooves she dashed deeper into the woods.

She stayed hidden in the trees and watched Kazak, Bo, Liam and Thomas streak past. Waiting a long time to ensure they were gone, she started moving again.

Wiping a tear of regret and loss, Cini turned off the trail and took one that forked in another direction, towards the emperor's compound.

Days later, she reached Emperor Boris Radisalvo's castle.

Leaving her horse tied in the woods, she made her way to the palace, blending in with others that lined up to seek to speak with the emperor.

She waited all day until she reached the doors.

Several guards were in place. A deputy was in charge of allowing people in, or not.

He looked down his long condescending nose at Cini. "Madam, your credentials and letter of introduction," he held out an arrogant hand. Cini had none of that.

Pleading, "Sir, please," she put on her biggest smile, and pleading eyes. "I am Princess Činnosti Brymiente. I come from Chalon-sur-Sônn. I must see the emperor, we need his help desperately. Prince Gavrill Andreyev has taken over our village, imprisoned the people, he is killing them."

She took a breath, "Please, I request Emperor Radisalvo's aid to defeat him and restore my-"

"Madam," the deputy's scorn abrasive in his voice, he sneered down at her.

Taking in the huge clothes held up with ropes, the girl was unkempt, dirty, undoubtedly a prostitute looking for cozy work inside the palace. "Run along now, before I call the guards." He made shooing motions at her as he looked around Cini to the next in line.

"Next-"

"No! Sir, I beg you, you don't understand, many will die, be enslaved, please-"

The deputy lowered his face but looked up at her with bored yet annoyed eyes. "I said, move on you little vagrant or I will have you arrested."

He smiled at the next person in line who was dressed to the nines and reeked of cologne to cover his unwashed body. The man held his papers out to the deputy with a cocky sneer.

Cini was roughly and rudely pushed aside.

People crowded around her, she was shuffled back down the line.

Aghast, frightened, angry, there was nothing she could do. Cini watched the people in line to see if she could do something different, but, they all had calling cards and letters of reference or introductions, and none were dressed like she was, as a dirty street urchin.

"What am I to do?" she wailed silently.

The sun was almost set, she made her way wearily back to where she left her horse.

After mounting the horse, they travelled a couple of miles when they came upon a farm that had many barns.

Sneaking onto the land, she got the horse water and hay, then made herself a bed in the straw. She lay depressed for a few minutes. Then she gave herself a pep talk.

"You can't give up, Cini, girl, you made it this far. Your people need you. You crossed dangerous country alone and outwitted a shrewd experienced hunter, a heavily medaled warlord. You can do this, you can."

Sinking into the straw, she sighed with determination. Tomorrow, yes, she would go again tomorrow and make the deputy hear her. Let her speak to the emperor.

Smelly old hay poking into her from all over, as her eyes closed, she saw Kazak, enraged…and sad that she'd left him. Her heart broke for what she had to leave behind.

Cini never believed she would learn to care for the big, tough grizzly man, but, she sighed again with want, with need, with loss. The beast had wormed his way into her heart. She would never forget him.

Her lips bunched in despair. So many women wanted him, he was probably being comforted by many as she lay there thinking of him.

The picture of Bonatella in his bed, his huge body hovering over her flitted into Cini's imagination. Tears sprung. She wiped at them angrily, with bereft frustration. She could not let herself dwell on Kazak. He was in the past, her future was saving her village.

Her brain told her to move on, get over him, but her heart cried itself to sleep.

Every day for a week Cini returned to the palace to plead her case.

Then on the seventh day, the deputy came out angry, and said, "If you do not move on, woman, I will be forced to have arrested. The goals are horrendous, not meant for a dainty woman like yourself. If I lock you up, you will never see the light of day, ever again." He huffed and puffed and waved his hands at her to shoo.

His voice hard and firm with dire warning, "You will leave this very moment, and do not come back. This is your last warning." He stood with his arms crossed glaring down at her, fully implacable, immovable, unmerciful.

Devastated, filled with hopelessness, Cini had no choice but to find her way back home.

She cried nonstop the first two days, for the deputy refusing to allow her to see the emperor, thereby ensuring that her village was doomed, and because she knew she'd never see Kazak again.

Then, she bucked up. She had to admit defeat. She had no choice but give up.

Staying amongst the cover of trees, she kept going, days, weeks over a month to reach home.

Chapter Twenty-Two

Tromping through the forest, defeated, despondent, exhausted, starving, Cini tried to keep mounted on her horse, but every hour she was losing the battle.

She had only eaten sporadically when she came across an orchard or a farm field that she could slip in and out without being seen.

Finally, she came to a familiar area, she sighed with sad relief, she was home.

Months ago she had fled with brave confidence that she would get to the emperor, elicit his aid. He would send troops to defeat the prince, and she and her village would live happily ever after.

Instead, she'd been turned away flat from the palace. She had to return home in defeat to tell her people that help was not coming.

Would she explain that along the way she'd been captured by, and beguiled by, and forced to marry, the greatest warlord in the lands?

And, Cini wiped at the tears that gathered, she had fallen in love with Lord Kazak Adarken. She could never go back to him, he would be filled with hatred for her for leaving him.

She for sure had humiliated him, his wife had ran away from him. Drugged him, and then ran away. No, she dug her palms into her eyes to still the weeping, she'd burned that bridge.

She had to get off her horse and let him go when she was still a great way from home, if the horse came home the prince would know she was back.

Hugging the horse, her tears rolling down his neck, Cini apologized, hoped he would be all right and would make his way to another village and be safe there.

So weary she thought she would just drop dead in her tracks, her clothes in shredded tatters hanging from her thin frame, Cini trudged on until she reached a grove of trees that she knew sheltered a tunnel that led into the castle.

It was located beneath a towering tree, the branches so broad and leaves so thick it shaded a big area.

On her knees, Cini brushed away the dried leaves and other debris that covered the trap door to the tunnel. So weak from travel and hunger, it was a terrible struggle to get the door open.

It was dark inside. She carefully let the door close over her as she climbed down a set of wooden steps with railings dug into the hard earth.

So dark, she walked as if blind, feeling her way slowly so she didn't trip, or run into a wall. It was painstaking torture.

The soil of the earth chilled her to the bone. Damp dirt stench sifted up her nose until she felt as dirty on the inside as she was on the outside. Every other step she stubbed a toe.

Eventually, she reached the end. Another set of steps.

It took all her strength to climb up, get the door open, and struggle out.

Cini dropped onto the floor with the effort, and then it was all too much, everything went black.

Cini and the Beast

Voices, whispered yet shrill bandied around Cini, poking and jabbing through the cloud of unconsciousness that kept her gratefully, in dreamless asleep.

"Cini, baby, please open your eyes, it's Mama."

The dear familiar voice trickled into her ears to wake her sleeping brain.

Her tired eyes swollen with tears and loss, failure and hunger, cracked open slightly. Mouth dry as dust, Cini whispered, "Mama? I'm home?"

"Oh my baby!" Giselle exclaimed, gathering Cini up in her arms. Hugging her child to her breast, she cried, tears wetting Cini's hair, "Yes my beloved child, you are home, safe."

Cini's mother held her until she got her bearings. Her dry cracked eyes opened and she saw her sisters, Gretel and Heidi, a few other women of the village were there and Meli.

When her eyes lit on Meli, her best friend hurried to her and hugged her.

"God's love, Cini," Meli wept, "you are alive. There's been no word of you, from you, we thought..." Her tears caught in her throat, "We feared you were dead."

The young women hugged and cried until, her mother sat back and said, "Cini," she took a careful hope-filled breath, at first she scolded her youngest daughter. "You were so wicked to leave like you did, worry us to death, but, did you...get to the...emperor? Is he coming?"

Pained lids lowered over her despairing eyes, Cini shook her head, her filthy matted curls dragged across her back.

"No." Her hand went to her heart, her voice husky with hunger, fatigue, and searing sadness. The words choked from her throat clogged with tears, "No. He would not see me, the guards forced me to leave."

Her mother stared unblinking at her for a moment. Then she said to a woman standing by wringing her hands, "Eleana, please get food and drink for my daughter." To another woman she said, "Prepare a bath, and get her clothes."

Cini struggled to sit up, croaked, "No, I just need a minute to rest and I'll be-" Her eyes rolled back in her head and she fell back on the bed.

The women saw to feeding, bathing and helping Cini dress. After a rest, only Giselle and Meli stayed in the room.

Cini woke to Giselle sitting on one side of the bed, and Meli on the other.

Giselle was an older version of Cini with light blonde hair and green eyes, but she had slight lines on her pretty face. She was as sweet as Cini, but of course not as naive.

When Cini sat up, her mother said, "Now, dear daughter, you've been gone months. Surely you weren't at the emperor's that entire time? I know the travel there was dangerous and lengthy, but," she smiled at her daughter, grateful she was alive and home, "where have you been all this time?"

Not able to fight the tears that blurred her forlorn eyes, Cini told of her travels, how she stayed hidden in the forest and dressed as a man to safely blend in, until, the day Kazak captured her.

The pain so piercing slicing into her heart, Cini told them about Kazak and her time with him, her marrying him.

"Oh how romantic, like a fairytale," Meli gushed and grabbed up Cini's hand. She swooned over the beautiful ring Kazak had forced on her.

Cini and the Beast

"It's beautiful, Cini, was he so very handsome?" Her straight black hair hung like soft sable over her shoulders as she regarded her long lost friend with love.

Cini's smile bent wryly. "Not exactly." She described the barbaric warlord. His scarred face, long hair, beard, blazing blue eyes that struck fear into the fiercest of men, his amazing body.

"So strong, Mama, so powerful, vigorous, utterly fearless," her words disappeared as the tears tightened her throat.

"Ah, my daughter," her mother soothed with a soft smile, "you love him."

Her big green eyes flooded with tears for what can never be, Cini nodded. She looked away as fat tears rolled out and plopped on her clasped hands.

The three women sat silently while Cini quietly wept.

When she got a grip on her emotions, she asked, "What happened here? It is so…quiet."

Usually the castle was bustling with energy and noise.

Mother and Meli shared a sorrow look.

Her eyes lowered at first, then Giselle said, "When the prince took over, he imprisoned your father and brothers, he imprisoned all of the men so they wouldn't be a threat. Those that resisted," she looked away her eyes filled with pain, her breathing heavy, "were killed. Some tortured, then murdered."

"Oh my God," Cini murmured with fear, and escalating resentment. "But, the fields, the animals, who is tending them? Certainly not the soldiers?"

"No," her mother shook her head with twisted lips. "No, they only rape and pillage, steal and destroy. No," her sigh filed with sorrow, she told her, "the women do all the work guarded by the soldiers. The prince feels they will be less apt to fight or try to flee because...the children..."

Cini's eyes flew to her mother's tormented face. "The children?"

"Yes," Giselle nodded weary from the horror that was now their lives. "Prince Andreyev...." She gulped down a sob, "He has also imprisoned the children to keep the women from resisting. If anyone does anything, at all, against him, a child is..."

"Is what?" Cini's heart stuck in her throat.

"Butchered," Meli said flatly. The young woman herself was wan and thin, her hands trembled with the constant threat of violence. "They cut them and strangle them in front of everyone, slowly, so we get the point and don't even resist for a heartbeat."

Her hands covering her mouth, Cini could say nothing in her shock. Her worst nightmares had come true. And she had stood by helpless, no, she was being kept safe and comfortable, cooking as she pleased while be seduced by an untamed barbarous warrior.

Her body tingled against her will as the picture of the big hard man jumped into her thoughts. Shaking her head, no, she could never think of him again. She had been safe and comfortable while her kinsman were tortured, raped and killed.

"Cini," her mother's voice soft, hopeful, "your warlord, maybe he can...I mean maybe you can ask him to help us?"

A snort and a shake of her head, more tears threatened. "No. He would never help me. If he ever found me, he would kill me. He's a great warlord, a famous knight, I humiliated him by deserting him."

She shuddered at the picture of Kazak, enraged, filled with vengeful violence, standing over her as she knelt and pleaded for her life. His eyes blank and merciless, swinging his mighty sword to take off her head-

"Cini, stop." Seeing her despair, Giselle hugged her daughter. Stroking her daughter's hair, she murmured, "We will continue to pray, we will find a way." Over her shoulder Cini saw Meli's miserable, resigned expression. No, they were doomed.

Days passed. Staying in back rooms seldom used for anything but storage, Cini hid while sewing in semi-darkness.

She felt like she had been sentenced to living and working in a cave, never to see the light of day again. She couldn't come out and about, if the prince knew of her presence, she shivered, hell would un-freeze and Satan would be upon her.

Her mother, Meli, and her sisters snuck her food.

Her mistake was, the dirt was so ground into her body, her hair a rat's nest, even Meli held her breath when she came near her, Cini could stand the filth no longer.

Under the cover of night, she crept out, slipping down the long corridor, sliding her hands along the rough stone walls to guide herself in the meager light of a few lanterns on the walls, she made her way to one of the bathing rooms.

It was heaven. Cini sat in a tub of foaming warm water she'd heated over a hearth. She'd scrubbed her body and her hair. But, she didn't dare linger.

Reluctantly, she left the luxury of the warm perfumed water, dried off and went into her sister's room to find something to wear.

Dressed in a pale yellow gown with frilled collar and short puffy sleeves, she found some sturdy slippers, and crept back out and down the hall brushing her drying curls.

A hand snatched out and snared her hair.

Twisting her locks around his fist, a man said, "Ah, glory be, the tales are true. The bird has returned to her nest." He swung Cini around to face him.

Pulling her hair back, her neck arched forcing her to look up at him.

A soldier, weathered skin, nose bulbous and red-veined from constant drink, breathed beor in her face as his breath spit and misted at her.

"Goy," he smiled exposing a few lonely teeth. "I would love to fuck you bloody here and now, my little princess, but Prince Andreyev would have my head. Come, let's see what my reward is for bringing you to him."

Cini had no chance to beg or fight. The man was huge, heavy-chested, and although he reeked of ale, his grip was hard and sturdy, and he easily and quickly dragged her down corridor after corridor.

When he reached enormous double wooden doors with gold hinges and handles, he knocked hard with confidence.

The door swung open, another soldier eyed him with fury.

"What the hell, man, knocking on his lordship's door in the dead of the night? What the hell are you think-" His mouth dropped like a rock when the first soldier thrust Cini in front of him.

Blinking like a foolish goose, he stammered, "Tis her? Not really, no, is that the girl, the one the prince-"

"Ramson!" a voice bellowed from within the room. "What the fuck is going on out there? Who the bloody hell would disturb me in the middle of the damned night!"

Bare feet slapped on the wood floor covered with scattered rugs. And Prince Andreyev came into sight. His eyes bugged out at the sight of Cini being held in the soldier's firm grip.

Dead silence reined while he studied her, from her drying blond curls that rolled down her front and back, big green eyes bursting with fear, and over the breasts that thrust out of the light gown at him.

He swallowed hard, his tongue circling his watering mouth. His gaze traveled down further, to her tiny feet, then made the journey, slowly back up to her lovely face.

"Ah, the princess, my princess, has returned. Release her," he ordered.

The soldier let her go, she stumbled, then quickly righted herself.

She tried to regard the king with bold defiance, but her body betrayed her with its uncontrolled shaking. Even her eyeballs trembled in terror. It was all she could do to keep her spine straight, her head up.

The prince had gained some weight in the past few months. His chest was even bigger, thicker, his face more square, brown hair tinseled with grey floated around his shoulders.

His hands clasped behind his back, Andreyev slowly paced around her, looking at her from all directions. His heavy breaths loud in the room as the other two soldiers watched on.

He reached out and picked up a lock of hair watching the soft tress curl around his hand. Letting it go, the prince stood in front of Cini.

"You are disgustingly scrawny, gaunt. But," his eyes dipped down to her chest where his pupils flared. "You still have those amazing curves that I have never stopped dreaming of. Yes," he stroked a lock of hair off her shoulder, "we will fatten you up before the wedding."

"Wedding?" Cini shook the word out, trying not to show her fear, but it was of course to no avail. It was all she could do to not recoil from his meaty touch.

"Of course, wench, you think because you got away from me, for a brief time, that I have set aside my plans?" His dapper head shook with mirth.

"No, Princess, things will continue to go as I planned. We will marry, that will solidify my rights to this land. Eventually all of the residents will be exterminated, and my own people will come in and populate this area."

His grin spread huge and obnoxiously narcissistic. Then, he saw her face clear of her insane fright, her lips firmed into a taunting smile.

"What? What is it, girl? What do you know?"

When she didn't answer him, he grabbed her arms and shook her until her teeth rattled and her eyes wobbled. "Answer me, bitch, what is it?"

Cini held out her hand. "I am already married, you and I cannot marry." Pleased that she could in one small way thwart his plans, her smile broadened.

Andreyev glared in disbelief at the gold and ruby twined band. His eyes bulged with fury, face swelled into tomato red with his rage.

He hauled his hand back and slapped her so hard, Cini crashed to the floor. Enraged, he bent and grabbed her hair wrenching her to her feet.

"You fucking whore," he hit her again. When she fell, he jerked her up and hit her again and again and again, cursing her until she was a bloody beaten mess sprawled on the floor.

Kicking her violently, Andreyev roared, "You think you won, you bitch, I will see you burned at the stake! You will be an example to your people what happens when a subject of mine defies me, escapes from me, refuses me!" And he kicked her again, and again.

His raging voice sounded further and further away as everything grew dark.

Chapter Twenty-Three

Her body ached, she couldn't move a finger. Everything stung and burned with agonizing pain.

At first, Cini couldn't understand why she couldn't open her eyes, then, she realized they were swollen shut, and glued tight with her blood.

She lay on what felt like cold hard stone. She tried to gather her thoughts in her broken head, but was so dizzy with pain and a split skull, everything floated in and out, nothing stayed that she could latch onto.

She couldn't remember what happened, how was she injured, how did she get on these freezing hard stones? She dozed off and on, waking for brief periods of time. Each time she awakened, in agony, a bit of the past slipped in her bruised memory.

Little by little, as she lay broken, the pain so excruciating she prayed for the sleep to come back and take her away from it.

Then, she remembered, the prince had come to take over her village. She had fled to the emperor for help. On the way there, she had been captured, imprisoned, forced to marry the warlord Kazak. She escaped him, ran to the emperor, and was refused aid.

Then, she recalled, she traveled what seemed like forever through the rugged forests to get back home, where she learned Prince Andreyev had completely taken over the land. He had imprisoned the men and children, kept the women working while he brought in his own people to completely take over.

She moved a leg and cried out with a hoarse whimper at the blinding pain. Taking slow breaths to dispel the pain, she couldn't breathe deeply, her ribs were likely fractured or even broken.

The beating the prince had given her sunk in as she remembered his viciousness, his violent brutality. He must have had her deposited here after she passed out.

She forced her aching eyes to open and looked around. All she saw was stone. Not a window, only a door and that was a solid sheet of what looked like thick wood.

The prince's words filtered around her bruised brain.

He had said…thinking hard only hurt more. Swallowing to ease her dry throat, she remembered what he said he was going to do to her. He had said he was going to burn her at the stake.

As much in agony as she was, the thought of such shattering torture struck a quill of searing terror to her entire body. He would do it. The prince never made empty threats.

He couldn't marry her as he planned, so he would use her to sooth his revenge and rage. He would murder her by fire, use her as an example.

So dry from lack of liquids, she had no tears left, only the burn as they fought to dislodge and flow down her battered cheeks.

Time passed, Cini had no idea how much. There was no light, and no one came to the cell. So broken, she could only lie there.

As bad as the pain was, it kept her mind present, otherwise she would lose it, go insane from the fear that either she would just die there of starvation, or blood loss, or she would be tied to a stake and set on fire, alive. None was desirous.

Worst of all, she was helpless to save her village.

Eventually, between the hunger and the unbearable pain, delirium set in. It was good. She was floating on a cloud, and she could see Kazak coming to her.

He wasn't angry with her, he loved her. He knelt down on the cloud, and petted her hair. He spoke in a language she didn't understand, but his face was kind and loving, his voice was soft and pleasing. He loved her.

Cini felt tranquility suffusing her, covering her like a happy blanket, her eyes drifted peacefully closed as he bent to kiss her-

A sound jarred her, jolting her awake. The pain and terror came flooding back.

She wasn't on a cloud with Kazak loving her, she was lying almost upon death in a frigid, damp, stone cell, and the only door just opened. She couldn't move her neck to look.

Two soldiers came in. They crouched beside her.

One said to the other, "Blimey, he made a bloody mess of her, eh? She won't likely live long enough to die in the fire."

The other soldier chuckled at his words.

"Yah, too bad. No enjoyment in that execution, eh? Maybe the others to be raped and executed along with her will bring more entertainment. All right," he touched her shoulder, "she won't be walking, you want to carry her, or shall I?"

Cini and the Beast

The first man grunted, "I'm bigger, I'll do it."

"Yah," the other snickered, "you just want to be the important guy that brings her to the gallows."

The soldier lifted Cini in his arms and stood up with ease. He looked down at her.

She was barely conscious, her face scrunched up in dire pain. "Too bad the prince is determined to kill her, when she heals, she'll be a right beauty, I would take her for wife."

The two men chattered on the way from the cell, and all the way outside.

Their boots tramped and shuffled across the tall grass to a dirt path that wound around the castle and down the road just a ways.

"Looky, pretty girl," the soldier carrying Cini chortled, lifting her slightly so her head was raised. "Everyone has come to see you! Aren't you pleased! You're famous!"

Through swollen, bleary eyes, Cini gazed around.

It appeared every villager was present.

The two men marched through the crowd. Mostly sad, defeated, frightened faces, many beaten and battered like hers, gazed hopelessly at her as she passed.

The men had been brought out to witness her execution, they were chained together.

The day was crispy cool, a taut breeze flailed Cini's hair around the soldier who carried her.

Grey clouds blocked some of the weak sun. A few sheep bleated in the distance, but it was mostly quiet. The frightened villagers whispered to each other, the atmosphere starkly bleak and oppressive. A perfect desolate day for an execution.

The soldier tramped through the people, the metal on his boots clanged with his heavy sure steps. He didn't stop until he reached a wooden stage.

At the top of the stage there were two women. Both crying, their frantic wails pleading, struggling against the ropes that bound them to wooden stakes.

Behind them were stacked and tied, branches and kindling. Between the two women was an empty stake, about six feet high, it was clearly for Cini.

A hoarse cry croaked through her broken chest, she tried to struggle, but she was too injured to even lift her head, the prince had beaten her too badly.

In any case, even if she wasn't hurt so terribly, she could never get away from the burly soldier who held her much less the others that circled the stage, top and bottom, waiting, for her.

"All right, little sweetness," the soldier's beor breath slunk up her nose, "it's almost over. Soon, the pain will be gone and you will be, let's hope," he chuckled, "in heaven. But," he shrugged, "ya never know, eh?"

He carried her up the many steps to the platform.

Waiting for her there, was Prince Andreyev. His face was shining with triumph, and creased with vengeful wrath. The soldier brought her to him.

Andreyev gripped her chin lifting her head, she winced in pain.

"You stupid bitch," he stuck his furious face into hers. "You could have had everything, me, the land, I will own it all and you could have ruled it all by my side." His eyes for a fraction of a second filled with regret, then hardened, sieved empty of pity or compassion.

He leaned back to see her more completely. Sucking in a deep breath, he said so quietly no one else could hear, "You can still set aside your marriage, we will solicit the emperor's assistance to dissolve it. And you can marry me. What do you say, Činnosti?"

Her eyes so pained and weak, she could only open them halfway, sucking in a shallow agonizing breath, through blood saturated lungs, she whispered, "*Never.*"

His face struck with black rage, the prince stepped away. "Fine, burn in hell you bitch." He stalked to the front of the stage, cleared the insulted fury from his angry face, and smiled at the audience.

"Greetings my subjects." He looked around and frowned as the silence remained.

His voice gruffer, harsher, he repeated, "I said, greetings my subjects." His inhuman eyes traced callously over the people. Seeing the murder in them, the people spoke up quickly.

"Yes, Sire," they rattled at once, quickly. "Greetings, welcome, we praise you, your highness," on and on until the prince held his hands up for quiet.

"Ah, that is better. I expect that every time I address you. Anyone not complying," he nodded to a soldier stationed in the audience.

The soldier instantly withdrew his sword and sliced it across the neck of the man standing next to him. The man collapsed with his head barely attached.

The audience cried out in horror, they all looked at their self-appointed king with renewed terror.

"All right," the king smiled, puffing out his pompous chest. "Now that I have your attention. You see today's entertainment and lesson. Those two women," he gestured to the women already tied to the stake.

"You know Mary on the left," he nodded to the haggard woman who had been whipped, her dress hung in shreds, her hands secured behind her.

"Well," he shook his head sadly. "I ordered beef for dinner, alas, she prepared mutton." He turned back to the audience and decreed, "I will not stand for incompetence or my commands not followed to the letter." It took effort to hold back his smile at their shocked gasps of disbelief and deeper terror.

He pointed to the woman on the right, her hands bound to the stake. "Willemena, mutinously did not please me in bed. Again," he smiled at the people, "I insist on full and utter subservience."

He scanned the vast crowd through narrowed eyes. "Does anyone have a problem with that? Speak up if you do, but know that to displease me will result in either that," he nodded to the women, "or that," he motioned to the beheaded man bleeding out on the ground.

Not a sound was heard. It seemed even the animals feared for their lives.

Andreyev looked around, then nodded with triumphant satisfaction. "Good. Now," he strode back over to where the soldiers were securing Cini.

One held her up while the other bound her. She had no strength in her broken legs, they had to tie the rope also under her breasts and arms to keep her upright.

"Of course, you are all aware this villager, your *princess*," he said the word as if it were repulsive, "dared to flee the village. Against my orders." His pride didn't allow for him to say that she also fled him, and even now to save her life, refused to be married to him.

"You will soon see what happens to those that defy my orders." He went over and stood near Mary on the left of Cini.

"Because of their impudence and defiance, they will be illustrations to show who their leader is, they will suffer the public humiliation of sexual violation, and then agonizing death. Bartholomew," he gestured to a soldier that had moved in front of Mary, "will desecrate this criminal by fucking her, and James," he nodded to a soldier who placed himself by Willemena, "will violate this one.

"They will bear their insubordination on the inside as well as the outside. And then I," he smiled at Cini who raised her swollen eyes to him, "will fuck your princess, for you all to witness her shame. And then," he turned to make his statement more dramatic, "all three women will burn, alive."

"Go, Bartholomew," he motioned to the soldier.

Bartholomew bowed to his king, then stepped to Mary. Grasping the shreds of her gown, he tore them off her until she stood completely naked.

She cried, pleaded, "Please, no, Sire, I will do better, please, don't-" Bartholomew slapped her to quiet her, then undid his breeches.

Moving behind her, and although her hands were tied, he shoved her to bend over and thrust ruthlessly into her.

Mary's screams rent the air, she wailed and wailed with each horrible thrust until he was spent.

Then he stood back and did up his pants and stood at attention beside the weeping Mary. Her head hung down, tied naked to the post, her nude body shook with her sobs.

"James," Andreyev said to the other soldier.

James bowed, and did as Bartholomew had. He ripped the clothes off Willemena, undid his pants, then did the opposite of Bartholomew, he bent her backwards as far as he could with her restrained, and drove roughly inside her.

Because he leaned over her, her screams were muffled. When he was done and standing at attention, the rest of the soldiers eyed Cini with greedy hope. But, the king moved to her.

"Look at me, Princess," he commanded.

With great effort, Cini boldly raised her head and looked him in the eye.

"Ah," he smiled. "Good, the fight has not yet left you. I always liked that about you, that gutsy, never back down attitude. Well, I wish things had gone differently," a brief regret flickered through his eyes was quickly replaced with wrath, "but they didn't." He paused.

"You have nothing to say, Princess? No begging for your life to be spared?"

He lowered his voiced, "It is not too late, say yes, and I will consider not burning you after I defile you on this stage."

The king wasn't sure if he really meant it, he just wanted to hear her plead for her life and break down, back down, give in and concede to marry him.

Struggling to keep her head up, face black with bruises, battered beyond belief, tears blurred the green of her swollen eyes. She stared directly at him, rasped, "Never."

Brows slashed down, his lips bunched at her brave but foolish rebellious stance. "Fine then. You have chosen your fate."

Andreyev moved right up to her, grasped the tatters of her gown and ripped down the front to the ropes under her ribs.

Chapter Twenty-Four

Kazak kept Bo, Liam and Thomas out for days, weeks, searched all day into the night until the twilight passed and they could no longer see into the dark depths of the abundant forest.

The woods obscure with teeming groves of dense trees, scrubby shrubs and jungle creatures, he knew the animals stayed concealed in the shadowed thickets watching them.

There were a couple of times his skin rippled with a strange feeling. It felt as if she...Cini...was also watching them from the cover of wide leaves and broad trunks. But, he would shake off the feeling and they would carry on.

When they'd covered so much land, trails, that she could have possibly been on, and Kazak realized she couldn't have gone any further without them finding her, he sat slumped on Falium. She somehow had gotten around him and completely disappeared.

Hooves clopped up, the snort of a horse beside him, he didn't have the energy to look over.

"Kaz," Bo said quietly, "it's time to give it up. She's gone. She either went over a cliff or was taken by a predator."

Kazak raised his head and squinted around the vast land spread out around them heavily dotted with masses of woods.

Shaking his head tiredly, his gruff voice low and rough with weariness, anger and grief, he said, "She had her horse. If an animal took her there would be traces of, evidence left of..."

"Nay, *mea frăţe*," Bo said, "if big cats took the carcasses deep into the-" He broke off at the narrowed red eyes of his friend glowering bleakly at him.

"One more circle around, Bo," Kazak growled with coarse anger, "then we go back."

Bo nodded, glanced over with a slight dip of his head to Liam and Thomas.

Same as all the other days, they searched another hour or so, then returned fruitless to the castle where Kazak left his steed for the stable boy to care for and trudged up to his room to drink his dinner.

Not bothering to disrobe or shower, Kazak flopped on the bed with his drink, and lay there sipping, while, like every other unsuccessful night of searching for her, he relived his and his wife's brief time together. The liquor could never dull the pain of reliving the memories.

His rage struck anew like a lance recalling when he had awakened and realized she'd drugged him.

The mad dash to search the castle, then hear the stableman tell him her horse was gone and the knowledge that she had left him hit him like a brick to the head, a dagger to his heart.

He gathered his men and immediately and struck out to search for her.

Then, every night, finding not a trace, the horse's clomps as sluggish as he felt, he returned to the castle to drink more, and remember more, and the memories started all over again.

How beautiful she had been lying naked beneath him. How terribly, like his own breath did he desire her, need her, miss her.

He had known that night she smiled at him and encouraged him to drink the brandy that something was wrong.

She was a virgin, he knew he had to go slow, prepare her to take him, especially as big as he was and as small as she was. But, his head had been so fuzzy, he couldn't think, she kept urging him to do it- and he did.

And she screamed in agony as he thrust his huge shaft inside her tiny virgin's channel. Gods, he covered his head at the remembered sound of it, at the look of her in terrible pain, because of him.

Then, her whisper that she drugged him, she didn't think he would get inside her so fast, she'd have time before he actually penetrated her.

Cursing, Kazak drank himself into oblivion until it was time to go back out and try again, to find word, any trace of her.

In between, he studied his rusty English, practiced with Bo. When he found her, he wanted her to understand his words, telling her why he was beating the life out of her.

Their horses' hooves crunching the drifting leaves as the four warriors trod along yet another trail, Bo, Liam and Thomas said nary a word of complaint.

They would follow Kazak to the burning depths of hell if that was where he went. They were brethren in battle and in heart, they stuck together no matter how hopeless the search went.

They paused for a meal at a mud lodge in a small village.

The men thumped down on wooden benches and drained their beor, chomping on bread and meat. Two of the emperor's soldiers dropped down beside Kazak. The beor buzzing his ears, their conversation floated around him.

One of them was laughing, telling the tale of a breathtaking prostitute, an extremely thin, frail actually, filthy young urchin, petite but so curvy trying to gain entrance to the palace.

How startling, crystal green her large exquisite eyes, how plush the tiny lips, how plump and high her youthful tits, how if he wasn't on duty he would have taken her for a tumble-

Kazak's fist was in his uniform and he wrenched him to his feet.

Got in his face and bellowed, "Tell me of this girl!"

Chapter Twenty-Five

"Gavrill Andreyev!" A deep, harsh voice called out.

The murmuring, weeping crowd suddenly hushed.

Andreyev paused, his fist still gripped in her dress, turned slightly. "What the hell?"

"Gavrill Andreyev!" the dark baritone called out again.

Andreyev let go of Cini's gown, and turned to face the crowd.

Taking a step from her, he held a hand over his brow squinting into the crowd to search for whomever was so brazen and foolish to throw his life away by calling out his name while he was in the throes of teaching his people a lesson by debasing rape and slow, horrendous execution.

The crowd shuffled and swayed, then slowly it parted as a man on an enormous ebony horse arrogantly pushed through.

Moving through the people, he sat with fearless aggression, dressed in black leathers and chain mail covering his tunic and breeches. He was huge, broad shouldered and brawny. His spine straight, head high, face fierce, blue eyes piercing yet inscrutable. His jaw was cleared of the beard.

"Who the hell is that?" the king questioned in furious awe.

Her voice so weak it was barely audible, Cini whispered in wheezing gasps, "That…is my…husband."

Before the king could give an order, Kazak kicked his steed so it bolted forward, he stood up on the saddle, and tossed a rope with an iron bar over a tree limb that hung over the back of the stage.

The bar wrapped twice around the branch. The horse kept running towards the stage, Kazak jumped, and swung on the rope up onto the stage.

Landing on his feet, he stuck the end of the rope under the back of his belt. The soldiers were too startled to move.

"What the fuck, who the hell are you?" Andreyev bellowed, "Guards!"

As he opened his mouth to order his men to take out the bold dark stranger, Kazak said calmly, "I am Lord Kazak Adarken, and I have come for my wife."

"You-" Andreyev started.

Kazak belted him in the mouth and the prince buckled to his knees. Stunned, shaking his head to clear it, he opened his mouth to call his guards to destroy the insane brute, but Kazak bent, grabbed his shirt and jerked him to his feet.

He hit him again and again, his huge fists pounding savagely fast and furious, so fast Andreyev couldn't block the blows much less deliver any of his own.

"You harm my wife?" Kazak snarled, intense rage speared furor in his homicidal eyes. "You die-" He hit him again but as he reached for him to beat him to death, the prince stumbled backwards and toppled off the stand.

The crowd paused speechless, then erupted in an ear blasting cheer.

The soldiers on the stage came out of their stupor and wielded swords at Kazak.

Without removing his own sword from its scabbard, Kazak narrowed his eyes at them and commanded, "Do not move." He stomped over to Cini pulling a knife from a sheath at his thigh.

The confused soldiers recognized the ruthless lethality in the warlord's eyes, and froze.

Her head wavering from the effort to keep conscious, Cini watched her enraged, butchering husband coming at her with a knife in his hand.

She couldn't keep her head up any longer. The thought of burning alive made every cell in her body sting in clamorous screams.

But, seeing her warrior husband, a nightmare of death resonating in those blazing blue eyes, Cini's brain frothed over with blinding terror of his vindictive wrath.

At least maybe he would kill her fast, that would be better than the slow, agonizing burning to death. Yet, as petrified as she was, her heart surged, she never thought she'd see him again.

As she passed out, she saw him raise the knife; a tiny whimper seeped out as he slashed it down.

Kazak cut her binds, she slumped into his arms. He lifted her over his shoulder, grabbed the rope, and swung off the back of the stage and leapt onto his horse that Bo had brought around.

Bo gave him a wink as Kazak settled on his saddle, lifted Cini to straddle him, wrapped his arms tightly around her broken body, and then, surrounded by his troop of warriors, Kazak barked the command to go.

Thunderous hooves pounded over the land, sinewy legs racing as fast as possible.

It wouldn't be long before the aggrandized king, if he survived the fall and the beating, would order his men after them.

Sure enough, less than ten minutes and they could hear the shouting of the soldiers as they gave chase.

Kazak strung an arm around Cini to hold her tight to his chest, and kicked his horse to go faster.

The warriors rode hard, the stallions' hooves trampling anything in their way like stampeding cattle.

Kazak led his men past a line of trees that bordered the beginning of the forest. They thundered towards the trees with the prince's men on their tails, and then they ever so unnoticeably slowed.

Rushing into the woods behind them, the prince's men hooted and hollered with glee that they were about to catch the marauders-

Suddenly the forest was filled with screams and bellows, curses and cries.

When Kazak found where Cini had gone, he had done reconnaissance of the entire area. He only had a vague idea what was going on.

First thing, was to get his wife.

Earlier, he had his men dig wolf pits. Now while his own men dashed around the hidden pits, Andreyev's men chased after them, and not seeing the covered ravines, raced right over- and dropped into them.

Those that saw and tried to stop before going over, panicked, trying to hold their horses back, but Kazak's men had burrowed under the area right before the pits.

The thin earth crumbled, the men screamed as they tried frantically to jump for solid ground, but they all fell into the ravine, one on top of the other.

The few that didn't fall in, realized they didn't have a chance against the warriors, turned tail and ran back to the castle.

Bo's laughter in his ears, Kazak's long hair billowed in the wind behind him as they continued their race to safety.

When they felt safe enough to slow down, Kazak looked down at Cini. She was barely recognizable, her face battered so gravely. Her hair matted with her blood, she was unconscious. Her skin almost transparent, she was so thin, only skin and bones.

"Bo," he called out.

Pulling back on his reins, Bo let his horse fall in beside Kazak, he glanced down at Cini and blanched.

"Gods, Kaz, what did he do to her?" Shaking his head sadly, his voice rough with emotion, "She doesn't look like she's going to make it, *frăţe*."

Kazak's head lowered to her, he murmured, "She better, she needs to be strong enough to survive the beating I have planned for her, before I put her to death for leaving me."

Bo's head slashed to his friend, his eyes wide, then narrowed. "You heard why she left. She needed to help her people. You would have done the same."

Still looking down at her, Kazak mumbled, "I would have trusted me. She should have trusted me to help her."

Bo studied his angry, hurt, friend.

Kazak had been uncontrollable with fury when he had come to and found she had tricked him, drugged him, and fled.

He and his men spent months looking for her. The longer it took, the blacker Kazak's mood. No one dared even breathe in his presence. Every time they returned unsuccessful to his castle, Kazak stalked straight to his chambers to drink and brood.

Finally, at one point on the trail, while at that pub, they ran into another soldier of the emperor. He had been there at the same time Cini was pleading to see the emperor, to beg him to hear her case and help her village.

The soldier told them who she was and where she was from, and his vague understanding why she was asking for the emperor's aid.

If only they had let her plead her case. The emperor would have sent Kazak himself to rescue the village. But his guards were too afraid to let the unknown girl get past them to the emperor.

Now that he knew what was going on, Kazak had led his men to find her village and plan how to take her.

He had been horrified when he'd seen her on the stage. The two women flanking her had just been brutally raped, and the king-prince had ripped Cini's dress and was about to assault her too before setting his beaten wife on fire, to burn alive.

He wanted to kill the prince then and there, but Andreyev had fallen off the stage, and it was more important Kazak get Cini away, get them all away before the prince's men could come after them. They could return later when they were prepared to fight.

Looking down at her bundled in his arms, her dress hanging off her, bruised eyes closed, skin so pale, he said, "Bo, we cannot make it back to the castle, she is too frail, she will not last until we get there. We need to find a place to stop, tend to her wounds."

"*Bine*, I'll have the men set up the tents," Bo said.

His eyes on Cini, her breathing was so slight he wasn't even sure if she still lived, Kazak said, "Nay, she needs warm shelter and food, medicine."

"*Da*, I'll search ahead for a village." Bo made a tsk sound and his horse speeded up.

They found a village with a two-story house big enough to accommodate all the men.

Kazak carried Cini to a round room far in the back. It was encircled with windows, he hoped the sun would help her heal. Bo had made sure it was a good solid place.

The wealthy people that owned it were in another country visiting relatives, the servants were eager to accept Kazak's money for good service. They were happy and grateful to wait on the infamous warriors that had given them protection at times.

Except, most of the servants were petrified of the large man with the harsh face and shadowed fierce eyes. He barely spoke to anyone, just grunted orders at his men.

Kazak had Bo find the most comfortable room with the most comfortable bed. Which was the round room. He carefully laid Cini on the big bed then sat on the mattress beside her. His weight sunk the thick mattress but Cini didn't stir.

He gazed at her face, so badly beaten, his stomach sickened, his brain screamed to get on his horse right now and go back and make that prince pay with his hide until he drew his last breath.

But, a sigh escaped, he reached over and brushed her blood soaked hair off her face, right now he had to see to his wife.

His eyes slid down, her torn dress showed more than it covered. The full creamy mounds of her breasts half exposed tantalized him, but he could see even her torso was heavily bruised, making his stomach revolt even more.

Kazak got up and left, found a servant and told him he wanted water and cloths, oils and ointment, bandages, medicine, and clean clothes.

Their heads down, scared to make eye contact with the fierce lord, the servants brought bowls of warm water and set them beside the bed. They didn't dare spare a glance at the poor miss he'd carried in.

The word was she was his wife and he had just saved her as she was being executed, and, when, if, she was well, he would kill her himself for betraying him.

As soon as they set everything he asked for down, they scurried out holding their breath, fearful that the man with the raw pain and dangerous ferocity in his icy eyes would slaughter them too.

Gingerly lifting Cini, he placed a blanket under her and another over her, then peeled off her ruined gown.

Kazak dipped the cloths in the water then, very carefully, he cleaned the blood from her poor broken body, his heart bleeding along with her wounds.

His throat too tight to swallow, he couldn't believe someone would hurt such a tiny, delicate, sweet woman like Cini. His gut roiled with the urge to go back and tear Andreyev's limbs from his body, one at a time, slowly.

He drew the cloth down her bruised arm, wiping away the blood. Cleaning her little fingers one by one, his breath caught. He held her hand, she still wore his ring. The backs of his eyes stung and blurred. She still wore his ring. Even her wedding band was caked with blood.

When he cleaned and then dried her, he carefully slipped a clean gown on her, covering up that luscious body that even at death's door, still made him instantly hard and hungry for her.

He set the bowls of dirty bloody water outside the door for the servants to dispose of. Just as he finished, Bo came in with a tray of food.

"Hey," he greeted Kazak in a quiet voice. "How she doing?" He'd seen the bloody water and his stomach pitched.

Setting the tray on a table, Bo went to look at Cini.

"Damn, Kaz," his whisper filled with terrible sorrow at seeing the shape she was in.

Kazak sat back down on the mattress. "I know. Help me get some water into her." He rolled his arm under her back and lifted her.

Bo grabbed a cup and dipped it in the basin of water and brought it to Cini's lips. It was difficult, and took patience, but they got some water down her.

"I have to wait until she is awake to feed her," Kazak sighed pulling the blanket up to her chin. He stroked her hair.

"Yah," Bo smirked, "get her strong enough to take your punishment, huh?"

His eyes on Cini, Kazak nodded.

"*Bine*, well, I'll leave you two in peace." Bo went to the door and said with a grin, "There's a lusty redhead that looks promising, but, let me know if I can do anything else."

Kazak didn't look at him, just nodded wordlessly, he didn't hear Bo close the door behind him. He looked at the food, he wasn't hungry.

Kicking off his boots, he climbed in the bed beside Cini. Curling towards her, he gently slid his arm under her to hold her.

With Cini in his arms, hearing her soft breathing, Kazak was asleep for the first time in minutes since the day she left him.

Chapter Twenty-Six

𝕴t was days and still Cini didn't wake. Kazak was beside himself, he feared he would be digging her grave any day now. He'd finally found her and now he was going to lose her all over again. He could not bear it.

He was pacing in their room, Bo and Liam sat sprawled in chairs, drinking ale and watching him traipse back and forth.

Searching for something to break Kazak's hopeless mood, Bo said, "So, Kaz," he glanced at Liam who shrugged, "they'll be practicing soon for the spring games what do you say-"

Kazak swung on him, roared, "*Føkk* the bloody games-"

A whimper and movement from the bed stopped him. His mouth open, he swung around.

Bo and Liam stood up.

Kazak hurried to the bed. Cini's lashes flickered, her head rolled, she moaned.

"*Mea miera*," Kazak knelt by the bed, and carefully caressed the side of her healing face. "Činnosti," he said softly, "wake up, sweet wife."

Cini's head turned towards his voice. Her lashes wisped, a trace of green peered from below swollen lids. Cracked and hoarse, she croaked, "*Dominio*? What-" She winced as pain waved over her face.

His brain staggered, she had at last woken, he had to fight to remember his English. "Tis Kazak, Činnosti, your husband."

"Ka-" The green eyes flickered in fright. "Please," she croaked, "don't hurt me, please," tears eked out the corners of her bruised eyes as she feebly tried to squirm away from him, but only cried out in pain.

"*Nu*, do not move, Činnosti." He gently set his large hand on her thin shoulder to hold her from moving and hurting herself more. He didn't notice Bo and Liam silently slip out of the room.

"*Mea babia*," Kazak murmured, softly stroking her shoulder, "my baby, you have been...hurt, do not move for more injury."

Cini blinked back frightened tears of pain, her pale face whitened further at the sight of the big man crouching over her. Her dreams meeting her nightmares.

She had wanted so badly to see him again; it was like a stabbing in her heart every time she thought of him, which had been incessantly. But, she so feared his deadly furor.

"Please don't hurt me...Kazak. I had to do it," her husky inhale filled with pain. "I had to go, please understand," her voice scraped out raw from her parched throat.

"I know, Wife. Rest now, you need strength." He petted her until her lids closed again and she was again asleep. Yet now her breaths were deeper, more regular.

Kazak crawled on the bed and leaned his back against the wall, crossed his ankles and continued to stroke her head, her hair, her arm.

It was another few days before she was even able to sit up, and she could only do that with Kazak's strong arm bracing her, lifting her.

Still she shrank from him, he frowned. They didn't speak, even while he fed her. He dipped bread in thick warm stew and brought it to her lips.

She couldn't lift her arms and was embarrassed that this vicious warlord that could break a man's neck with one move, was feeding her calmly and gently like she was an infant.

When she'd had enough, he got up and set the bowl on a table.

Watching him, she croaked, "Kazak, why are you...caring for me when...you're just going to...kill me?" Her voice wobbled and croaked, she stared at his broad back as it stiffened.

When he turned she flinched. Was he going to beat her now that he helped her get well enough to- to what?

He didn't move. Inhaling deeply, he raked his fingers through his long hair then expelled the heavy breath.

She was suddenly startled. "Your beard, you shaved your beard?"

His hand went to his jaw. He had shaved it but already there was black scruff from the days of being with her. Too intent on Cini's health, he bothered with little other than eating to keep himself strong to care for her.

Gaze of steel on her, he clawed his thick fingertips through the scruff.

With a short, mirthless smile and nod he said, "*Da*, we searched so long and hard for you, it was too hot, too uncomfortable-" he broke off remembering the terrible days of looking for her and the hopelessness that besotted him every night while he tried to sleep after fruitless days of not finding her.

Cini saw the darkness creep over his face, harden his jaw, hood his eyes. He took a step to her, she shrank back against the pillows he'd stacked behind her.

Seeing the fear rigid in her body, the fright in her eyes, he still moved to the bed.

"Kazak, please," her voice quivered.

Perceiving, yet ignoring her anxiety, Kazak sat down on the bed facing her. The gravel in his deep voice softened, "Wife, I will not hurt you. Never."

He had told himself and his friends he would beat her and then kill her when he got his hands on her. But, he had said that to bury the aching anguish from her leaving him that engulfed his soul, sucked at his heart so, that he thought it would stop beating and he would lose all breath.

And then day after dreadful day of not being able to find her and fearing the worse, so afraid he couldn't think, couldn't keep a thought in his head amongst the pictures of her lying dead somewhere. Murdered by soldiers or ravaged by a bear or jungle cat.

Then, when he finally found her, retrieved her, saw the critical condition she was in, he was afraid that just as he found her she would die in his arms.

He lifted his hand and touched her still bruised cheek. "Do not be afraid of Kazak, ah, of me."

Still terrified of him, she didn't flinch but her brow furrowed. "Your English, you're speaking better English?"

A smile gentled his hard mouth. "*Da*, when you first came, I had not spoken it for a long time, was, uh, as Bo says, rusty. I study and Bo help me practice."

He shrugged a thick shoulder. "I practice all the time while looking for-" His mouth shut.

Clearing his throat, he shifted his position on the bed, leaned over Cini to place his hand on the other side of her on the mattress.

Her body stiffened, there was no way she could try to get away from him. He had her fenced in with his big body.

He reached for her hand and raised it. Fiddling with the ring on her finger with his thumb, he rolled his eyes up at her and said softly, "You wear Kazak's ring, you not take it off."

Lifting her hand to his mouth, his gaze leveled on hers, he kissed her hand, then each dainty finger, then held her palm to his mouth.

Leaning against the pillows, Cini's body relaxed a hair, she smiled. "Kazak, believe it or not, I didn't want to leave you."

Shaking her head at his frown of doubt, she said, "No, Kazak, no, I didn't want to go. I wanted to..." her smile crooked from the split lip, she looked up at him, "stay with you, Kazak."

He sat there, huge and strong, his gaze hard on her. His eyes wandered over her bruised face, then down the front of her, the tips of his ears turned red, he quickly raised his eyes back to hers.

"You...wanted to stay with Kaz- ah, with me?" Still holding her hand, he caressed the top of it with his thumb.

Ducking her head, she peered up shyly at him, nodded. "Yes." Her hair slid forward covering part of her face, curls rolled over her shoulder.

Then, her eyes narrowed at him, was that moisture in his eyes? "Kazak," she reached for his face, he leaned back and brushed his hand over his eyes.

They both sat silently, watching the other.

Clearing his throat, his voice a gruff rasp, Kazak asked quietly, "You want to be wife, uh, my wife? Live together, with…babes?"

She laughed then winced when it hurt. Her hand went to her sore lip. "Yes, I want that so badly Kazak. Is that…I mean, do you want that too?"

His answer a hungry growl, he leaned in and ever so gently kissed the side of her mouth that wasn't torn.

Shifting back, he laid his hand against her face. "*Da*, Kazak want, ah, *I* want you, Činnosti. I married you, I searched for you, because," his eyes flit back and forth across her face.

"I wanted you, I…" his lids lowered over his brilliant blues, then raised. "I wanted the rest of my life to be with you, Činnosti, Wife."

The tears flowed, her voice broke, "Oh, Kazak."

He leaned in and carefully took her in his arms, held her as she pressed her face into his shoulder and sobbed.

His arms wrapped around her, Kazak nestled his mouth and nose into the top of her hair, inhaling her scent with such unbearable relief his body contracted with the excruciating pain of it.

He would not have to force her to stay with him! She will lie in his arms, in his bed of her own free will. Perhaps there truly is a benevolent God!

Dying to crush her in his arms, hold her so tight against him, feel the soft body he'd missed and longed for, he had to force himself to keep his hold loose so as not to damage her further.

He always became so excited when he held her, he tended to forget his own strength, that she was so small, so feminine, his delicate fairy.

He murmured against her hair, "You stay now, Wife, for always, with…me."

When she stiffened, he drew back, black brows a hard V, "What, Činnosti?"

Eyes flooded with churning tears, she lowered her long blonde lashes over them, took a shuddering breath. Then she boldly raised them to look straight into his gleaming orbs so intent on her.

The relief mingled with happiness that she would stay with him of her own volition, that she *wanted* to, shimmered damply in his eyes and his mouth lifted to almost a smile.

But, Cini said, "Kazak, I can't do as I want, live a happy life with you while Prince Andreyev destroys my home, kills my family, friends, neighbors, everyone at Chalon-sur-Sônn. I…"

She lifted a shaking hand to wipe at her eyes. "Please understand, I have to go back. I have to do something, I-"

"Do what?" he roared, gripping her upper arms as anger fraught with fright of her ever leaving him again rose to choke him.

"What can you," his gaze swept down her with sarcasm, "a fragile, young woman, alone, with no weapons, no soldiers, what can you possibly do to save your village?"

The tears of helplessness, hopelessness streamed down her face, she lowered her head into her hands weeping.

He held her arms but loosened his incensed grip, rubbing her skin while watching her cry.

Then she looked at him through torrents of tears, determination tightening her soft features. "But I have to do something. I can't live here safe and happily with you while they-" she shook her head as sobs overwhelmed her, her head dropping again.

"Ah, foolish wife." Kazak put both hands on either side of her head and gently raised it. "You will do what you should have done in first place," he brushed at her tears with his thumbs.

"And," her eyes closed savoring his tenderness, "what is that? I went to the emperor, he refused to see me. I can only go back and try to figure out a way to make him-"

"Godsdammit Činnosti." He shook her but not roughly. "Stop that. You will never do anything alone again."

Cradling her face, he told her, "I am *dominio*, and husband, tis my duty to save wife's village. But," he kissed her softly, "you are beloved Činnosti, I would always do it for you."

Surprised, perplexed, her brows down, she said, "But, the emperor will be mad at you-"

He started speaking. His English was much improved but still as he spoke Cini added missing words automatically in her head.

"*Babia*, even if he was, I would still do it. However, if his *idjit* men had let you in to him, he would have aided you. It is what makes him a great leader. All life, villages, are under his protective dome. It is why we are here, why we patrol the Spider Thread Trails, to protect the people. If he was aware of your village's troubles he would have immediately sent his *dominio*, me, to rescue your people.

"Even not knowing you were Kazak's wife, he would have commanded me to take my men to your village, destroy Prince Andreyev, and restore all back to safety and peace."

He pecked the side of her mouth. "Now, you no longer worry, fear for your people. We will return to my home in Thondragu at Salbaji Keep, where you will continue your...what you say," he thought, "recuperation, and I will lead my men to your village to-"

Louise Furley

"Oh no, Kazak, I am going with you. No," she held a hand up as his skin darkened, eyes narrowed. "They are my people, I will be there to fight with you."

Shaking his head angrily, he said, "Nay, I will not allow it. There will be no more danger for you, you will stay safe at castle."

"Kazak, I will either go with you, or I will go on my own. You think you can keep me at the castle?" She smiled with the shake of her head. "You already tried that, a few times, and I got out. So, I go with you, or without you. What will it be?"

His eyes narrowed further in menace, a severe look that struck terror in the toughest of men, but only met her bruised face, lush mouth firm in determination. A loud rough sigh of resignation expelled from his exasperation.

Giving in, he said, "*Bine*."

Before she could rejoice, he went on, "However, you will never leave our home unless you are with me. But," now he held his hand up to stop her objection, "if wife insists on going, Kazak will teach wife how to fight, will have a sword made that Činnosti can wield, and will train before go."

Eyes flying wide with surprise at his words, her mouth swept into a smile, then she winced at the pain of it from her wounds.

Cini said enthusiastically, "Great, great, I'm game. But we need to do this as soon as possible, while the people still live, all right?"

"*Da*," he nodded. "As soon as you can stay on two feet without fall." He smiled, his love for her shining like a sun emerging from a dark eclipse, the warmth completely enveloping her.

220

"Hmmm," she smiled back. Then, Cini stroked her hands over his face. "Can we...uh, make love now? Can we," a blush overtook her, "you know, do it right?"

A happy glow brightened his eyes before lust clouded them, but he shook his head.

"Nay. Not yet. Činnosti is, uh, you are too ill. When better," he bent and licked part of her cheek that wasn't injured. "We...what you call, properly consummate our marriage, *bine?*" his brow wriggled with a leer.

His hands itched to touch her breasts, feel the supple weight of them, clutch her pure plump femininity in his needy fingers.

He craved to slip his hand down between her legs to caress her woman's folds. He smothered a shiver that rolled through him at the remembrance of how beautiful her body was, how her silk oozed onto his hand as his fingers penetrated her sweet channel.

But, his gut twisted, bruises glared from her neck to cross over her cleavage. He would die before he ever hurt her again.

Chapter Twenty-Seven

As soon as she was strong enough to travel, Kazak brought her back to the castle. Every day Cini was a bit better.

As much as the people clamored for her cooking, Kazak refused to allow her to go to the kitchens. He wanted her safe, and he was a jealous man of her time, he wanted her with him.

One early eve, since she was very much on the mend, the bruises had faded, and she walked without limping, Kazak escorted her down to dinner.

As they entered the dining area, a hush rolled over the chattering diners, and as one, they all rose, and bowed.

One of the warriors lifted his head and said in Romanian, "Blessed be Lady Činnosti Adarken, long may she live, may she and our revered Lord Adarken be fruitful with babes. And," he grinned, "may Lady Adarken make those rare smiles our lord has recently been sprouting upon his face, permanent!"

The crowd roared their approval and agreement,

Cini looked around like she had at their wedding. Everyone was beaming at the couple, genuinely showing their elation. She tugged Kazak's sleeve. He bent to her.

"Husband, what did he say?"

With a happy, peaceful smile, Kazak translated.

Cini glanced all around with surprise.

These people seemed to truly care for Kazak, and, now, accepted her and cared for her too. Her heart filled and overflowed with joy.

She was unaware, that the women, such as Bonatella that were nastily jealous of her and mean to her, Kazak had banished from the castle. He wasn't going to let anything, or anyone, hurt her again, physically or mentally.

Every day Kazak gave her combat training. He was serious with her training, but in the back of his mind, there was no way he would ever let her near a battle, near any soldiers other than his own, and he would certainly never let her be even in the vicinity of Gavrill Andreyev.

But he knew better than to tell her that. His tiny delicate wife had a spine of steel and was as stubborn as their worst mule, and if he advised her that he wasn't going to let her anywhere near the fighting, she would chew his ear off telling him that oh yes she was.

Kazak had sent a troop of warriors to Cini's village. Some were to surround the perimeter of the village staying hidden. Some slipped in and out of the castle through the tunnel Cini had told them about.

The rest inserted themselves carefully into the village homes, staying inside so the prince's soldiers wouldn't know they were there.

When all was ready, Kazak led his men to travel to Chalon-sur-Sônn.

He kept a very angry Cini at the very back protected by Bo and Thomas. She felt it was her place, her duty to be at the lead as they attacked the prince's soldiers.

It was a lengthy journey through the dense cover of woods. They stayed off the trade routes, they didn't want their presence announced before they got to the village.

Kazak had some of his female warriors from another division come and travel with them, he wanted to make sure Cini had a wall of warriors around her at all times, even when she relieved herself.

As they traveled south, it was a bit warmer as winter hadn't yet fully hit the upper part of the continent. At night they slept in tents.

Kazak and Cini had their own private tent, they snuggled under blankets. He wanted her 100% healed, and in total privacy, before he claimed her again, but that didn't mean they couldn't explore each other's flesh and he could pleasure her like he'd done before.

He had to cover her mouth with his own to smother her screams and groans of rapture as he taught her how to enjoy her body, and how he could make it sing. And she grew familiar with the sight and feel, and taste, of his manhood.

The closer they moved to the village, the more agitated Cini grew. After all, these were her people, her family, her friends, and if they couldn't save them, everyone there would be ill-fated.

Reaching a familiar copse of trees, Cini had excitedly advised that the woods were the beginning perimeter of the village.

Kazak directed his warriors to their assigned duties. In groups, they would spread out and surround the village making contact with their comrades, and get word to the men stashed inside the castle and the houses.

When they set up camp, Kazak had two female warriors and two males, one being Liam, bring Cini to the settlement, her mouth was already setting into a hard line.

"No Kazak, no way. I know what you're going to do, and I am not staying here!" Cini rode her horse to where Kazak was giving orders.

When she reached him, her mouth opened to tell him she was not staying- and he suddenly reached up, grasped her around the waist and lifted her off the horse and onto her feet.

Holding onto her arm, Kazak, who Cini had not seen him change, was now wearing chainmail, motioned to the two female and two male warriors. They dismounted and surrounded Cini and Kazak.

"No, Kazak!" she shouted. He slapped his mouth on hers, a hand cupped the back of her head, the other splayed across her back.

After a heated kiss that left Cini dizzy, Kazak released her, quickly stepped back, and the four warriors instantly surrounded her like a fence.

"*Da,* Wife, you will stay here. There is no argument." His hands clasped behind his back, he watched Cini's face turn dark red, she sputtered furiously, and tried to get past her human pen.

"Damn you, Kazak, I will not stay here, you can't make me!"

The soldiers didn't touch her, but they were all, including the women, too big and brawny for her to move aside. Tears of frustration blurred her eyes, "Please, Kazak, I need to come with you," she wailed.

"Nay, Činnosti. You have briefly trained, but you are not a warrior. I will not allow you to be in danger, you will stay here. We should be back in, a day, two at the most."

He took one last long look at her infuriated beautiful face, then pivoted and strode away with her yelling at his back.

At his signal, Kazak led his men into the forest. It was a few hours of travel just to get through the woods.

When they emerged, he gave a shrill whistle and all of his warriors swarmed from the woods like killer bees from a flaming hive to surround the prince's soldiers.

There were so many warriors, they totally took the prince, the self-appointed king's soldiers by surprise. There was some sword fighting, but the soldiers were quickly killed, too injured to move, or taken captive and restrained.

Kazak led his men through the village to the castle. The soldiers that protected the outside of the castle came at them shrieking and hollering to bar the entrance.

But Kazak's men were already stashed inside, and they fought the soldiers from inside so the door was unbarred, wide open for Kazak and his warriors to barge into the castle.

Bo swung his sword left and right, up and down, slashing, stabbing in and out, he fought his way through the main part of the castle to a set of stone stairs.

He battled more soldiers as he made his way up the stairs. Kazak's order was to keep going up until every inch of the castle was cleared of the prince's soldiers. Then he heard a woman screaming.

He burst into a hallway with an open alcove a few dozen feet away. Two soldiers had ahold of a young woman, a gorgeous, very young woman with long raven hair. Wide blue eyes radiated her terror, her lush mouth was open to scream.

Each man held one of her arms and they were hustling her against the wall.

When she screamed again, one of the men wrapped his beefy hand across the front of her neck and shoved her hard to the wall, pinning her there with a curse. "Shut up, woman, we just want a little fuck before we join the fight. The less you struggle the faster we'll be on our way."

She screamed again, tossing and twisting her slender body to fight free. The other man shoved her long skirt up and was moving between her legs.

"Now, now, boys," Bo said cheerfully, strolling down the hall towards them. "Vomen are not fair game in this war, so kindly step away from her and battle with someone your own gender."

The men halted and glared at him.

The one with his hand around the girl's neck scowled. "Get bloody lost, boy, before I run you through with my sword. You want the bitch, you wait until we're done. Now, take off."

The second guard turned back to the girl and shoved her skirt up to her waist. He pushed a foot between hers to keep her long willowy legs apart.

Bo kept moving to them, his sword in his hand, the cheerful smile gone. His handsome face hardened into a killing mask.

The closer he got, the more the soldiers noticed the blood spattered all over him and his chainmail, his sword was dark with blood. They both released the girl and stepped in front of her.

"Go the hell away, boy, this is your last warning," the first soldier threatened, raising his sword.

Bo ran up to the men, but went kitty-corner to the side drawing them away from the frantic girl.

The two men shouted raging words and struck at Bo. Now his grin was back as he fought the soldiers.

It took him less than twenty seconds to dispatch them both. The corpses dropped to the floor, one head rolled towards the girl.

Screaming, she scrambled against the wall to get away from the head.

Bo darted in front of the dead men, sheathing his sword.

"All right, sweetheart, tis done. I pose no threat to you, I swear-"

Lovely lips parted in a gasp, huge bright blue eyes like round pools widened at him, just before they rolled back in her head and she swooned.

"Bloody hell," Bo mumbled and raced to her to catch her before she hit the floor.

Chapter Twenty-Eight

Kazak fought his way up to where Cini said Prince Andreyev would likely be hiding from the fray.

He tried to lift the handle to open the heavy wooden door laden with iron studs and bands, but the gold handle was locked from the inside.

No matter, he lifted his sword and slashed at the handle until it broke off, then he put his boot to the door and shoved it open.

"Ah, Princess Činnosti's husband, I presume?" a nasty, sardonic voice said calmly as Kazak entered the room. "We meet again, eh?"

Kazak scanned the room without moving his head, barely moved his eyes. So trained, he knew everything and everyone that was in the large, lavish chamber.

Intricately carved dressers and tables filled the room, lush braided carpets covered the floor, and the only occupants were the man, and the toddler he held. The toddler was crying.

Taking in the scene, "Gavrill Andreyev I presume?" Kazak replied laconically, moving cautiously into the room and towards the man.

Puffing out his barrel chest, the fifty-year-old snarled through his heavy lips, "Yes, I am Prince, uh, *King* Gavrill Andreyev," he answered with all pomposity, and set the toddler on the sill of an open window.

His face was covered with faded bruises and lacerations from Kazak's brief beating that day on the podium when he rescued Cini. Kazak would have ensured he'd drawn his last breath, but the prince had been lucky, he'd fallen off the platform and Kazak had to leave him to get Cini to safety.

Andreyev commanded, "You will come no closer, or I will push this child out the window."

Kazak slowed his step as the king set the child so more of his body was outside the window than in. Kazak's frown heavy, voice growling deep, he questioned, "What tis your game, Andreyev?"

"You will soon find out. Now, remove your armor."

At Kazak's questioning glance, Andreyev's voice roughened as he wiggled the child, "Now. Take it off now or the child goes over."

Still Kazak hesitated, the prince gave the child a little nudge, the baby wailed, his little chubby legs kicking into open air.

Kazak removed his chainmail, letting it clunk on the floor.

Andreyev then ordered, "Now the sword, and the daggers at your back and up your sleeve, also the ones in your boots. Hurry, the child appears to be slipping out of my fingers."

The frightened toddler shrieked and kicked harder. Andreyev had to quickly grasp him with both hands before he tumbled to his death.

Kazak quickly divested himself of all of his weapons, then stood with his arms out. "That is all. Now, what are you going to do?" he demanded.

"This-" Andreyev laughed full of evil, purely heartless, and let go of the baby giving him a little nudge as he darted away from the window.

"You *føkker*-" Well aware the prince had pulled his own sword and would be behind him, Kazak had no choice but to rush to the window as the baby toppled out of it.

He managed to throw half his body out the window to grab the baby as it fell screeching in mid-air.

"Ah, perfect," Andreyev muttered, as he raised his sword to cut off Kazak's head.

As he swung the sword, his triumphant roar broke off with a squawk, then a gurgle. Choking, he struggled to reach behind him to get at the dagger that was stuck in the back of his neck.

Lifting the baby out of the window and holding it against his chest, Kazak swung around. His eyes popped when he saw Cini standing there, her hands covering her mouth, freaked out eyes bursting over her hands.

They both watched as the prince still fighting to get the dagger out, crumpled to the floor, blood gushing from his neck.

"Godsdammit, Činnosti," Kazak barked, striding to his mortified wife. Tucking the baby under his arm, he reached for Cini, and hauled her against his chest, wrapping his arm around her.

Into her fragrant hair he mumbled, "Will you never do as I command?"

He saw Andreyev's hand twitch, grasping his sword. Kazak set Cini aside, snatched up his own sword from the floor and jabbed it into Andreyev's back staking him to the floor.

Still holding the baby, he returned to fold Cini into his arms.

Keeping her face nuzzled into his powerful chest, Cini sobbed her fear and relief into his shirt, soaking it with her tears.

They made their way down the stone steps.

When they met other warriors, they all went outside, the village people roared with their grateful cheers.

Kazak saw that Thomas had a serious wound to his back, blood was flooding out, he was sinking to his knees.

Kazak handed the child to Cini, tore off his shirt and hurried to him, using his shirt to stall the flow of blood. He yelled out for assistance.

Men ran over to aid Thomas.

When the blood was staunched and a læce, a field medic was stitching Thomas' wound, Kazak stood, and went to rejoin Cini. As he neared her, he realized the crowd had hushed.

Cini's parents were there, standing on either side of her, their mouths open, eyes round with disbelief.

"What?" Kazak asked as he reached them.

"Your back," Cini's father, Garund Brymiente exclaimed, his voice rich with astonished awe. "The sign of the royal House of Rôhnan is tattooed on, no wait," Garund moved behind Kazak. His hand up, palm out a few inches from the markings on Kazak's back.

"No," Garund said in quiet amazement, "not a tattoo, but, it is a part of you."

Frowning, Kazak turned to face him, queried, "What are you talking about?"

An elderly woman stepped from the crowd. "I can answer that. I could not speak before, when Prince Andreyev still lived, but now," she wiped her wet eyes.

"Speak, voman, what the hell are you talking about?" Kazak ordered. He took the child from Cini and handed it to her mother who was holding her arms out, tears rushing down her cheeks.

He glanced over as Bo, holding a young woman's hand came out of the castle to join them.

"Meli!"

"Cini!"

Joyous, the girls rushed to each other and hugged fiercely.

Smiling at the happy girls, Kazak turned back to the elderly woman with a commanding frown. "Speak, what about the markings on my back?"

His back was facing the crowd. His tanned skin covered with sweat did not hide the ancient Russian streaks and the Siberian tiger paw etched over his shoulder.

The old woman spoke softly, the crowd hushed to hear her. "I am Victoria, my Sire. It is my deepest pleasure to see you return to your home."

Murmurs in the crowd rose as they agreed with her.

Victoria said, "Many years ago, King Øysten Rôhnan, well, he wasn't king then, he was a lord of the realm. Your father was king. King Leopald Rôhnan. Øysten was your uncle and he desired to be king and had your parents murdered so he could be next in line to receive the title of majesty.

"But, there was you, you weren't much older than that babe there," she nodded to the toddler now sleeping in Cini's mother's arms.

"Lord Øysten had to get rid of you, but a sorcerer in the village had warned him that if he killed you, the evil spirits would have him perish on the spot. But he needed you out of the way."

An old man nodded, he said, "Cini's father, Garund, a distant relation of the Rôhnan family, became king when

Øysten died before Cini's birth. But that was many years later."

Everyone was in rapt attention. Kazak had moved back to Cini and dropped his arm around her shoulders and held her close to his side. "Go on," Kazak urged the elderly woman to continue.

Victoria nodded, pulling her cloak up closer around her wizened, withered body. "Yes. So, Lord Øysten secretly ordered his men to take you out to the middle of the vast forests, the deepest part of the treacherous jungle, and leave you there.

"You were so young, you were barely even speaking much then. The lord figured you would die quickly, but not by his hand. The forest would eat you alive in one way or the other. You would starve to death if a wild animal didn't get you first."

The crowed hung on her every word. Kazak's face was a blank mask of stoicism. He hugged Cini tighter, bent his head and kissed the top of hers.

She laid her head against his chest and he crossed both arms over her hugging her to him. He said quietly to the woman, "It would appear, that he was wrong."

"Yes," Victoria smiled, her withered face wreathed in wrinkles crinkled with her smile. "He apparently was. Somehow, you managed to survive. Lord Øysten had one of his people say you had wandered off while playing. Everyone searched for you for days, weeks, months.

"But we never found any trace of you. At a point, it was clear you could not still live, so your uncle was declared King. And you?" she nodded pointedly at Kazak to fill in the rest.

He hesitated, looking around at…his people. These were his people. He looked down at Cini's shining face tilted up happily at him. He and his wife were actually related, distant cousins it would seem.

Kazak faced the public, with a mix of other languages to fortify his English, he said, "I cannot tell you how I survived. I was too young to remember. They, a band of warriors, said they had come across me in the forest.

"They had no way of knowing who I was, where I came from, how far I had traveled. I spoke very little. Said only a few words, such as, three, and 'I *alb tirgis*' which means, I am white tiger.

"They assumed I was saying I was three years old, the white tiger they laughed at, saying I was being fanciful, a child with an ego, they would try to beat that out of me," he snorted with a shake of his head.

The warriors assumed since I said three, and that judging the growth of my body I was really around four, that it had likely been a year that I was in the forests. No one knew who I was." He looked to the old woman. "The missing heir to the throne had apparently been long forgotten."

"No," Victoria said with a sad smile and a shake of her head. "Not a'tall. You merely emerged somewhere else from the jungle, far away from your home."

Kazak pondered that.

Then he went on, "The warriors kept me with them, raised me as a warrior from that age." He didn't have to describe how vicious and brutal his childhood was. He was spared nothing, he was beaten, whipped, pounded into the warlord he was today.

The crowd could see it in the violent mist in his brilliant blue eyes. The mist cleared when he gazed upon his wife, who smiled so lovingly up at him.

"So," Victoria, the old woman said, "you, are our true king."

Hugging Cini, Kazak knew who he was, he was Lord Kazak Adarken. He had been created by aggression, battle, violence. He asked with faint curiosity, "What is my birth name?"

The oldest people in the village gathered closer to him, the ones who had known him when he had disappeared. The warriors that were his closest friends also grew near. Bo's face split in a huge grin between the news about Kazak being a true king, and, he looked down at the woman he had his arm protectively around, Cini's best friend, Meli.

"Jîn-kháu," Victoria said, deep respect for Kazak in her tone, her manner, she bowed to him. "You are King Jîn-kháu Lūi Rôhnan."

The old man repeated reverently, also bowing, "King Jîn-kháu Lūi Rôhnan. Long live King Jîn-kháu Lūi Rôhnan."

The crowd all dropped to their knees repeating his words.

Her eyes gleaming, Victoria said, "Aye, and long live Queen Činnosti Rôhnan!" and she went to her knees.

Around Kazak and Cini the crowd knelt and chanted, "Long live King Jîn-kháu and Queen Činnosti!"

Kazak turned Cini in his arms to face him and his mouth fell to hers.

After a soft kiss, he leaned back cradling her face with his hands. He said, "Long live my beautiful wife, Queen Činnosti," and he devoured her mouth.

Chapter Twenty-Nine

𝔚eeks later, the villagers celebrated their new king, and queen, and their freedom from the tyrannical Gavrill Andreyev.

There was a formal ceremony crowning Kazak king, and then Cini as his queen.

At the feast that Cini oversaw, musicians played and sang, people ate and drank and danced all night.

Kazak had his kingdom by birth, and also one Emperor Radisalvo rewarded him with for his years of fealty and hard work cleaning up the Spider Thread Trails and protecting all the towns along the routes.

Kazak and his team were also hugely rewarded for their valiant rescue of Cini's village.

Leaving the celebration before it even started winding down, Kazak and Cini slipped into their chambers.

He had his hands all over her the second he closed and locked their door. His fingers went right to the strings of her dress. Smiling down at his wife, Kazak tugged the strings and watched as the dress slid down her body.

"Činnosti," he murmured, dragging his palms up the front of her to grip her plump breasts. Groaning at their heaviness in his big hands, he bent, his lips closing over a pink nipple and then he pushed the dress the rest of the way off her, leaving her naked, the way he liked her best.

Cini stood back and plucked at the buttons on his shirt. When she got them all undone, she groaned as her palms splayed over his thick chest, sifting her fingers through the matting of black hair.

Kazak moved his hand to cup her mound and smiled at the moan purling up her throat. He slid his hands under her and lifted her to set her gently on the bed.

Cini lay on her back, hair spread as a golden sun, her hands up by her head on the mattress.

"Nice *babia*, so nice, but," Kazak bent and took an ankle and moved it apart from her other leg. "Perfect. Do not move, *babia*," he instructed.

Keeping his eyes on Cini stretched out in all her nude glory for him to consume with his eyes, Kazak shrugged off his shirt, and unfastened his breeches, kicked off his boots and then his pants. He climbed on the bed pulling Cini into his arms.

They lay in the large bed cuddled in each other's arms. He brushed loose tendrils of hair from her face, caressed her soft skin, then cradled her head as he kissed her with love and simmering heat for his beautiful, reckless, courageous wife that he knew would never leave him again.

"Wife," he said, gazing in adoration at her.

"Hmmm?" she murmured, her fingers stroking through his long hair.

"Where shall we live? I have two kingdoms and enough land to build my own country." He skimmed his hand from her face, down over her plump breast.

Enjoying her fullness kneading in his big fingers, he squeezed the supple flesh and tweaked the pert nipple before moving lower over her taut belly he planned to fill with his babes, then down to tease her sex.

"Uh!" Cini gasped with pleasure as his fingers plundered her woman's folds, stroked her swelling damp slit then pinched her hardening bud. "Um," she gulped, shifting her hips to urge him to touch her more.

"It uh, matters not to me, Husband, my home is where you are," she pulled his head down so their lips could mesh again and strike that heat like flint on rock, burning them in the wildfire of their lovemaking.

She writhed with ecstatic moans as he sank his thick fingers inside her silky sheath, wet and waiting for him.

"Kazak, now, I need you now, bring me home," she cried as his fingers strummed and thrust inside her, sharply rousing her to needy delirium.

His smile as wide as all outdoors, Kazak rolled on top of her, nudging her slender thighs apart with his strong legs. As he pushed inside her, his mouth against hers, Kazak said, "My precious wife, and my home is where you are."

Epilogue

Three years later

Kazak stood beside Bo, a cup of Cini's blueberry infused wine in his hand. His gaze filled with love arrowed unwavering upon his beautiful wife who was across the keep, near the castle.

"The castle finally appears completed," Bo commented, sipping at his own plum Brandewijn. His cup in one hand, he held several small, seeded chocolate cakes in his other hand, benefits of course from Cini.

They stood companionably contemplating the enormous structure. The stone castle was four stories high with several jutting, rounded turrets. Chimneys spiraled grey smoke along numerous slanted slate roofs.

The keep surrounding the castle was bustling with Kazak's merry people. Under sunny skies, goats, chickens and pigs meandered the dirt ground, as dogs and children played and ran amongst the people going about their daily tasks.

As usual, leather was being stretched in one area, women washed clothing in another, fowl hung drying from trees. Newly created quilts pinned along clotheslines regaled legends told in dramatic colors.

Wooden and stone huts lined the main avenue then sprawled out exponentially for miles in all directions.

Sheep like miniature clouds dotted the green meadows and hills in the distance.

Kazak's soldiers on regal horses trod down the middle of the compound, hooves kicking up small clouds of dirt behind them.

Children chased after the horsemen yelling cheers at them. The soldiers smiled amiably at the little ones that were so eager to grow up to become one of Kazak's courageous, heroic knights.

Cini's best friend, Meli had exited the castle and was chatting with Cini.

A tiny toddler stood on chubby wobbly legs as Cini crouched and wiped his face with a cloth. The boy clearly didn't like it as he swung his face this way and that to avoid the cloth.

Biting back a grin, Cini gently admonished him as she continued cleaning his plump cheeks and bow mouth. Meli bent and ruffled the child's hair, as black as his da's.

Kazak slew a glance at Bo. Bo's attention was rapt on Meli. His lips pressed in a tight frown.

"Ah," Kazak murmured. In Romanian, he said, "Melisandra Maciel has not come around to your engaging ways?"

His lips pushed out further. Bo said glumly, "She avoids me like the Sansic Plague. Her father is ordering her to marry some damned Lord of Rimshire Roans to connect the two families. Meli is terrified of her da. She won't go against his commands."

Kazak's attention returned to his beloved wife.

Still crouched, Cini laid her palm over her swollen belly while still holding onto Kaiden, their rambunctious son.

His eyes on Cini, Kazak said, "So? What was it you were always telling me about my wife?"

His bulky arms crossed over his massive chest, his gaze on Meli, Bo muttered, "What? What pearls of wisdom had I offered to you?"

With a smirk and a chuckle, Kazak reminded him, "You told me to take what I want. It is my, your, right as the Emperor's knighted warriors, to take any maid upon this land as ours, with or without hers or her family's consent."

He nodded towards his obviously happy and content pregnant wife as she tussled with their recalcitrant toddler. Indeed the roses shone brightly on her rounded cheeks, and although she fought with their unruly child, her smile was radiant.

"Worked out perfectly for me, *mea frắţe*. I saw, I took, she flourishes in my arms," Kazak bragged proudly, happily.

"Hmm," Bo ruminated, rubbing his chin thoughtfully. "Perhaps you are right." He grinned at his friend. "I mean, I was right." His gaze back to Meli, he mumbled, "When the time is right, I believe I shall pluck that ripe blossom and hasten her away on my steed."

"Uh huh. Just remember the battles I had to endure with my own feisty lass. The clever escapes and whatnot. It wasn't easy, my brother, to convince her it was a life with me she wanted."

"Perhaps not, but was it worth it?"

A grin spread across Kazak's tough, scarred face. "Oh *da*, every bit. Every bit, Bo. Just be prepared, my brother, you're looking at a long skirmish. Meli is deeply entrenched in her family's ways and she fears her da dreadfully. You are going to have a fight on your hands."

Finally a grin broke through Bo's glum countenance. "Oh, I love a challenge, I look forward to it." He rubbed his palms together. "In fact, I can't wait. By this time next year, I guarantee that Meli will be swollen with my babe."

Beside him, Kazak broke out in a loud laugh. Something he had never done before he'd met his Činnosti, and he was joyfully learning that he loved to laugh. Delightfully, his small family kept him grinning all day long.

"Anyway," Bo said, his mind was already working on how he planned to capture his prize. Meli would not be going with him easily. He needed to find a place where he could keep her secure and hidden until he married her and got his own bairns on her.

Maybe he should get her pregnant right away, she'd be less inclined to fight him and try to escape. Yes, that's a plan.

He said to Kazak, "You built the castle big enough to hold many bairns. Good job." He smirked at his friend. "And you plan on keeping our Cini swollen with your babes, eh? What do you think you are having next? A boy or a girl?"

"She is *my* Činnosti, not ours," Kazak frowned at Bo.

Then his brow lifted. "My wife is hoping for a *femelă* this time. She wants to name her Jenja after her grandmother. I care not what it is, as long as the babe and Činnosti are healthy and happy."

"*Yah*," Bo turned to Kazak with a broad smile. "It is good, my friend, to see you finally get what you deserve. A kingdom, a beautiful, kind, sweet wife who loves you, and a house full of rowdy bairns."

Nodding happily, Kazak clapped a huge hand on Bo's back. *"Da,* and now tis your turn, *mea frăţe."* He didn't wait for Bo's response, he strode quickly towards the castle.

Bo's hands dropped to his lean hips as his eyes narrowed across the keep.

Meli hugged Cini and was heading down the lane to return to her own home. She must have felt his eyes upon her as she looked up.

Seeing his eyes daggered on her, a blush rose over her lovely features. She shook her head at him with a frown of negativity and hurried off. Her body was willowy with soft curves, slender legs that carried her quickly out of sight.

"Yah," Bo muttered, his scheming grin widening. "Tis my turn. Run and hide whilst you can, my future bride. Our time will come." His eyes flicked to Kazak who was striding purposefully towards his wife.

When Kazak reached Cini, he grasped her arms and helped her stand up straight. This action freed his impish son who, like his mother had years before, tried to scamper away from the great warrior.

"Halta," Kazak ordered. He snatched the boy's arm stalling his escape. First he bent and kissed Cini's burgeoning belly then he swung his son up onto his shoulders.

"Da, da, gallop! Da gallop!" Kaiden demanded, lifting his tiny body up and down on his father's shoulders as if riding a stallion.

Clutching the child's leg, Kazak said, "Later, boy," and laughed at his antics. He wound a brawny arm around Cini's shoulders as he walked his young family into the castle.

Smiling with brilliant lust in his eyes at his wife, Kazak said, "Mama and Da are going to play by ourselves for a while."

Cini grinned up at her handsome husband. "I already asked Sarah to keep him occupied, my Lord. Our chamber is warmed by fire, and cozy with new quilts on the bed."

She cocked her head shyly at him. With a sultry lilt in her voice and desire in her green eyes, Cini said, "I've waited hours for you to finish training. Now is my time."

Love beaming from his piercing eyes, Kazak replied, "*Yah*, Wife, tis our time." He leaned over and kissed her cheek. "You have brought color and laughter, boundless joy and warm bright light to my cold dark world. I love you with my whole heart, my beloved Činnosti."

Her head tilted up, Cini returned the adoring gaze. "And I love you as well, Kazak, with my entire being. You've made me so happy."

He kissed her again before leading her inside. "There is more to come, my bride, much more."

The End

Dear Reader, thank you for purchasing Cini and the Beast! *I know you could have picked any number of books to read, but you picked this book and for that I am extremely grateful.*

I hope you enjoyed this novel, and if you did, please leave a review where you purchased it, and look for other exciting titles in my name!

About the Author

Louise Furley loves writing romance with a huge helping of suspense. She finds it exciting to study new lands and learn everything she can about the area and the natives that call it home.

Her idea of fun is researching ideas, studying enigmatic modes of science, archeology, and different ways to kill someone.

Her Significant Other finds the last to be particularly notable. He remains wary yet gives Louise his full support with her writing adventures.

Sunny Florida is home where Louise is a graduate of St. Thomas University with a master's degree in Mental Health.

This degree is essential for exploring the deviant soul, and understanding the mind of a killer, while finding it exhilarating, frightening and sad all at the same time. With artistic license, Louise can be judge, jury, and sometimes executioner!

Louise is the author of numerous published novels. When not researching or writing, she is dreaming of unique plots, and discovering fresh ventures she hasn't yet experienced in the world.

Ride along with her as she travels new and thrilling journeys!

www.ingramcontent.com/pod-product-compliance
Lightning Source LLC
Chambersburg PA
CBHW050026180626
46810CB00002B/593